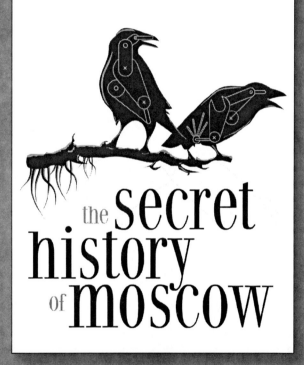

Weird Tales®

MARCH–APRIL 2008

SUBSCRIBE AT WWW.WEIRDTALESMAGAZINE.COM

WEIRD TALES was the *first* storytelling magazine devoted explicitly to the realm of the **dark and fantastic.**

Founded in 1923, WEIRD TALES provided a literary home for such diverse wielders of the imagination as **H.P. Lovecraft** (creator of Cthulhu), **Robert E. Howard** (creator of Conan the Barbarian), **Margaret Brundage** (artistic godmother of goth fetishism), and **Ray Bradbury** (author of *The Illustrated Man* and *Something Wicked This Way Comes*).

Today, O wondrous reader of the 21st century, we continue to seek out that which is most weird and unsettling, for your own edification and alarm.

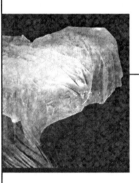

FICTION

POETRY

COVER ILLUSTRATION | **Newel Anderson**

EDITORIAL & CREATIVE DIRECTOR Stephen H. Segal FICTION EDITOR Ann VanderMeer
CONTRIBUTING EDITORS Scott Connors, Elizabeth Genco, Darrell Schweitzer
EDITOR EMERITUS George H. Scithers EDITORIAL ASSISTANTS Nivair H. Gabriel, Tessa Kum
CONTRIBUTING ARTISTS Molly Crabapple, Ming Doyle, Vance Kelly, Ira Marcks,
Daniele Serra, Star St. Germain, Oliver Wetter

PUBLISHER John Gregory Betancourt
ADVERTISING SALES Evelyn Kriete ASSISTANT TO THE PUBLISHER Renee Farrah

All writers of such stories are prophets

FEATURES

VOL. 63, NO. 2 | Issue 349

DEPARTMENTS

WEIRD TALES ® is published 6 times a
year by Wildside Press, LLC. Postmaster
and others: send all changes of address
and other subscription matters to Wildside Press, 9710 Traville Gateway Dr.
#234, Rockville MD 20850–7408. Single
copies, $6.99 in U.S.A. & possessions; $10
by first class mail elsewhere. Subscrip-
tions: 6 issues $24 in U.S.A. & posses-
sions; $45 elsewhere, in U.S. funds.
Single-copy orders should be addressed to
WEIRD TALES at the address above.
Copyright © 2007 by Wildside Press, LLC.
All rights reserved; reproduction prohib-
ited without prior permission. Typeset &
printed in the United States of America.
WEIRD TALES ® is a registered trade-
mark owned by Weird Tales, Limited.

The eyrie

A VIEW FROM UNEARTHLY HEIGHTS

JUST A FEW months after I first came to work here, I picked up a phone call that turned out to be from the personal nurse of one of our subscribers, who was calling to make sure her patient had renewed in time and wouldn't miss an issue. "Her *Weird Tales* is very important to her," the nurse said. "She started reading it in 1927." >>>

Onward to the Next 85 Weird Years

Welcome | BY ANN VANDERMEER

IT GIVES ME great pleasure to help present the 85th anniversary issue of *Weird Tales*, which contains a wealth of new fiction. Historically, *Weird Tales* has been as forward-thinking and inventive as any magazine in the field. In addition to publishing the work of luminaries such as Ray Bradbury, Robert Bloch, Robert E. Howard and H.P. Lovecraft, *Weird Tales* found a home for Tennessee Williams' first published story, as well as work by the likes of Theodore Sturgeon, Robert Bloch, and Mary Elizabeth Counselman.

In this issue, you will find fiction by Michael Moorcock and Tanith Lee that honors the tradition of *Weird Tales*, but also an acknowledgment of such exciting new writers as Sarah Monette, Rachel Swirsky, and John Kirk. Perhaps most importantly, under my editorship, *Weird Tales* will actively encourage fresh talent like Ramsey Shehadeh, whose first published story, "Creature," appears within these pages. I think "Creature" marks the debut of

a major new writer — you'll be seeing more from Ramsey in future issues.

As the new fiction editor, and only the second female editor of *Weird Tales* in eighty-five years, I am fully aware of the history behind and importance of this institution. I plan to respect its literary past —including its long reputation as ground-breaking and trend-setting. This is the *Weird Tales* of the twenty-first century, and I hope you will find that the fiction delights and entertains you while also taking chances. Nothing gives me greater enjoyment than discovering a wonderful new story and presenting it to you, the readers. You make this magazine fantastic, and I hope you enjoy it — not only the fiction, but the entire publication. Our team has worked hard to revitalize *Weird Tales* all the way through, from the nonfiction to the artwork.

Finally, I need to thank a few people. Thanks to my good friend and colleague Paula Guran for recommending me. Thanks to John Betancourt, Stephen Segal, and Sean Wallace for offering me the position. Thanks to George Scithers and Darrell Schweitzer for their graciousness in passing the torch. I'd also like to thank my husband, who makes all things possible (and worth it), my family and friends, and all of the writers and artists who continue to make *Weird Tales* the best magazine around! ❧

>>>

I blinked. So many things were remarkable about that statement, I didn't know where to begin remarking. I finally settled on: "But it sort of didn't quite exist for thirty years in the middle there."

"Oh, I know," the nurse said. "But as soon as she heard it was coming back in the '80s, she signed up again right away."

Such is the power and allure of great weird storytelling. It sticks in the mind and becomes habit-forming — for the simple reason that it is *unique*, just as the cover of this magazine has trumpeted (on and off) since its very first issue, 85 years ago this month. In that time, authors have debuted and faded; artists have sketched and painted; typefaces have angled and cursived and heavyweighted — but through it all, one thing has remained constant: *Weird Tales* has done its damnedest to try and hit every reader with *something* that would leave them thunderstruck, speechless . . . weirded out like never before.

Of course, we've hardly been alone. Freaky and bizarre storytelling isn't something that's limited to the pages of a pulp fiction magazine. Genius may be both rare and unique, but it's certainly not localized; for every H.P. Lovecraft in cultural history there's also an M.C. Escher, for every Margaret Brundage a David Bowie. That's why we decided to kick off our 85th anniversary year by embracing the whole of the weird spectrum and presenting our wide-ranging list of "The 85 Weirdest Storytellers of the Past 85 Years" (page 24). Thanks to the many readers who helped us shape this list — not least by showing us you wanted it to be "the most influentially weird storytellers" rather than "the weirdest storytellers you've never heard of."

Thanks, also, to the illustrious editors who've worked to make founder Jacob Henneberger's vision a reality: Edwin Baird, Farnsworth Wright, Dorothy McIlwraith, Sam Moskowitz, Lin Carter, Darrell Schweitzer, John Betancourt, and George H. Scithers. We're trying to do you proud. — *Stephen H. Segal*

LETTERS TO THE EDITOR

Letters may be emailed to letters@weirdtales.net or snail-mailed to *Weird Tales*, 9710 Traville Gateway Dr. #234, Rockville MD 20850-7408. Letters may be edited for publication.

WEIRD TALES 85th ANNIVERSARY CALENDAR

Events & Noteworthy Dates in Mid-2008

I-CON | *www.iconsf.org*
SUNY at Stony Brook, N.Y. | *April 4-6, 2008*
WEIRD TALES fiction editor Ann VanderMeer is an official guest at I-Con, the three-day Long Island festival encompassing a wide range of fantasy, horror, and science fiction, from literature to movies to comics.

LIBRARY OF CONGRESS | *www.loc.gov*
Washington, D.C. | *April 11, 2008*
The Library of Congress's noontime "What If" lecture series will feature editor emeritus George H. Scithers and editorial director Stephen Segal discussing the magazine's literary and artistic history.

NEW YORK COMIC CON | *nycomiccon.com*
New York, N.Y. | *April 18-20, 2008*
Come participate in the WEIRD TALES panel discussion and group signing, featuring an assortment of magazine contributors and fans as well as several of our honorees from the "85 Weirdest Storytellers of the Past 85 Years!"

THE 66TH WORLD SCIENCE FICTION CONVENTION | *www.denvention3.org*
Denver, Colo. | *August 6-10, 2008*
"Things to Do in Denver When You're Dead" strikes us as a promising motif. Hmm: Warren Zevon wrote that song, and Colorado is home to WEIRD TALES contributor and werewolf novelist Carrie Vaughn, so — whatever we end up doing at Worldcon, expect lupine involvement . . .

Weirdism

AN UNEXPECTED LEGACY

Nonfiction | BY S. GEIGEN-MILLER

PHOTO: MARC OPPERMAN / MODEL: RYAN HILL, VIOLET CROWN RADIO PLAYERS

I WAS BEGINNING to suspect that weird fiction, like crime, is a weed that bears bitter fruit. I'm a writer — a fourth-generation writer. But I'm unusual in my family: I write fiction. Weird fiction. My mother and father are journalists, as is my grandmother. And when I look at the success, the acclaim that they have achieved by writing non-fiction — practical, factual, serious nonfiction — in comparison, my taste for writing stories of the alien, the fantastical and the bizarre, has always seemed, well . . . weird.

So yes, I was thinking about weird fiction, and about my family history. H. P. Lovecraft would have approved. His passion for history and genealogy is well-known, although in his writing, interest in the subject tended to lead to the discovery of black magic, hideous atavistic mutations, or Yog-Sothoth being a branch on the family tree.

Even so, I was thinking about my great-grand-father, Victor Lauriston. He was a journalist too, and a historian. His history of Kent County (around Chatham, Ontario, his home) is still considered definitive. He was a beloved and acclaimed local figure; there's a school named after him.

But he also wrote fiction, and that's something we have in common, a tie binding me to a man I never knew, who died when I was a baby.

I've never known much about my great-grand-father's early career, his career in fiction. I've read two of his novels, and I knew that he'd written short stories for various magazines at some point. I always sort of assumed that they were earnest literary efforts printed in earnest Canadian publications to earnest critical acclaim and no real audience.

This is why it pays to look into your family history, and Yog-Sothoth be damned. Because, after my thinking, I did a web search on my great-grand-father, and I found resources that listed some of the short stories he had published. In magazines like *Detective Story* and *Wild West Stories*. Magazines like *Black Mask* and *Argosy*!

My great-grandfather wrote pulp. He was in on the ground floor of creating the genres — the alien, fantastical, bizarre genres — that have fascinated me for my entire life.

And there was another magazine. He was published in it only once. His story "A Changeling Soul" appeared in the January 1925 issue.

Of *Weird Tales*.

Some of the other writers published in that very same issue were Frank Belknap Long, and E. Hoffman Price, and yes: Howard Phillips Lovecraft.

Lovecraft probably could have done justice to the dizzying sensation I felt at perceiving a legacy across generations connecting me — he would probably have written, "Across the yawning abyss of time" — to my great-grandfather.

My family, as I said, has done very well writing non-fiction, and I've always felt like the odd one out, scrambling to achieve some kind of success, plugging away writing stories and comics in genres that are considered very nearly as déclassé today as they were in my great-grandfather and H. P. Lovecraft's day.

But now, my life-long love of weird tales has turned into a family connection to *Weird Tales*, the magazine that started it all. I can see that weird fiction is indeed like a weed, a hardy, resilient weed — or an atavistic mutation. Because fascination with the bizarre, the alien and the fantastical may be weird, but it's also perennial. It never dies, just keeps coming back, a passion that recurs again and again, linking people across generations. And my writing, my striving, is part of history — my family history, and the history of weird fiction itself — and that makes it seem almost epic in scope.

I wish I could have had the opportunity to congratulate and to thank my great-grandfather for that. I'm pleased to have the chance to congratulate and thank *Weird Tales*. ❧

Stephen Geigen-Miller is writer and co-creator of the comics *Xeno's Arrow* and *Cold Iron Badge*.

The Library

Books | BY SCOTT CONNORS

CURRENCY OF SOULS
by Kealan Patrick Burke
(Subterranean Press, $40)

Ever since Lord Dunsany first shared with the world the adventures of Mr. Joseph Jorkens, stories whose narration is set within the comfortably circumscribed confines of the private club have been a trope in the fields of fantasy and science fiction. Generally speaking, they provide a backdrop for tall tales that more often than not turn out to be true, but the familiar setting allows the listener—and the reader—to dismiss them as more of the ramblings of the club eccentric. The setting has transmutated into bars and pubs, ranging from Gavangan's Bar (L. Sprague de Camp and Fletcher Pratt) to Callahan's Bar (Spider Robinson).

Kealan Patrick Burke, as it happens, knows something about bars, having edited the anthology *Taverns of the Dead*. There is nothing at all comforting about the setting of his novel *Currency of Souls*. Milestone is a near ghost town in Big Sky country that can barely support a single bar. Every Saturday night the regulars at Eddie's Tavern gather together, but it is not fellowship that brings them together. Each of them has killed someone, even the town sheriff. The guilt that stains their souls has lead them to become reluctant foot soldiers in the private crusade of Reverend Hill. The good Reverend is an exceedingly unsympathetic example of that sort of preacher who is fixated upon the Old Testament god of vengeance, but who seems to have skipped over the New Testament's ideas about mercy. He wields the promise of eventual salvation over each of them like an overseer wielding a bullwhip, sending them out to punish those whom he has deemed worthy of extermination. But tonight the intended targets of his wrath unexpectedly walk in upon this mournful flock, and suddenly they become real people instead of nameless targets. This unwelcome development calls into question the Reverend's credentials as a vessel of divine justice.

As might be expected given its setting, Eddie's Tavern hosts a colorful assortment of characters, but that is about the only conventional device in this off-trail and intriguing novel. Burke takes the conventions of the bar story and uses them against the reader's expectations, taking the plot in directions that are totally different from what might be expected. No sooner are we introduced to many of them than they end up dead, including Reverend Hill! But the old saying about "the devil you know" holds true, and if the "good" reverend seems reminiscent of every crazy preacher in horror movies, from Robert Mitchum in *Night of the Hunter* through Kane in *Poltergeist II*, his replacement arouses both loathing and sympathy in the reader.

One might expect *Currency of Souls* to be a variation upon the Faust theme. It does deal with supernatural bargains, but the habitues at Eddie's are trying to regain their souls, not barter them. As unattractive as Reverend Hill and his successor may appear, they offer the apparent opportunity for atonement, although whether or not they ever deliver on that promise is unclear. This is an excellent example of a book where character drives the plot, and not the other way around: there are some twists that are genuinely surprising but flow naturally out of how Burke describes the characters' actions and history, in particular the town sheriff and his strained relationship with his son. If the book begins by questioning the justice of the powers behind their actions, some of that doubt is resolved by the end of the book, which may prove unsettling to some—and that may well be the whole point.

THRILLERS 2
Edited by Robert Morrish
(Cemetery Dance, $40)

This long-delayed horror series offers a select group of writers a showcase for their shorter, less commercial fiction. International Horror Guild Award winner Gemma Files provides a fine opening with "Pen Umbra," an extremely effective tale of how an art student's participation in a psychic experiment may have left her vulnerable to ghostly intrusions. In "The Faces That We Meet" Tim Waggoner examines the extent to which we will ignore that which we find disturbing in our loved ones to keep a family together, while "The Long Way Home" offers an apocalyptic vision of a mother's love. R. Patrick Gates attempts to combine humor with horror in his four tales, usually with mixed results, but he succeeds brilliantly in the surreal "The Tell-Tale Nose." Caitlin R. Kiernan's blend of deft characterization and eldritch atmosphere are displayed in two excellent tales of cosmic dread. "The Daughter of the Four of Pentacles" is a prelude to *Daughter of Hounds* (reviewed in *Weird Tales* #346) which raises some unsettling questions about our circumscribed position in the universe, while "Houses Under the Seas" handles its Lovecraftian roots with a poignant sensitivity that intensifies its impact. *Thrillers 2*'s effective mix of styles and themes offers a sampler of the best that modern horror offers.

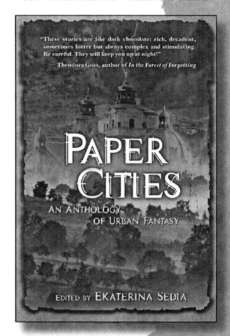

ASTOUNDING HERO TALES
Edited by James Lowder
(Hero Games, $16.99)

Subtitled "Thrilling Stories of Pulp Adventure," this original anthology attempts to capture some of the same sense of wonder that we now associate with the pulp magazines of the 1930s and '40s. The editor has perhaps cast his net a bit wider than necessary, since he appears unable to decide if he wants to emulate the hero pulps, the weird menace pulps, or the fantastic pulps. Nevertheless, there are some stories included that are well worth reading. The best of these is William Messner-Loebs's "Wolf Train West," which manages to combine both a scathing indictment of economic and social policy that might make those who look back upon those "simpler" days with nostalgia feel uncomfortable with both a strong (and appropriate) supernatural element and an unexpected and rousing heroic rescue that manages not to feel contrived, but somehow downright numinous. Robert Weinberg's "Kiss Me Deadly" is a fine combination of hardboiled detection

and the supernatural. Thomas M. Reid and David Niall Wilson have written fine homages to the lost race and sports pulps, respectively, with "Bandit Gold" and "Slide Home." The latter might well be the better of the two, since it managed to engage my interest despite my total lack of enthusiasm for baseball. Other contributors include Darrell Schweitzer, Will Murray, Hugh B. Cave, and John Pelan.

A DAMASK OF THE DEAD
by John Gale
(Tartarus Press, $50)

This well-produced Tartarus Press volume will interest fans of one of the most revered writers ever to write for this magazine, Clark Ashton Smith. John Gale's collection of prose poems is titled *A Damask of the Dead*; a damask is a lustrous fabric in a satin weave, often grayish-red in color. Like Smith, Gale's brief vignettes are a phantasmagoria out of the *Arabian Nights* or William Beckford's *Vathek* — and also like Smith, death is a pervasive theme that >>>

TALES OF THE LING MASTER, VOL. I-IV
"Blaster" Al Ackerman and E.J. Barnes
(http://world.std.com/~ejbarnes/lm.html,
$1 each digest-sized zine volume)

Weird fiction has its small-press heroes and its cult figures, but few *underground* artists. Then there's "Blaster" Al Ackerman. Ackerman's stories don't appear in *Asimov's* or even *Weird Tales*, but some of his stuff has shown up in the zine *Dumb Fucker*, and is often shipped directly to readers via "mail art." He's hilarious, and a weirdo. (Then there's his work . . .) Anyway, artist E.J. Barnes has adapted several of his short stories, such as "The Squid Boys of Terre Haute" and "I, The Stallion", and has turned them into neat little comics zines. You can get the first four for only three dollars if you buy them all at once from the website. Barnes's art channels both R. Crumb and the sort of propaganda comics the nuclear power industry used to print and send to grade schools. Reading these little zines will comprise the funniest six minutes you've ever spent all by yourself. —*Nick Mamatas*

>>> imbues the entire work with a melancholy that manages to be more contemplative than angst-ridden. Several of the stories deal with the sorcerer Lord Kandra, brother-in-spirit to Smith's archmages Malygris and Maal Dweb, who contended eons ago with Death for immortality but has now grown to regret his apparent victory. Loss, regret, and the verdigris of uncounted ages permeate Gale's enchanting pieces. To describe them would be as ineffectual as describing the taste of chocolate or the exultation of new love, but a brief sampling of his style serves to display the author's virtuosity:

> *I closed my eyes and a cool touch of lips came to my brow, like a breeze, fingers through my hair . . . my eyes and there was my loved one as of yore. O such joy surged through me, not once questioning this impossibility. I had surely slipped back in tome to the halcyon days when we were together. But no, I think . . . Yet I do know that the robe of pale ruby came away from the shoulders to expose the jasmine skin and that I was held there to my lover's chest while the tears flowed from my closed eyes and I felt in that chest no pulse of the heart . . . held there, then still weeping we lay down amongst the fragrant sheets and . . .*

While Gale certainly counts Smith among his literary ancestors, there is no pastiche in his treatment. If he treats some of the same themes, then his handling of those themes is his own and not a mere aping of Smith. His style is just as elevated as Smith's, yet in some ways it is simpler: there are not so many Latinate words, but the effect is curiously almost as if he had. All of Tartarus Press's books are printed in extremely limited editions, but Gale's slender volume is limited to a mere 250 signed copies. It reminds me very much of Smith's own collection *Ebony and Crystal: Poems in Verse and Prose. A Damask of the Dead* surely belongs on the same shelf. ❧

TO SUBMIT BOOKS FOR REVIEW:

Fiction: *address to Scott Connors, 4277 Larson St. #52, Marysville CA 95901.* **Nonfiction, comics, weird art/music, etc**: *address to Weird Tales, Attn: Reviews, 9710 Traville Gateway Dr. #234, Rockville MD 2085-7408.*

A Cthulhu-Steampunk Mashup, with Amulets

We have fantasy and SF authors such as Tim Powers and K.W. Jeter to thank for the concept of "steampunk" — retro-tech SF via a Victorian sensibility. Since its origin, the steampunk aesthetic has percolated out of literature into the world of artistic craftsmanship. We sent author Cherie Priest to chat with fellow Seattlite **MOLLY FRIEDRICH**, a steampunk artist who's been incorporating bits of Lovecraft's Cthulhu mythos into her unique medallions, more of which can be seen online at **http://porkshanks.deviantart.com**. (Original commissions available.)

In your Lovecraftian designs I see a really neat fusion of biological nightmares meeting mechanical structures. How did this marriage of preternatural form and clockwork precision come about? I think it blends well because the precision of the watches becomes a strange sort of Dada when applied to this new form. The inner workings of the watches are inscribed with all kinds of fancy scripted words and perfect geometry that speak of arcane arts and strange magicks, but none of it makes sense in context — which really invokes the undercurrent of insanity that I love so much in Lovecraft's writing!

The gears, wires, and vintage feel of your pieces fit gorgeously with the aesthetics of steampunk. Tell us about some of your influences. The biggest influence on my affection for the steampunk culture is that I grew up around a welding shop. When I was a kid, I often went to visit the shop my grandfather owned and operated, and I would get lost for hours in box after box of bolts, nuts, and washers. As far as I knew, goggles really were appropriate everyday wear. I grew to accept the grime, appreciate the feel of rust, and love the smell of burning torches. I saw in my grandfather the ultimate expression of creativity — the ability to take some sheet metal and an arc welder and turn it into anything. I try to live with that kind of can-do DIY mindset.

Speaking of steampunk, I hear rumor that you're taking up the aesthetic as a full-time gig and going full-time, full-blown steampunk style. How's that working out for you? And what does it typically look like? I love the streamlined and the down-to-earth silhouettes of Edwardian styles (as compared to the more forced look of the Victorians). Plus, I love how the proportions of hats just went crazy in that time period. I think that the larger, more dynamic headwear of the time blends better with the otherworldly aesthetic I am personally going for than those tiny precious hats of the preceding years. Don't get me wrong, I love the way most steampunk ladies rock their look, I just prefer a bit more pulp fantasy and occult style fashion mixed into it. I'm still in the early stages of developing my wardrobe for daily wear; but it's not quite where I want it to be yet, because I want to make most of it myself

I love the look of the original suffragettes — definitely ladylike, but badass in a primordial way. Right now I like long layered, faux-bustled skirts or walking skirts with petticoats paired with a tall Victorian boot. Sometimes its just altered jeans and massive stompy industrial boots for those days I'm feeling more on the "post-apocalyptic" side of things. For tops, I generally go with tank tops or vests that capture the more fantastical skypirate-y side of steampunk. I also have some period-style clothing from which I ripped off the arms. I customize pretty much everything with new details or radical alterations.

PHOTOS COURTESY MOLLY FRIEDRICH / PORKSHANKS.DEVIANTART.COM

LEFT: Friedrich's "Eldritch Secrets" pendant has a hidden chamber. RIGHT: "Unquiet Dreamer."

I've used wind-up pocket watches regularly since I was a teen. I'm definitely a brass addict, whether it's buttons, buckles, or just incorporating true hardware like lynchpins into something as a D-ring. I love antique-looking clothes, but the mad scientist in me can't stop experimenting on it! Steampunk culture really lets me play with odd asymmetrical embellishments like belts with split Y straps, bandoliers, vintage army canvas pouches, and of course the ol' standby: goggles.

You do some awesome custom-mods for things other than jewelry. Do you have any favorite projects you'd like to talk about? And what do you think inspires you to do this — to convert sleek, modern objects into bulkier (if more charming) devices? I'm sick of disposable culture. Sleek, new, plastic . . . and broken in a year; it's just played out! I'd love for our whole society to reject planned obsolescence, because it's filling the ground with processed material and it wastes precious resources! We treat our objects with the same reverence as people. When they die, we stick them both in the ground and let them rot, but the nutrients never get back into the earth. All the metal and plastic we throw away will still be there in a thousand years, only it'll probably smell funny. I wonder if someday we'll mine our landfills the way we mine for gold. I'm all for re-cycling, and that is why I try to use found objects and old parts in my work. I choose disassembled watches simply because they are so beautiful and unique.

My own interpretation of fashion is that most of the last century was a diversion. It was an exercise in mass-producible goods and lowest common denominator couture. My heart is yearning for a time when clothes were handmade and individual, but I certainly don't yearn for the stifling society they had. The "punk" in steampunk is a very key part of it to me; it's shorthand for all of the advancement we've made as humans since then.

What's next? One of your pieces was called "The Spawn of Innsmouth;" might you be considering Lovecraft's other stories as source material? My dream is to do costuming for stage or film. But for now, I'm really enjoying making jewelry! Eventually, I want to work more with animated features and clockwork-style gears that actually function in some way. I am trying to delve further into things thematically. I want each piece to look like it has a story; like a cursed artifact or an amulet to awaken Those Who Slumber In The Deep. I want to capture a post-apocalyptic vibe with materials like bones, detritus, and rust. I've stared into the seer's ink and I see lots of tentacles in the future! ◉

BRIEF CROSS SECTION *of* MODERN INNSMOUTH

MASSACHUSETTS.

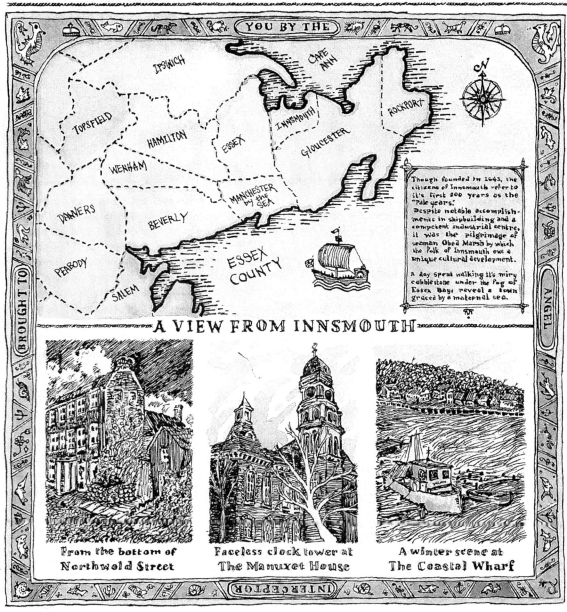

Though founded in 1643, the citizens of Innsmouth refer to it's first 200 years as the "Pale years."
Despite notable accomplishments in shipbuilding and a competent industrial centre, it was the pilgrimage of seaman Obed Marsh by which the folk of Innsmouth owe a unique cultural development.

A day spent walking it's miry cobblestone under the fog of Essex Bay, reveal a town graced by a maternal sea.

A VIEW FROM INNSMOUTH

From the bottom of
Northwold Street

Faceless clock tower at
The Manuxet House

A winter scene at
The Coastal Wharf

ADAPTED TAILOR SHOP, specializing in unlikely garment modifications.

NOVELTY PIPE, depicting historic Innsmouth figure, Obed Marsh.

GROTESQUE *BURLESQUE

A nod to Innsmouth in this WORLD FAMOUS excentric taboo journal.

JOIN US!! INNSMOUTH FASHION REPERTORY · 27

HUMOROUS POSTCARD & WOODEN SPOON.

ORDER OF DAGON, unofficial versions of the sacred writ are a hot ticket.

BOOTLEGGING, rum runner sloop 'Obed's Glory' proudly stacks it's contraband right on deck.

STYLE & INFLUENCE & TRADE & TRINKETS &

* FISH & POTATO PLATE, Local favorite at Breakwater Tavern.

INNSMOUTH AS USUAL

1. **TYPICAL INNSMOUTH RESIDENCE.**
Notice the focus on the basement.

2. **CITIZENS IN SUNDAY DRESS.**
Mr. & Mrs. W

3. **DECORATIVE FLATWARE.**
Honoring the water elemental.

4. **'DAGON'S FAVOR' TAPESTRY.**
Reference to be defined.

5. **CORAL ANTLER SCEPTER.**
The marriage of land & sea.

6. **OBED MARSH FIGURINE.**

7. **'OLD MINISTER' CARD.**
Figure in ceremonial regalia.

8. **ANTIQUE LANTERN.**

1

WORN-RIDDLED WALLS

GAMBREL ROOF (partly collapsed)

SLOPPED FLOORS

2

How about lunch?

3

FORK. braided in the extensions of Cthulhu.

SOUP SPOON, stamped with the icon of Mother Hydra.

KNIFE, for the Father Dagon
A celebration of his agricultural influence.

4

5

6 ♣

7 ⁕

8

♣ local card game.   ⁕ often preceded by epithet (Lost or Herald)

BY IRA MARCKS

A Compleynte on the Deth of Sir William Thatcher, Sumtyme Ycleped Ulrich Von Liechtenstein

BY GEOFFREY CHAUCER

Of late, ich haue been soore depressid to heere of the deth of myn freend Sir William Thatcher, yclept Ulrich of Liechtenstein for a certayn tyme, with whom ich did travel in Fraunce about XXXX poundes ago. Ich haue sat in my room going thurgh oold joustinge programes and thinkinge of thos jours d'alcyone.

Thogh my pen is but a sely thing, bettir fit for ditees and smal jokes and puns, yet ich koud nat but trye to write sum few lynes of rym for the memorie of my good freend, the which ich share heere. Ich knowe that newes of his deth hath long ben known, and many wyse folk have seyd thinges of hym, yet tak this rym-doggerel for my part.

Yif al the woe and teeres and hevinesse
And eek the sorwe, compleynte and wamentynge
That man hath heard in thes yeeres of distresse
Togedir were y-put, too light a thynge
It sholde be for this yonge knightes mournynge.
Withouten hym this world can no wey plese,
Fulfild it is of shadwe and disese.

In sorwe and teeres and eek in hevinesse
Stand Roland, Wat, and Kate, his compaigyne,
(And eek mynself, the forger of noblesse):
Sir Deth wyth falshede and wyth sorcerye
Hath slayn thys knight who never feered to dye,
Of honor nat of lyf took Ulrich kepe.
A see of teeres nys nat ynogh to wepe.

Proud Deth, yower trophie is our hevinesse,
Your heraud may ful loude yel and crie,
For thou hast slayn the flour of hardinesse:
Sir Ulrich knewe the herte of chivalrie
And evir daunce he coud to melodye;
A silent yere he spent oones in a toun
In Itaylye to understonde a roun.

This feble world fulfild of hevinesse
Offreth us nat but wo, o welaway!
No thyng it hath may us give restfulnesse
For yisterday was noblere and moore gay
Than thys clipt peni that we hold today.
On Ulrich spende yower XII last silver teeres
Syn now departid aren hys golden yeeres.

He chaungid hys sterres, ros out of lowlinesse,
Bicam the man that fyrst did make me thinke
Our dedes nat our birth bring gentilesse –
And when ich was depe in the dice and drinke
He bought my pants ayein, it is no nay
May hevenes blisse repay that charité!
For blessed on erthe are al who had the chaunce
To walk the gardyn of his turbulaunce.

Geoffrey Chaucer is the wryter of *The Canterbury Tales* and, in deede, also of *A Knight's Tale*. He hath a blog: **http://houseoffame.blogspot.com**

HOW *to* RAISE *a* SOUL *from* *the* DEAD

(A MODERN SCIENTIFIC INQUIRY)

BY CSILLA CSORI

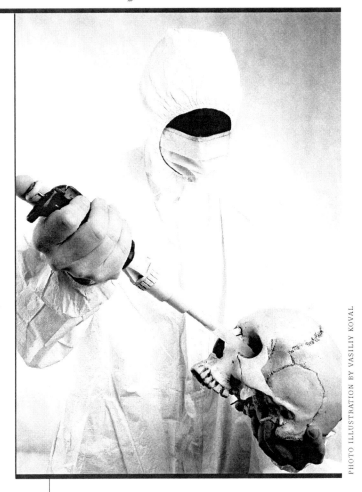

PHOTO ILLUSTRATION BY VASILIY KOVAL

Since mankind first sat around a fire telling scary stories, we've had tales of people coming back from the dead in one form or another. Modern tellings substitute science for the supernatural, but these stories continue to capture our imagination and leave us wondering, is it possible? Would such a person be the mindless zombie of countless horror movies, or a resurrected Lazarus?

These questions will not always be academic. People used to be considered dead when their hearts stopped, but not anymore. Every day, people whose hearts have stopped beating for brief periods of time — sometimes their hearts are even stopped on purpose during surgery — are brought back to life, and they are essentially the same person as before. The next logical step is to consider what would happen if we could overcome brain death. Would the revived person be the same, have the same personality, and retain all of their memories?

In Frank Herbert's *Dune* series of science fiction novels, we are introduced to the *ghola:* a body resurrected through medical means. Our ghola, a man named Duncan Idaho, has a consciousness of his own but no memory of his former life or his death. He is most definitely not a mindless zombie, and, in fact, is resurrected with the capability to learn new skills which he didn't possess in his previous life. He is a person, but is he the same person, the same Idaho who lived and died before? Not at first. Although certain voices and places seem familiar, he doesn't regain any actual memories until one traumatic event unlocks the past, and all of the memories from his former life come flooding back at once. If the brain is like a computer, then it is as if his memories are stored in a hidden file system to which he does not have access. Once he acquires the key to unlocking that system, all of the files (or memories) within are opened to him at once, and he knows himself as Idaho.

The news is full of stories in which authorities confiscate a suspect's computer and recover a hoard of incriminating files which the suspect had deleted. If a computer can retain deleted files, what about a human brain? Should this analogy of recovering information from a damaged brain give us hope for the Terri Schiavos of the world? If we could repair and regrow brain cells, would her personality still be in there somewhere, fully intact and just needing the right key to unlock it? To answer these questions, we need to examine how a brain stores and retrieves memories, and how this process compares with computer memory.

Like a computer, your brain has storage systems for short-term and long-term memory, and a central processing unit, known as the hippocampus, which connects the two. Your hippocampus filters data — determining what is relevant — from short-term memory to long-term memory. However, the manner in which data is stored and then accessed later is different, and that is where the key to recovering lost memories lies.

Most computer users are familiar with hierarchical file systems, which are basically made up of a main directory (or folder) containing files and subdirectories. The subdirectories can, in turn, contain both files and additional subdirectories. Users navigate up or down the hierarchical structure to locate a specific file in a specific directory. You might expect that all of the files in a particular directory are stored next to each other in the computer's memory, but this is not always the case. In fact, a single file may be broken into fragments and stored in several loca-

tions. This fragmentation occurs when files are edited and increase or decrease in size. On a brand-new disk (or other chunk of storage), the computer's operating system starts at one part, writing data in an orderly fashion, and if the data never changes, it continues until the disk is full.

But data files are almost never static; users are constantly adding on to files, deleting entire files, and otherwise changing the amount of memory needed to store a subdirectory or a particular file. As data is deleted, chunks of memory become available for new information, making holes in the nice, orderly system. When a file increases in size, if there is not enough memory in the original location to store the entire file, then the computer will look for an additional chunk of memory to store the second piece of the file. This process can be repeated many times, and a single file may end up stored as several pieces spread out over the disk.

The exact method a computer uses to keep track of all the pieces differs between operating systems, but it basically uses some kind of master reference table. When a user deletes a file, the actual data is not erased — only the entry in the reference table gets deleted. This tells the computer that the particular chunk of memory on which that file is stored is now available for writing new data. But the old data will sit there until it is overwritten, so that is why it is possible to recover deleted files from a computer.

Does the brain work in an analogous way, allowing us to recover lost memories? Your brain also stores pieces of memories in different locations; but, unlike a computer, it does not store information sequentially. Different types of sensory signals, such as sight, sound, and taste, are processed in different regions of your cortex and routed to your hippocampus. After filtering, the hippocampus sends these bits of information back to their respective regions and creates neural links between them. These links are strengthened by repetition (for example, by repeating a list) and by emotional factors

This essay appears as "Memory (and the Tleilaxu) Makes the Man" in *The Science of Dune*, published January 2008 by BenBella Books. Learn more online: **www.benbellabooks.com**

such as the personal relevance of the information. Your hippocampus keeps track of all of the links and associations, indexing and cross-linking with similar information. It seems similar to the master reference table in a computer operating system, but it is much more complex. Even though a computer may break a file into several pieces for storage, it still considers a file to be one discrete unit. The computer has no way of examining file content and determining that the letter you wrote to Grandma last week is in any way connected with the photo of her hugging you as a child. Your brain's reference system, on the other hand, is able to cross-link information from memories that are widely separated in time and location, and makes connections based on everything from strong emotions to mundane details.

This interweaving of one's memories strengthens associations, but it can also muddle memory recall and make it unreliable. When you recall the memory of an event, you are not opening a single file containing all of the data. Rather, you are dynamically reconstructing the memory from its various components. The process is associative, so one thing, like a particular song or smell, can trigger an associated piece of the memory, which triggers another, and so on. The ease and accuracy of your recall depends on the number and strength of the neural links, which, in turn, are dependent on such factors as how long ago the event occurred, when you last remembered it, and whether it is similar to other events in your memory. In the process, pieces of memories can get confused and mixed in with one another.

For example, a married couple who has had several arguments over money may mix up what was said during which argument when trying to recall one particular confrontation. If they later have to testify in court as to what was said, they may give different accounts and yet each will believe they are telling the truth. In addition, the process of memory reconstruction is further clouded

Every day, people whose hearts have stopped are revived. The next logical question is: What if we can beat brain death, too?

by current emotions and motivations. So, unlike a computer file, which is the same each time you open it, your memory of an event will differ at different times in your life.

Consider again our ghola, who has no memory of his former life. If those memories are still stored in his brain, how might they be accessed? Amnesia is often temporary, with people gradually recalling some or all of their missing memories. Our ghola's brain has been repaired, so there is no physical damage preventing access. If the neural links are intact, then it should be as simple as placing him in an environment which will trigger the old memories. It is unlikely that everything would return at once. A familiar face or voice would bring back a flood of associations, and, over time, the entirety of his memories should return. Of course, he is not exactly the same person, especially after the trauma of remembering his own death — but he is, for all intents and purposes, Idaho.

However, it's not that easy, because our ghola's memories are locked away in that hidden file system. In searching for a physical cause for the block, you might suppose that there is something in his hippocampus, or CPU, that is preventing access, but it is not that straightforward. Once the associations between neurons — the neural links — reach a certain strength, they become independent of the hippocampus, and the neurons can trigger each other directly. So his oldest, strongest, and most well-connected memories are not controlled by the hippocampus at all. In fact, damage to the hippocampus has the opposite effect on memory than what our ghola is experiencing. Rather than causing retrograde amnesia — the inability to recall past events — a damaged hippocampus causes anterograde amnesia — the inability to acquire new memories. Without the hippocampus, short-term memories can never be translated into long- term memories, and they are lost forever. (Drew Barrymore's character in the movie *50 First Dates* and Guy Pearce's character in *Memento* are two examples of people suffering from anterograde amnesia.)

Therefore, there is no simple physical explanation for a total memory block in the presence of familiar surroundings. Due to the distributed, associative nature of memory, there is no central switch to turn on and off, no single access point which can be hidden or encrypted. Even in cases where a person suffers from severe retrograde amnesia due to lesions on the brain, such as in Alzheimer's disease, early childhood memories generally remain intact.

Perhaps our ghola's memory loss is not due to a physical cause, but a psychological one. The trauma of dying is surely something he would want to block out. Although rare, there have been cases where people suffered from amnesia after being the victim of a violent crime, but the amnesia was associated with a confused state and only lasted a short time. What remains, then, is the complex and controversial subject of repressed memories, a concept which is often associated with childhood abuse. Can a memory be forgotten, either intentionally or subconsciously, and then be remembered later? According to the American Psychological Association, both phenomena do occur, but the mechanism is not well understood. The accuracy of recovered memories is questionable; as the brain reconstructs those memories from their component parts, the person's emotions and intent influence the result. Memories are not perfect recordings of events, but rather, impressions colored by our emotional state both at the time the memory was formed and at the time it is remembered. To further confuse matters, it is pos-

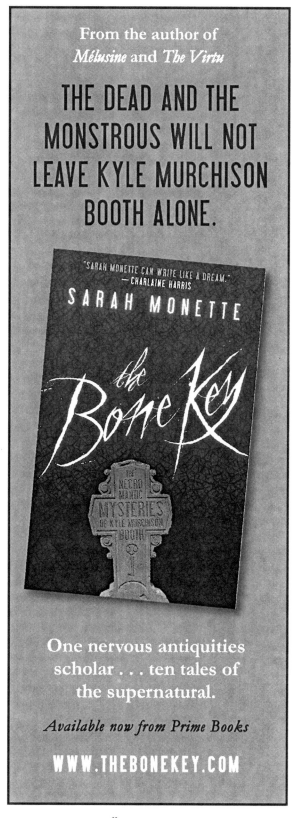

sible to construct false memories of events that never occurred.

Even though the concept of repressed memory is possible, it does not offer a satisfying explanation for the total amnesia our ghola is experiencing. In recorded cases of repressed and recovered memories, the phenomenon was localized to those memories associated with the traumatic event. Our ghola might not remember the circumstances of his death, but he would not suppress the memories of his entire life. So a psychological cause for his type of memory loss is no more likely than a physical one.

We have looked at the question of access, of how memories are recalled, and whether they could be hidden from the conscious mind until triggered by a single event or whether memories would return in bits and pieces over time. But this assumes that the intact memories are in the brain to begin with. The next question is of storage, of whether old memories would remain in the brain at all. The answer depends on the type of ghola, since there are two distinct methods for creating them.

In the time when *Dune Messiah* is set, the process of creating a ghola requires the entire body of the original person. A ghola is literally a corpse brought back to life. The dead flesh of Duncan Idaho is placed in a tank where his damaged tissue is repaired, and a person emerges, alive and conscious. This person has no memory of his past, but since he has the same brain, he still has the neural connections (the file system of memories) created by all of the events of his life. Time is the greatest limiting factor, since neural links weaken with disuse. If a lengthy period passes before our ghola is exposed to memory triggers, some of his past may be lost. But his oldest and strongest memories will remain for a long time, and chances are good that he will regain at least some of his former identity.

However, by the time *God Emperor of Dune* takes place, technological advances have changed the process dramatically. The many subsequent Idaho gholas we meet are not the same body repaired and resurrected again and again. They are grown from mere cells of the original person, and there can be more than one of them alive at any given time. In other words, they are clones. This has completely different implications for the possibility of memory retention, because it requires the transfer of memories from one body to another.

Like any clone, the adult gholas of Idaho are created using DNA as the means of coding information into the copy. What we know about the way memories are stored and retrieved in the brain involves neurological and chemical processes. There is no research to indicate that DNA stores specific memories, such as the events in a person's life. As our ghola grows in his tank, his DNA dictates the basic structure of his brain, but it does not stimulate the neural links which are key to the creation of memories. When he emerges, even though he is physically an adult, he is essentially a newborn person. Unfortunately, our Idaho clone has no inherent memories of the original Idaho's life.

What about transferring memories, downloading them from the original into a copy? Preserving the original brain indefinitely poses a problem, so it is more practical to download memories into a permanent storage system, such as a computer disk or flash drive, and upload the information into our ghola as needed. This system requires a working interface between the computer, the hippocampus, and other parts of the brain; but once that is achieved, it is a matter of sending signals through the brain and recording the position and strength of electrical impulses. This gives us a snapshot of the physical structure of Idaho's brain at the time of his death.

If we re-create this physical structure in our ghola's brain, is it the equivalent of uploading Idaho's memories? More than a question of physical and biochemical requirements and limitations, the heart of this query asks what makes us who we are.

What about transferring memories? Preserving the original brain indefinitely poses a problem.

If we can create physical clones of Idaho and give them all the same memories, experiences, and personality, then what makes any of them a unique individual? If the clones are perfect recreations, do terms like "original" and "copy" even have any meaning? The conclusion of these questions may have to wait until the first ghola emerges from his tank and speaks the answer.

Until cloning reaches that level of technology, our first type of ghola — the resurrected person — is the kind we will have to deal with. It is not just a subject for speculative fiction, but a topic for present-day discussion. As medical science advances, the moment when a person is beyond resuscitation gets pushed further and further back. Like Miracle Max in *The Princess Bride*, our doctors can determine if a person is just "mostly dead," and therefore partly alive. Machines can assist the heart and lungs to function until the body heals sufficiently to work on its own. Unfortunately, brain science has not yet advanced to the point where we can repair damaged brain cells, but that, too, is in our near future.

What will a real-life ghola, a person returned from brain death, be like? Will he remember any of his past, or will he be an entirely different person? In addition to impaired function, people who suffer from non-lethal brain damage often experience memory loss and even changes in personality. Repairing damaged cells would clearly return them to normal functioning, but what

about memories? A cell which sustained only partial damage would retain some of its neural connections. A newly grown brain cell would not, but if it were connected to undamaged cells, the links from those healthy cells might be sufficient for the memory connection. Memory recovery would depend greatly on the extent of initial damage, but the distributed nature of memory works to our benefit here, as it's unlikely that all areas associated with any particular memory would have been damaged.

When medical technology provides us with a method for repairing and regrowing brain cells, the diagnosis of brain death may cease to exist. Just as people who suffer cardiac arrest today can have their hearts restarted, people who suffer severe brain damage may someday have their brains jump-started, or otherwise brought back online. For the person returned to life in this manner — our real-life ghola — this means that he has a chance of regaining at least parts of his memories, especially if he is in familiar surroundings which will trigger memory associations.

And that's really all our ghola needs: a chance of recovery, the hope that his memories may trickle back and that he will regain some semblance of the person he was before. ✍

Csilla Csori is a programmer/analyst at the San Diego Supercomputer Center. She works primarily on database and software development for business applications, and she also moonlights as a gremlin hunter for her colleagues when their computer programs start acting funny. Recently, she released version 5.1 of ProBook grant application software she authored for the University of California. It's one of those pesky projects that started small but took on a life of its own, and now, like *Doctor Who*'s Cybermen, keeps coming back to demand more upgrades. She gained an interest in brain function in college, where she earned extra cash by volunteering for cognitive experiments at the National Institutes of Health.

REFERENCES

American Psychological Association. "Questions and Answers about Memories and Childhood Abuse." Learning and Memory. Aug. 1995. http://www.apa.org/topics/memories.html.

Dubuc, Bruno. "Memory and the Brain." The Brain From Top to Bottom. http://thebrain.mcgill.ca.

THE 85 Weirdest STORYTELLERS of the past 85 years

Readers wrote us in record numbers last autumn when

WeirdTalesMagazine.com asked you who, in *your* book, are the weirdest of the weird: the most influentially strange authors and artists and talespinners of all kinds to work their magic on the world in the 85 years since 1923, when *Weird Tales* was born.

WE ASKED THAT you not limit your suggestions to just fiction writers, and you responded enthusiastically, naming hordes of filmmakers, songwriters, cartoonists, and more. We took your ideas, added a few of our own, called some top fantasy professionals to put in their two cents, and then dove into the long and arduous process of winnowing the list down to a mere 85 names. What you now hold is a true distillation of the bizarre, from *Weird Tales* greats and surrealist visionaries to cutting-edge performance artists. In the end, 85 turned out to be a frustratingly small number; still, we'll stand by these honorees. They deserve their kudos, the freaks. We had so much fun re-experiencing the works of all these strange creative minds, we don't want it to end. After all, isn't introducing you to weird storytellers this magazine's whole mission? So we've set up a new page on WeirdTalesMagazine.com titled "Share Your Weird," where you can tell other readers about your favorites who *didn't* make this list. Let the weirdness flow!

THE 85 WEIRDEST

DOUGLAS ADAMS
(1952–2001)

He imagined a spaceship whose engine was powered by highly unlikely coincidences; a temporally bifurcated alien who convinced Leonardo to whip up six more copies of the *Mona Lisa*; and a bathrobe-clad hitchhiker who lamented to a friend, "You're turning into an infinite number of penguins." Across a multimedia array of novels, screenplays, and radio dramas, Adams was Grand Master of the absurd; we would weep over his premature evacuation from the planet, but we're still too busy laughing at all he wrote.

CHARLES ADDAMS
(1912–1988)

The TV series based on Charles Addams's life and odd creations brought weirdness to prime time, well before the term "goth" was but a bloody tear in a suburban teenager's angst-filled eye. But thanks to his 40-year career as a cartoonist for *The New Yorker*, not even the well-read and well-bred were safe from Addams's dark visions. Legend has it that one of his cartoons was used to gauge lunacy levels in asylum patients.

LAURIE ANDERSON
(1947–)

The angelic techno-poet of the 21st century, blown backward into the 20th by a wind called tomorrow. She conjures the earthbound skeletons of prehistoric whales, writes odes to Hansel and Gretel, and builds digital audio triggers into her violin bows, all the while enchanting us to re-envision the moments of our

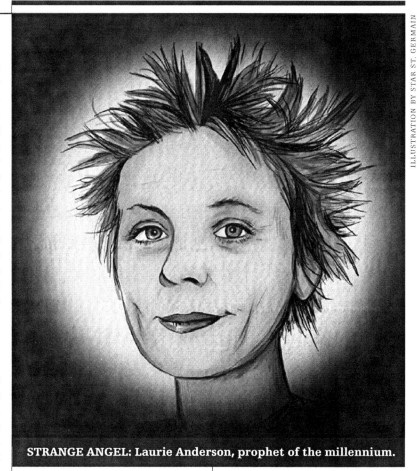

STRANGE ANGEL: Laurie Anderson, prophet of the millennium.

lives. There's no substitute for her ineffable stage performances, but listen anyway to *The Ugly One With the Jewels* and *Mister Heartbreak*, for starters.

J.G. BALLARD
(1930–)

Stuck on a traffic island, starving in a high-rise, loving in a mangled wreck of flesh and steel, and what's not to love? J.G. Ballard was raised in a prison camp and grew up to want to fuck Ronald Reagan. His vision is bleak and darkly realistic for all its weirdness. Though much of his fiction mines postmodern culture for satire, his roman a clef novel *Em-*

pire of the Sun offers something else: a boy trapped in a new world he doesn't know, after the old one was swept away. Hmm — maybe that's *not* so different.

NICK BANTOCK
(1949–)

Ominous. Foreboding. Reading Bantock's indescribable postcard-scrapbook-collage-novel *Griffin and Sabine* is like listening to the familiar rhythms of reality give way and break under the discordantly building cacophony in the Beatles' "A Day in the Life." Bantock brings two gifts to bear in his 15-year wave of groundbreaking literature: that talent for conjur-

ing the massing Fates, and the ability to weave a narrative through text to visual art and back again in a way most writers, illustrators, and cartoonists could never even conceive, much less pull off.

CLIVE BARKER
(1952–)

Clive Barker burst onto the horror scene in a way nobody else ever could: with a six-volume short-story collection, *The Books of Blood*. When other horror writers would turn away, Barker marched forward, showing off blood and intestines as if such grue were worthy of the Louvre. And his interest in the visual arts was always apparent: in the 1990s he wrote baroque fantasies, and his *The Abarat Quintet* is copiously illustrated with his own paintings. Barker's work in film also led to endless *Hellraiser* sequels, for better or for worse.

ART BELL
(1945–)

When Bell first broadcast paranormal talk on his syndicated radio show *Coast to Coast,* topics like UFO abductions and Bigfoot were thought the province largely of kooks who can't sleep at night. Bell proved the number of sleepless kooks in the United States reaches around 10 million on any given evening. Arguably, no one has done more to establish modern America's most prevalent myths, fantasies, and mysteries. From unexplained lights in the sky to shadow people lurking in our bedrooms, Bell has presided, shaman-like, over a national campfire of the strange.

BJÖRK
(1965–)

Those of us of a certain age and demeanor who recognized Björk Guðmundsdóttir's weird genius in her early days look back over her 20-year songwriting career with a certain smugness. That swan dress at the Oscars? We saw it coming! Silver-tongued, smart, and refreshingly in touch with her inner primitive, Björk uses the surreal to explore arguably the weirdest landscape of all: what it means to be human. But watch out for those giant rampaging teddy bears.

DAVID BOWIE
(1947–)

The first space alien rock star, Bowie has at various times portrayed a dehydrated space traveler, the Goblin King, a vampire, the Elephant Man, a spooky clown, a blue-skinned religious zealot, and Nikola Tesla. He brought rock & roll rebel attitude and artistic credibility to movie roles and lyrical ideas ("Look out your window, I can see his light / If we can sparkle he may land tonight") normally the province of geeks. He made weird cool.

WHERE OTHER HORROR WRITERS WOULD TURN AWAY, CLIVE BARKER MARCHED FORWARD.

RAY BRADBURY
(1920–)

With *The Illustrated Man* and *Something Wicked This Way Comes*, Bradbury confirmed forever the ineffable link between the fantasy crowd and the tattoo crowd. With *Fahrenheit 451*, he unsettled us all with the repugnant vision of firemen whose job is to set things on fire — the fact that said things were books just made it all the more horrific. His storytelling genius was cultivated in *Weird Tales*; it's gone on to profoundly affect humankind for generations thereafter.

MARGARET BRUNDAGE
(1900–1976)

At the very peak of *Weird Tales*'s classic run in the 1930s, the magazine's visceral appeal was arguably due as much to Brundage's lush cover paintings as to the incredible stories within. She showed us violently smoldering viragos bearing whips, decades before the boom in the gothic fetish craze; she showed us a "Bat-Girl" in black leather, years before the comics gave us such a character; she showed us art-deco skulls long before anyone ever imagined a heavy-metal album jacket.

WILLIAM S. BURROUGHS
(1914–1997)

Just another scion of the ruling class who shot his wife (and paint cans against canvases), did an enormous amount of drugs, appeared in both *On The Road* and a Nike commercial, declared that

language was a virus from outer space, taught at a city college, wrote novels by typing up pages and then cutting them to ribbons, outlived virtually everyone he knew, and retired to Kansas a fine old-money gentleman. You know — one of *those* types.

TIM BURTON
(1958–)
Skulls and curlicues collide in rickety Victorian mansions while pale outsider heroes encounter terrible yet cuddly beasties. Mired in death but bathed in amusement, Burton's films transform a singular gothic vision into something universal. While quite a few folks make strange movies, what sets him apart is that he makes strange *blockbusters*, from *Beetlejuice* to *Batman* to *Edward Scissorhands*. Sure, there's some Edward Gorey in there, but admit it, there's some Spielberg, too.

KATE BUSH
(1958–)
A touchstone of surrealism in modern pop music, Bush's narrative songs evince a fierce intellect and dream logic. She's well infused with the fantasy genre, addressing it directly in tracks like "Hammer Horror" and "Strange Phenomena." Her two magical-realist masterpieces, "The Ninth Wave" and "A Sky of Honey," address the nature of reality itself. And at her most wonderfully abstract, in "Suspended in Gaffa" or

"Sat in Your Lap," she uses powerful imagery, redolent of genre, getting into our heads like the best psychological writers.

OCTAVIA BUTLER
(1947–2006)
African-Americans who enjoy genre fiction are often labeled "weird" by their peers. But it's extraordinary authors like Butler who make the attraction to speculative literature seem a little less strange. Not only does she concoct a unique stew that's part fantasy, part horror, part science fiction, but stories like "Bloodchild" and novels like *Kindred* and *Fledgling* give us characters imbued with a distinct sense of Otherness that is, simultaneously, very familiar to any reader who's been labeled as "Other" in real life.

ANGELA CARTER
(1940–1992)
Next time you see one of Gregory Maguire's reworked faerie-tale novels on the shelves, take a moment to thank his predecessor, Angela Carter. The English author spent the '60s and '70s ripping apart old-fashioned concepts

DAVID CRONENBERG
IS A FILMIC BRAIN
SURGEON WHO'S
FALLEN IN LOVE
WITH THE TUMOR.

of fantasy and myth and putting them back together in stranger, more modern shapes, from the short-story collection *The Bloody Chamber* to the novel *The Magic Toyshop* to the werewolf movie *The Company of Wolves*.

NICK CAVE
(1957–)
His voice thunders at you with an undeniable allure. You will never, never understand Cave's songs on the first, second, or fifth listens, and you will sometimes question why you're still trying — and yet, you can't quite turn him off. He twists mythic language into an apocalyptic sound of fury and decadence, populating his world with killers, wanderers, and fallen angels. It's as if he could fall apart at any minute — but is haunted by his muses to continue his drunken stumble through your head.

LON CHANEY SR.
(1883–1930)
Chaney wasn't merely a great actor; he was the first person in Hollywood to truly understand the emotional force that could be wrought by enhancing a human performance — his own — with weird visual tricks. The "Man of a Thousand Faces" almost singlehandedly invented effects make-up; as the Hunchback of Notre Dame and the Phantom of the Opera, he made monsters sympathetic. Ray Bradbury said it best: "He . . . acted out our psyches. He somehow got into the shadows inside our bodies; he was able to nail down some of our secret fears and put them onscreen."

CREATOR-CHARACTER CONFLATIONS: Neil Gaiman as the dream king, Tim Burton as the emo Edwardian, and David Bowie as the fancy mystic lord.

CIRQUE DU SOLEIL
(founded 1984)

There aren't any other ensembles on this list — but really, how do you *not* credit this entire troupe of craziness, this symbiosis of human bodies that move like the digits of a single limb? Cirque du Soleil is singularly weird: who on Earth would use a circus as the storytelling medium for a discourse (*Alegria*) on humanity's struggle against tyranny? Who expresses surrealistic millennial dreaming (*Quidam*) with a posse of acrobats? Having seen them, who'd go back to dancing bears?

JOEL & ETHAN COEN
(1954– , 1957–)

Like the two genres to which so many of their films pay homage, it's the dialogue — snappy, rapid-fire, off-kilter — that strings together the dark screwball comedy noirs of the Coen Brothers. From Gabriel Byrne's smart talk in *Miller's Crossing* to the yah-sure-yer-darn-tootin of *Fargo*, the words take center stage. Well, words and White Russians and wood chippers and hair jelly and hula hoops and extortion and blackmail and kidnapping. Always with the kidnapping.

ALICE COOPER
(1948–)

With buckets of fake blood, electric chairs, boa constrictors, coffins and (of course!) guillotines, Alice Cooper put flesh on the bare bones of "shock rock." His traveling carnival may have horrified parents, but what looked like violent self-indulgence was a much-needed escape valve for a collective psyche that was ready to blow. Cooper gave voice to disaffected teens, form to nightmares nobody wanted to mention, and carved a bloody path for later acts to follow.

DAVID CRONENBERG
(1943–)

Like a brain surgeon who falls in love with the tumor, Cronenberg sets out to explore the mind and winds up exploding some heads – sometimes those of his characters (*Scanners*), usually those of his viewers. Each film is a sci-fi psychology dissertation written in hallucinatory gore, where men transform into flies (*The Fly*), grow vagina-like maws in their belly (*Videodrome*), or fornicate with the leg-scars of car accident victims (*Crash*). Foul but fascinating, and never without a purpose.

R. CRUMB
(1943–)

Sure, he's the comics king of '60s counterculture, but it's R. Crumb's trippy jaunts through his unfettered hindbrain that lands him firmly on our list. With devil girls, sexed up cats, exploding heads and more, Crumb's lowbrow art spills the contents of our animal minds and exposes what most of us are too inhibited to admit. With his landmark anthology *Weirdo*, Crumb unleashed a whole new cult of weird artists on the world.

ROALD DAHL
(1916–1990)

Lemony Snicket may be all the rage now, but it was Dahl who proved once and for all that kids need weird, too. Dahl's work knew no boundaries. We bet *Willy Wonka And The Chocolate Factory* still gives you nightmares; the Alfred Hitchcock Presents episode you've never been able to shake (say, the one with Steve McQueen and the lighter) is based on one of his short stories. There's even an erotic novel . . . but let's not go there.

SALVADOR DALI
(1904–1989)

When Dali expressed his support for Spanish dictator Francesco Franco, the other surrealist artists expelled him from their group. Dali's response: "I myself am surrealism." He had a point. From his paintings (melting pocketwatches) to his filmmaking (ants in the hole in my hand) to his theatrical public quirks (stole Velazquez's mustache), Dali may have defined weirdness for the 20th century more than any other single figure. Plus, "Visage of War" would have made an incredible *Weird Tales* cover.

SAMUEL R. DELANY
(1942–)

Delany writes science fiction for people who don't read science fiction, fantasy for readers interested in the '80s AIDS crisis, and pornography for those who may

THE SURREALIST: Salvador Dali defined his own world.

never have sex again. He's declared that reading is an act of writing and vice versa. Have we mentioned he's had thousands of lovers, rocks a Santa beard, and is seriously dyslexic? We're not being coy here; more than once someone has held up a copy of *Dhalgren* and asked us what it means. "Delany's dyslexic," we tell them, "to such an extent that the world's geography is inside

out." And then they begin to understand . . .

PHILIP K. DICK
(1928–1982)

Philip K. Dick was the surviving twin, and spent his entire life looking for something — fiction, drugs, love, fame, God — to make him whole again. The worlds of PKD's novels are shattered and detourned, ridiculous and sublime, proximately paranoid and yet sometimes ultimately redemptive. Dick died before his time; his vision of consumer spectacle, political thuggery, and the slim possibility of transcendence fit the late twentieth century perfectly, leading Hollywood to eagerly borrow, and screw up, any number of his great stories. Philip K. Dick saw such rat-bastardry coming.

STEVE DITKO
(1927–)

If this were an "85 Awesomest Storytellers" list, it would certainly showcase Stan Lee and Jack Kirby; since it's the "85 Weirdest," we've got to honor Steve Ditko. As an artist, he gave us Spider-Man's gallery of gruesome grotesques — the Green Goblin, Dr. Octopus, *et al.* — as well as the comics medium's greatest eldritch mystic, Dr. Strange, who faced a pantheon of Lovecraftian horrors. And let's not forget the philosophical weirdness of Ditko's most mysterious creation, The Question.

HARLAN ELLISON
(1934–)

Harlan Ellison decked guys in the Army, marched in Selma, had gang-fights with a hanky clenched between his teeth, fights for truth and justice, has never lost a lawsuit, can push his index fingers through a coconut thanks to his decades of typing, and is a friend to all and protector of young children and animals. Just ask him. Oh, and he's written, what, like, 2,000 short stories? "I Have No Mouth, and I Must Scream" is pretty good. "Shatterday" and "Jeffty is Five," too.

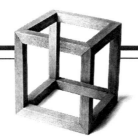

M.C. ESCHER
(1898–1972)

Let's face it: math isn't just confounding and painful for most of us word nerds — it's weird. Nobody captured the weirdness of math, time and space better, or rendered it more fantastically, than M.C. Escher. He took abstract notions of physical transformation and made them real places to see, touch and get lost in, complete with dimensionally transcendent staircases. But what lurks just beyond the walls? In Escher's worlds, what he *left out* is brain food of the weirdest kind.

VIRGIL FINLAY
(1914–1971)

Weird Tales's premier interior story illustrator in the '30s, Finlay influenced a generation of fantasy artists, who passed his influence along, unheralded, to the next generation. His forever unmatched scratchboard technique melded on the page with his

---

SAMUEL R. DELANY

IS SO DYSLEXIC

THAT THE WORLD'S

GEOGRAPHY TURNS

INSIDE OUT.

---

unerring ability to zero in on the most arresting angle in the most compelling scene in the most unforgettable narratives. Without Finlay, our monsters and heroes would never have reached the same extremes of unearthly beauty and unspeakable horror.

CHARLES FORT
(1874–1932)

While others have claimed more fame, Charles Fort could be the single most important person in the history of weird: an archivist who wrote books filled with strange occurrences culled from newspapers all over the world. Falls of fish, frogs, and blood. Visions of cities floating in the sky — not to mention spaceships soaring through them. But Fort was no paranormal apologist. He rejected all manner of dogma, from Catholics venerating the Virgin to closed-minded scientists who clearly didn't read the same newspapers he did.

NEIL GAIMAN
(1960–)

Among the great invented mythologies of the 20th century — the Cthulhu mythos, Middle-Earth, the *Star Wars* galaxy — must also be numbered Gaiman's spooky "Endless" cosmology of the landmark graphic novel series *The Sandman*. From there, Neil has gone on to become the most beloved weird storyteller of a generation, the Bradbury of the multimedia age, spinning tales like *American Gods, Anansi Boys,* and *Coraline*. To top it all off, he seems to have personally actualized the life of Jubal Harshaw. Sir, we salute you.

THE 85 WEIRDEST

TERRY GILLIAM
(1940–)

Gilliam's marvelous and surreal animations for Monty Python featured cut-up Victorian photos and bulbous drawings of giant feet, but his movies are twice as unhinged. Gilliam's jumbled films invite us into fantastical parallel dreamworlds where anything can happen and usually does, whether it includes time-traveling dwarves (*Time Bandits*), bureaucratic cities of documentation in triplicate (*Brazil*), an incomprehensible Dr. Gonzo (*Fear and Loathing in Las Vegas*), or Matt Damon with a goofy haircut (*The Brothers Grimm*).

EDWARD GOREY
(1925–2000)

Serial killers, doomed ballerinas, unlucky children and countless visions of Victorian and Edwardian terror, with just enough space to make a good mind turn bad. Flip through the pages of Edward Gorey's tales and you'll find the starts of things most awful and the ends of things even worse. But you'll never see the damage go down, thus leaving the things most horrifying to your imagination. The best weird artists do it on the inside.

GUNTHER VON HAGENS
(1945–)

He invented the science behind the original *Body Worlds* exhibit, which opens up preserved human bodies for educational display; he's also the final word on its striking aesthetics. While his competitors have been accused of using corpses from unethical sources, von Hagens's own exhibits hold documented proof of informed consent for the use of all the bodies. Which still leaves a healthy debate over the morality of showing dissected remains to paying onlookers — but, undeniably, it is powerful storytelling, and it is among the most profoundly weird.

JIM HENSON
(1936–1990)

Think Jim Henson and you think Muppets. Think again. His experimental filmmaking ranged from *Timescape* to *The Cube*. Though his interest in puppetry started as a way to get on television, he stayed with it because of the stories it allowed him to tell, and the weirdness from his film work shone maniacally through. Even with the Muppets. Like those dancing tubes with eyeballs in "Java." (*Wait* for it.) And hey, what exactly *is* Gonzo, anyway?

FRIDA KAHLO'S STARK SELF-PORTRAITS PUT THE INTERNAL ORGANS OUT WHERE WE CAN SEE THEM.

ROBERT E. HOWARD
(1906–1936)

For a guy who never travelled far from his home in Cross Plains, Texas, Howard had an uncanny ability to conjure believably authentic realms of the unearthly — as if he was tapped into Jung's archetypal consciousness, or drawing on his own past lives, or race memory. A world-builder of the highest order as well as the prince of adventure, Howard gave us stories and characters — from Conan to Solomon Kane — that tasted of truly weird flavors.

SHIRLEY JACKSON
(1916–1965)

When Jackson's story "The Lottery" was published, *The New Yorker* was assailed with hate mail — and with more than a few requests for the name of the town in which the annual stoning ritual takes place. People wanted to book snuff-tourism trips to next year's lottery. Jackson found the hell in other people and trotted it out for viewing; *The Haunting of Hill House*, which combines the fantastic and the domestic in a way few books have managed, is one of the most important horror novels of the twentieth century. Also, Jackson once ended a biographical sketch with the sentence, "I beat my kids regularly." P.S.: It's West Bennington, Vermont. See you next year!

FRANZ KAFKA
(1003–1024)

Somewhere, a parallel universe exists where Kafka survived his illness, agreed to have his stories translated into English, and became *Weird Tales*'s second su-

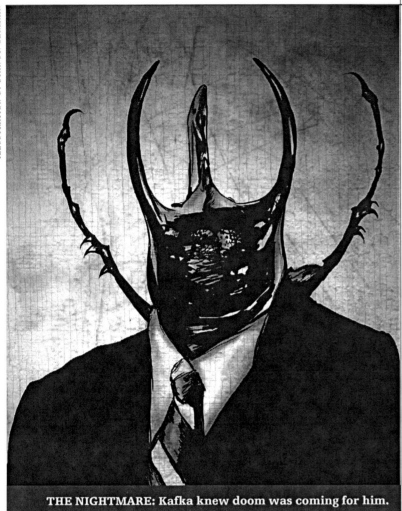

THE NIGHTMARE: Kafka knew doom was coming for him.

perstar alongside H.P. Lovecraft. As it is, he has to settle for posthumous recognition as one of the greatest authors of all time. In his works, a man turns into a giant cockroach; another starves himself to death for the amusement of onlookers; a third is held in endless thrall to a mysterious castle's bureaucracy; and a fourth, deemed a criminal, must have the judge's "sentence" carved into his flesh by a fiendish justice machine. But they are all the same man, and that man is Kafka.

FRIDA KAHLO
(1907–1954)

That brain you see hanging out in a ThinkGeek ad owes its existence to Frida Kahlo, whose stark self-portraits eliminated the boundaries of the body and put the four-chambered hearts, fetuses, and internal organs where we can see them. Frida's work is weird at its most personal. She wore her inner pain on the outside, beautifully rendered and impossible to ignore. Her paintings will make you flinch,

but just try to look away. Go on, we dare you.

ANDY KAUFMAN
(1949–1984)

Apparently, we were all in danger of never finding out what avant-garde comedy looked like. Quoth Andy Kaufman: "Here I come to save the day!" He didn't do stand-up, he did put-on, dragging both intentional and unknowing audiences into his bizarre narratives. (Okay, so some of those audience members were plants, but still.) From the Inter-Gender Wrestling Championship of the World to the spinning nervous breakdown of the crying Rotowhirl rider, Kaufman's pranks constituted sophisticatedly strange world-building.

STEPHEN KING
(1947–)

Look, everyone knows about Stephen King's weird fiction. So let's just move on and . . . consider the import of that fact. *Everyone knows about Stephen King's weird fiction.* Horror is supposedly the literature of the freak, the outsider, the weirdo — and, writing it, Stephen King became the most popular author in the world. So listen up, all you young freaks and geeks and rejects, we've got a message for you: Hang in there. Don't give up hope. Because, in the end, *you win.*

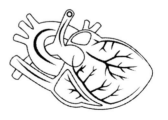

THE 85 WEIRDEST

STANLEY KUBRICK
(1928–1999)

Dairy-based Beethoven-fueled ultraviolent rape-a-thon? Acid trip space pregnancy? Thermonuclear protonazi doomsday over precious bodily fluids? Mask-clad Cirque du Scientologist orgy-palooza? Vietnammy soap-sock blanket party Pyle-on? Humberty Humberty cross-country lollipopping? Snow-induced secluded-hotel indoor unwelcome lumberjacking? Who is Spartacus? I am Spartacus. No, I am Spartacus. No, I am Spartacus.

MADELEINE L'ENGLE
(1918–2007)

Sure, Lovecraft and Doc Smith showed off their superperceptible four-dimensional beings first. An obvious enough concept, really, for anyone who'd read *Flatland* with a creative eye. But L'Engle portrayed an *angel* as that sort of alien monstrosity in a *children's book*, made it into a Christ figure, and had it fight off unspeakable cosmic horror all at the same time. *Bravissimi, maestra!* She introduced generations of preteens to the weird rehybridization of science fiction, horror, and myth — and tended lovingly to their souls along the way.

GARY LARSON
(1950–)

Countless imitators; only one Far Side. It was to single-panel humor cartoons what Weird Tales was to pulp fiction and The Twilight Zone was to television: a new brainspace where anything goes. Drawing upon Charles Addams's perfect sense of comic timing and his own encyclopedic

THE FAR-SEER: H.P. Lovecraft envisioned the colossal cosmos.

knowledge of zoological trivia, Larson gave us fourteen years worth of unexpected conceptual reversals — and has been immortalized by the scientific establishment for his efforts. Just Google the word "thagomizer."

TANITH LEE
(1947–)

Comic young-adult author, robust adventure fantasy novelist, gothic poetess: Tanith Lee has more writing personas than Sybil. But in her short fiction, much of it published in *Weird Tales*, all aspects of her various writing modes come together. Such pieces as "La Vampiresse," "Antonius Bequeathed," and "The Persecution Machine," with their death-defying mixture of prose poetry, genre trope reversals and ominous wit, could be written by no one else.

THOMAS LIGOTTI
(1953–)

He's often been called the latter-day counterpart to Poe or Lovecraft — and, as any songwriter who's ever been called "the next Bob Dylan" can attest, that kind of acclaim is a rough burden to bear. Ligotti does so with grace, horrifying and awe-striking his readers with very little in the way of the usual, gory, modern-horror tricks. His best-known story collection is called *The Nightmare Factory*, and considering the way his tales invade the consciousness en route to bizarre realities, that title sums it up quite nicely.

H.P. LOVECRAFT
(1890–1937)

From hoary arctic wastes to the inbred backwoods of New England, from tenebrous ocean depths to the forbidden realms beyond sleep, the imagination of Howard Phillips Lovecraft staggers the mind. His fiction repeatedly shattered the illusion that humankind sits at the center of the cosmos, and he influenced generations of storytellers and fans alike with his dreams and visions. Yet even with ancient terrors waiting to "press hideously upon our globe," his characters paused to give milk to a lonely cat. Considered Poe's successor in a line of horror greats, this solitary man would be astonished at his renown today.

DAVID LYNCH
(1946–)

Eraserhead's deformed baby. *Blue Velvet*'s severed ear. *Twin Peaks*'s nested mysteries. *The Elephant Man*'s freakshow redemption. Lynch has redefined modern cin-

ema by exploring the concepts of good and evil in his own, uniquely unsettling style. He challenges his viewers' perceptions of reality with the stories he tells; he's an iconoclast who refuses to compromise his strange and unique visions.

GABRIEL GARCIA MARQUEZ
(1927–)

Garcia Marquez's brand of writing, dubbed magic realism, serves as a lyrical reminder that in some cultures ghosts, spirits and unseen forces are just part of everyday life. The Colombian author's *One Hundred Years of Solitude* introduced the world to a romantic mysticism that could only be made convincing by prose of incomparable precision. Visiting with Marquez for the 468 pages it takes to finish *Solitude* should be a requirement for all those wishing to explore their own capacity for wonder.

DAVE MCKEAN
(1963–)

Few artists have so widened the possibilities for how to create graphical narratives than Dave McKean. And even fewer artists have the ability to pack so much storytelling into single images.

Yet McKean, known for his work illustrating writers ranging from Neil Gaiman to Jonathan Carroll to Tori Amos, possesses something rarer still: the uncanny ability to create images that spark an instant visceral reaction in the viewer. Powerful tools for a wielder of weird, these. We thank our lucky stars for his breathtaking body of work.

RAND & ROBYN MILLER
(1959– , 1966–)

When they designed, wrote, and produced the computer game *Myst*, the Miller brothers didn't just create a spooky, ethereal, otherworldly puzzle-solving experience reminiscent of a collaboration between Clark Ashton Smith and M.C. Escher. They also revolutionized videogame architecture, making first-person narrative the default gamer perspective. Another 85 years from now, literary historians will note that moment as the major paradigm shift on the road to truly interactive storytelling — weird or otherwise.

MICHAEL MOORCOCK
(1939–)

As editor of the British science fiction magazine *New Worlds* through the second half of the 1960s, Moorcock shepherded in a younger, weirder generation of authors more interested in straddling, crossing, and breaking literary boundaries than in defining them. And as creator of the dark, moody epic fantasy anti-hero Elric of Melniboné, Moorcock offered the new wave of readers a brooding, angst-ridden — dare we say emo? — mage-warrior-king whose fallibilities they could identify with.

ALAN MOORE
(1953–)

V. Watchmen. Promethea. Lost Girls. D.R. & Quinch. The Voice In The Fire. All those "Future Shocks" for *2000 AD* back in the '80s. The simple fact that he's held the title of Most Revered And Respected Creator In Comics (By Pros And Fans Alike), de facto, for over two decades. Need we say, uh, more? Okay: devotee of Glycon, a snake-deity-slash-sock-puppet that probably never existed. Performance art involving same. We rest our case.

CATHERINE L. MOORE
& HENRY KUTTNER
(1911–1987, 1915–1958)

The original *Weird Tales* power couple, the two authors met and married after Kuttner, not knowing C.L. Moore was a woman, wrote "him" a fan letter that was printed in "The Eyrie." Moore's heroine Jirel of Joiry was the first female protagonist in the sword-and-sorcery genre, not to mention the source for the classic *WT* cover "The Black God's Kiss." Kuttner & Moore's story "Mimsy Were the Borogoves" was just Hollywood-ized last year as *The Last Mimzy.*

GRANT MORRISON
(1960–)

We've met a few poseurs in our day; ergo, we assert: the comic book writer-rockstar-mage thing only works if you've got the skills to pay the bills. Enter Grant Morrison, who consistently transforms the surreal and non-linear into a crackling good story. It's tempting

to ask "How does he *do* that?" but we know that like the great magical texts, the secrets are hidden in plain sight. He could tell us, but then he'd have to kill us.

JOYCE CAROL OATES
(1938–)

Joyce Carol Oates publishes at will. In *The New Yorker* one month, in a mystery pulp or fantasy magazine the next. Novels, essays, poems, plays, reportage on boxing: she's written everything. In the future, there will be no Joyce Carol Oates scholars because nobody will have time to read it all. The gothic runs through her work like veins; Joyce is arguably the darkest and weirdest writer to be fully embraced by the mainstream since Poe himself, and even he only managed the trick posthumously. When she asks the question "Where are you going, where have you been?" the only answers are "Anywhere but here," and, "God, you don't want to know." But we do, and Oates tells us.

MERVYN PEAKE
(1911–1968)

A painter turned theatrical designer turned novelist, Peake's early success in the London art

OATES IS THE WEIRDEST WRITER EMBRACED BY THE MAINSTREAM SINCE POE HIMSELF.

world was interrupted by the horrors of World War II. After a nervous breakdown in 1942, he was discharged from the army and began to produce the works for which he'd be remembered: fantastic illustrations for Lewis Carroll, Samuel Taylor Coleridge, the Brothers Grimm and more; books of strange poetry starting with *Rhymes Without Reason*; and the weird fantasy cycle of the *Gormhengast* novels, which have inspired generations of readers and authors. (And The Cure.)

PENN & TELLER
(1955–, 1948–)

Stage magic has traditionally relied upon the audience submitting to the magician's illusive version of reality. Penn & Teller somehow succeed in breaking the illusion at the same time that they cultivate a deeper one, explaining the physics and statistics of the tricks even as they seem to overcome those earthly limitations. How does Teller make the rose bleed? How does Penn shoot a nail gun at his head and not die? And how has Teller refrained from speaking onstage for more than 25 years now?

BILL PLYMPTON
(1946–)

You have to love the artist who foists his particular brand of weirdness on an unsuspecting world in the sneakiest of ways. Take animator Bill Plympton, for instance. His brilliant celebrations of the body grotesque have sold you everything from tacos to operating systems. Infiltration via MTV before it sucked? Check. The 'toons even spawned a

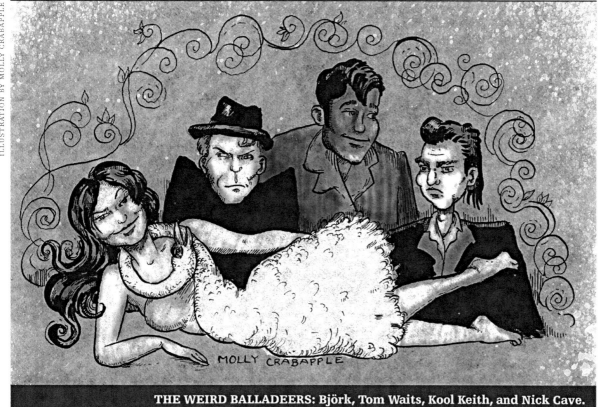

THE WEIRD BALLADEERS: Björk, Tom Waits, Kool Keith, and Nick Cave.

snarky comeback ("So's your face"). "More fun than nitrous oxide!" says a guy on the Internet. We couldn't agree more.

THOMAS PYNCHON
(1937–)

If not for space and time, everything would happen all at once. Maybe that's what happened to the reclusive Pynchon decades ago, as his books are chock-full of everything. Anarchism, *Boy's Own* fiction, Tesla, the aether, very very smart dogs, the Hollow Earth, and dirigibles — and that's just in his *latest* novel. More prized than read, Pynchon will likely go down in history famed as the guy who played himself on *The Simpsons* with a bag over his head.

ANNE RICE
(1941–)

She made vampires sexy again in the public imagination. In doing so, Rice pushed the door open a bit wider on the mainstreaming of goth culture, and she set the stage for the subsequent rise of Laurell K. Hamilton and, more indirectly, today's most popular new hybrid strange-fiction genre, the paranormal romance. Fanged exsanguination and dramatic fornication: a weird combination indeed.

ROD SERLING
(1924–1975)

For those baby boomers whose storytelling habits were formed in the big TV boom of the '50s and '60s, Rod Serling *equals* weird.

The Twilight Zone wasn't just the smartest, strangest, most soul-shaking television show ever seen, it was also the natural evolutionary successor to the original run of *Weird Tales*, picking up on the magazine's brain-twisting vibe and reshaping it to fit a form built of cameras, actors, and timely cuts and fades. Every lover of the weird should watch every episode of the classic Serling-helmed *Zone* — no exceptions. Just do it.

DR. SEUSS
(1904–1991)

Our "same planet, different worlds" award for weirdness must go to Theodor Seuss Geisel. His tales charm all but the grumpiest readers, but beneath those happy faces, bright colors and wacky inventions lay social commentary torn straight from the hundreds of cartoons he drew for the WWII leftist newspaper *PM*. Still unconvinced? Seuss taught kids to read and brought anapestic tetrameter to the masses. If that's not weird, we're not sure what is.

ALICE SHELDON, a.k.a. JAMES TIPTREE JR.
(1915–1987)

Imagine if Hemingway, master explorer of the male psyche, was really a woman writing under a pseudonym. As James Tiptree, Jr., Sheldon's muscular, intellectual science fiction turned gender in genre on its head in the late '60s, exploring taboo themes fearlessly. Tiptree's relentless and unforgiving worldview were famously considered quintessential masculine writing. When the hoax was exposed, the author carried on under the byline of Raccoona Sheldon, and the fiction was no less dazzlingly dark.

CHUCK SHEPHERD
(1946–)

Not only is 2008 the 85th anniversary of *Weird Tales*, it's the 20th anniversary of Shepherd's syndicated newspaper column, "News of the Weird." What started in the *Washington City Paper* as just another alt-newsweekly snarkfest turned into the world's premier tabulator of real people doing bizarre things. A million bloggers have emulated Shepherd's format, but he was there first, chronicling the depths of surreality to which actual reality can sink.

CLARK ASHTON SMITH
(1893–1961)

Clark Ashton Smith was the only one of his contemporaries that H.P. Lovecraft regarded with awe, writing that "In sheer daemonic strangeness and fertility of conception, [he] is perhaps unexcelled by any other writer dead or living." In the space of five years, Smith gifted the world with just over one hundred ultra-imaginative tales of "inconceivable fear and unimaginable love." (And that's not counting all the poems!) He managed to depict cosmic outsideness tinged with human frailty.

STEPHEN SONDHEIM
(1930–)

The stage musical tends to be a cozy, familiar, comforting form. Not in Sondheim's hands. *Into the Woods* put every classic Grimm faerie tale into a food processor and spit them all out bloodied and abused. *Sweeney Todd* brought the English language's most fiendish serial killer to colorful, dancing, singing life. And *Assassins* is a musical circus revue of would-be presidential hitmen. Take that, Ziegfeld and Webber!

REV. IVAN STANG
(1953–)

The prophet of the invertedly iconoclastic and surprisingly enduring Church of the SubGenius — a postmodern movement of "Schizophreniatrics, Morealism, Sarcastrophy, Cynisacreligion" — is also, presumably, its founder, despite his insistence that it was started in 1953 by a pipe-smoking clip-art face named "Bob." Stang's elaborately bizarre tracts have inspired the likes of Devo, Pee-Wee Herman, and John Shirley — not to mention declaring as holidays the Feast of St. Cthulhu (Nov. 10) and the Martyrdom of St. Kenny (Dec. 9).

OSAMU TEZUKA
(1928–1989)

Walt Disney, Hanna & Barbera, and Alex Toth aren't on this list — but if they had all merged into one, single, ultra-historic, gestalt super-cartoonist? Now that would be weird. And that's Osamu Tezuka. The father of Japanese anime, Tezuka effortlessly danced back and forth over the boundaries between storytelling styles and genres, remixing them as he went, from the all-ages android allegory of *Astro Boy* to the more mature mythic immortality quest of *Phoenix* to the demonic imagery of *Dororo*.

HUNTER S. THOMPSON
(1937–2005)

The creator of "Gonzo" journalism, Hunter S. Thompson showed us how the sausage of politics and culture is made. When he reported in 1972 that there were rumors that Presidential candidate Edmund Muskie was addicted to the drug Ibogaine, he also declared that he started those rumors in the first place, thus making him the most ethical journalist in the incestuous swamp on which he was reporting. A consummate outsider who hungered for insider status, Thompson was a fringe figure who parlayed a genius with words and an amazing ability to metabolize horse tranquilizers into a scruffy credibility. Unfortunately, he couldn't stay ahead of the Bad Craziness curve forever, and the world got too strange for even him to report on.

KOOL KEITH THORNTON (1964–)

Half of Kool Keith's weird art comes from his sophisticated, horror- and science-fiction-themed hip-hop recordings, starting with the pioneering acid-rap album *Dr. Octagonecologyst*. The other half comes from the multifold tangle of alternate identities he's created to perform said songcraft. Dr. Octagon becomes Dr. Dooom [sic] becomes Black Elvis becomes The Fourth Horseman — and through it all, Thornton threads an ever-evolving storyline of mad science and mad beats.

KURT VONNEGUT (1922–2007)

He made us weep for humanity's Earthbound woes by unsticking Billy Pilgrim in time and letting him be abducted by Tralfamadorians. He showed us what voodoo-inspired government-sponsored weapons research looks like on the road to unintentional Armageddon. He gave us secret paintings, underwater temptresses, and Fed-

ILLUSTRATION BY STAR ST. GERMAIN

PUNCTUATING HIS OPINIONS: Kurt Vonnegut has an asterisk.

eral Ethical Suicide Parlors. His book *Slaughterhouse-Five* was honored on *Time* magazine's "100 Best English-Language Novels" list, and his book *Breakfast of Champions* includes a drawing of his own anus. So it goes.

TOM WAITS (1949–)

Waits has built his oeuvre singing odd stories of life on the road, chronicling hobo existence, underground Americana, and downright weird folks through sordid lyrics and abrasive melodies. Every album is a singular experience, a collection of unique tales told in musical notes and gravel-throated vocals. His latest album, *Orphans: Brawlers, Bawlers, and Bastards* is a tour de force through the weird world of his creativity.

ALICE WALKER (1944–)

An odd name to see on this list? Perhaps — but here's the thing: While Walker is renowned for her realistic fiction (*The Color Purple, Meridian*), an examination of her career's trajectory shows that her earthly stories set the stage and built the audience for the author to deliver her later, weirder ones. *The Temple of My Familiar*, which uses myth and fable to weave together the world's dark realities; the children's fantasia *Finding the Green Stone* — these works fired the imaginations of readers who'd never heard the phrase "speculative literature."

KARA WALKER
(1969–)

Kara Walker summons ghosts. They are the opposite of most ghosts you're accustomed to. Instead of spectral white shades floating in the darkness of night, Walker's acclaimed art installations present void-black human figures against a background of white emptiness: life-sized silhouettes of the long-deceased, captured in their most obscene, degrading moments of abuse and torment. The topic is racial injustice; the aesthetic is weird through and through.

ANDY WARHOL
(1928–1987)

We haven't found any evidence that Warhol ever met fellow 85er Philip K. Dick, but they certainly should have recognized one another's reflections. While Dick was forecasting the future's fractured mindscape, Warhol was beta-testing the pre-release version he'd hacked together in his Factory for art. The experiments he conducted there — upon still and sequential images, upon the interplay between life and media,

POP WEIRD: Andy Warhol layered sincerity upon irony.

ILLUSTRATION BY STAR ST GERMAIN

even upon *Dracula* and *Frankenstein* — rarely failed to pinpoint a nexus of the strange and the strangely banal.

SYLVIA TOWNSEND WARNER
(1893–1978)

One of the most oddly overlooked giants of weird fantasy, Warner's epic literary life stretches from the 1927 novel *Mr. Fortune's Maggot* to the 1977 collection *Kingdoms of Elfin*. Within that half-century came volumes of poetry, a classic Arthurian biography — and yet Warner's most enduring tale remains her very first novel, 1926's *Lolly Willowes*, in which a gentle woman rebels against a life of conformity by turning to witchcraft. Warner was ahead of her time.

JOHN WATERS
(1946–)

They may have remade *Hairspray*, but nobody will ever remake Waters' hilariously outrageous early stuff. These ironic exercises in extremely bad taste feature an obese drag queen eating dog crap (*Pink Flamingos*) and a post-surgery drag king hacking off his new penis, after which, needless to say, it is eaten by a passing dog (*Desperate Living*). And that's just for starters.

ROGER WATERS
(1944–)

That *sound*. That unending subbass thrum, vibrating through bones and brain and soul as Pink Floyd's song "Welcome to the Machine" opens. It is the sound of dread, the sound of not-too-distant madness inescapably approaching; it may well be the sound of Cthulhu's first eyelid opening. Then there is the hallucinatory experience that is the film version of *The Wall*, brain-eating worms and all. And then there's the fact that Waters made the band perform *The Wall* live from behind an *actual wall*. Freak-o . . .

WIM WENDERS
(1945–)

The atmospheric film *Wings of Desire* saw two angels wander the streets of Berlin, contemplating love, suicide, and Peter Falk. Then writer-director Wenders brought us *Until the End of the World*, the story of a falling nuclear satellite intersecting with the saga of a genius who can record human dreams. In *The End of Violence*, Edward Hopper's painting "Nighthawks" comes to moving, breathing life while a surveillance agent probes Los Angeles from the digital ether. The soul and the machine: Wenders knows both well.

THORNTON WILDER
(1897–1975)

In *Our Town*, Wilder lulled audiences into a false sense of apple-pie warm-and-fuzzies before veering off into a third act of death, ghosts, time travel and lamentations. In *The Bridge of San Luis Rey*, he drew the ley lines of interconnectedness through, between, and beyond the victims of a single moment of violent tragedy. And in *The Skin of Our Teeth*, he stretched one family across the space-time continuum from the Ice Age to 1940s Atlantic City to an apocalyptic war. The first two works shaped whole genres; the third is merely the greatest play of the century.

ROBERT ANTON WILSON
(1932–"2007")

Robert Anton Wilson was killed and replaced with a clone in the mid-1980s. Prior to his assassination, Wilson worked at *Playboy*; the secret information he found in reader correspondence formed the basis for his political novels *The Illuminatus! Trilogy*, written with Robert Shea. After revealing the simple fact that "National Security is the chief cause of national insecurity," Wilson was liquidated for reasons of national security. The cloned Wilson revealed that it was a clone to the public and was widely disbelieved; its warranty was prematurely expired on January 11, 2007.

WARREN ZEVON
(1947–2003)

Never even mind his biggest radio hit, the classic lycanthropic dance tune "Werewolves of London" — Zevon's songwriting oeuvre conjures a twisted universe where upwardly mobile zoo gorillas steal the lives of urban yuppies, the ghosts of murdered mercenaries stalk their old battlefields, and Earth itself fades to the entropic assault of chemical pollution while love blooms in the mall. Unsettling, surreal, and wickedly funny, Zevon died too soon, but his specter haunts rock & roll forever. ❧

Portraits by Star St. Germain. **Group caricatures** by Molly Crabapple. **Text** by Michael Batz, K. Tempest Bradford, Scott Connors, John R. Fultz, Elizabeth Genco, Craig Gidney, Mary Robinette Kowal, Matt Kressel, Nick Mamatas, Stephen H. Segal, Paul Tabachneck, and Steve Volk.

The Heart of Ice

BY TANITH LEE

IN WHICH HOT
EMOTION LEADS
TO MANY VERY
COLD THINGS

O H, THE ICE MAIDEN. He has been hearing of her since he can remember. Her dark and coiling hair with the gleam in it of blue-green coal, her jewelry of icicles, her eyes that are like frost on lapis lazuli. But her skin is warm, the colour of honey, which from a distance can make her for an instant seem almost human. She dresses in the pale furs of winter beasts which she charms from their backs, leaving them naked but for shivery flesh and bones in the bitter cold. And then she clothes them instead in ice and they become ice-creatures, and her servants.

Nirsen worked in the town. He had been apprenticed at five years of age to the Kuldhoddr, who with his boys bought the unwanted things of the townspeople and hauled them to his yard, where they were sorted and turned into other things — such as broken pots into filling for wall-building, or spoilt furniture into firewood, or old garments into rags — and resold. Nirsen was by now nineteen and this was all the life he knew, the town life of buying, sorting, smashing, chopping, tearing, and so on. He knew the shabby house of the Kuldhoddr, where he slept in a shed off the yard with the other once-boy, now twenty, Jert. This one did not like Nirsen, had bullied him when they were children, and currently sneered and played adult tricks on him. The Kuldhoddr was himself a villain, and his wife a sow. The house, the work, the bad food, the winding narrow self-centred town, the whole of existence were foul to Nirsen. Even the red-cheeked girls that Jert leered after did not entice him.

Yet beyond the town lay the fields that in summer turned yellow, and in the winter black then white. Out there too lay the stretches of the river that were not choked with muck, but flowed in summer like ale with strawberry fish in themselves it, and in winter froze themselves to pewter. Beyond, the great forest began, ash and birch and pine, and this ran all the way to the distant mountains, far as outer space. And the summer woods were green and the mountains lavender, but in winter both were white and the home of the Ice Maiden.

Where had he heard of her first? Nirsen could not recall, but he must have been a baby then, for it was before the Kuldhoddr bought him (one more thrown-out thing) and clobbered and smashed and thrashed him into a new, more useful article.

Even in the house of the Kuldhoddr, however, the Ice Maiden was spoken of, as a sort of curse — "May the Ysenmaddn take him and hang his skin on her trees!" Or whispered to by the wife as she stirred her filthy soups on the fire: "Don't you be harming my poor fingers, Lady Ice." For it was a fact the wife had had a finger bitten off by the frost one year, and everyone knew the Ice Maiden made the frost. It spun from her blue eyes and dropped from her mouth in her cold sweet breath, but changed to needles and knives in the air. It would paint the round windows prettily over, but if ever the

Ysenmaddn caught you out of doors and you could not get away, she kissed you and froze you, and then her frost filmed over your eyes like the windows and blinded or crippled, or you were dead.

Amulets were put up to placate her on half the houses, though it was supposedly a Godly town. These were in the form of little man dolls all in a white spindly mummy-wrapping, like the rime, or they were polished awls, or the long teeth of wolves or foxes or the skull of a white cat or a white owl. She liked white animals best (if she took their coats she made them new ice ones that were whiter.)

Offerings, such as dead hares and round cakes were slung by the forest's edges or along the inner tracks, by hunters and wood-cutters. But few ventured into the trees once snow was down.

And now it was.

The russet town was muddy white, but the fields and forests and the mountains and the sky were whiter, like scrubbed china. And as they ran from smoky hot brazier to brazier at the corners of the streets, the children sang this rhyme:

Leave on our hands, Queen of Ice.
Leave on our feet, Queen of Ice.
Leave on our noses, Queen of Ice.
Yet take it all and leave us life —
Such a small price, such a small price.

One freezing night Nirsen went to the tavern on Killfox Street and drank a couple of cups. He spoke to no one, liking no one. As for the tavern girls he turned his face away, and then they called him names — High Nose, Little Cockeral. He had never been with any of them. They loathed him like an alien, as if he had two horns growing out of his head. But the drink was comforting.

When he got back he entered the yard beside the Kuldhoddr's house. The Kuldhoddr was away at the other end of the town, bargaining and drinking with some

merchants. In the kitchen window smeared a tiny orange chink of light. Nirsen rapped softly on the door. The idea of the fire's embers appealed before he slunk to the shed.

When no one answered he slipped the latch.

Inside the kitchen, ah now. The sow wife was riding with Jert, and each of them grunted and moaned in pleasure. Nirsen felt sick, for he hated them both as they him, yet too they broke his heart, poor things, trying to find joy in the glacial heart of winter and unkindness. He would have gone away and said nothing.

But Jert on some sudden impulse turned from his work and learned he and the wife had been seen.

He shambled up, pulling his clothes together, his face already a clenched fist.

"You," was all he said. But the single word was a malediction.

Then he sprang and Nirsen fell back on the stone floor under the weight of him.

There they struggled, and in the background the dishevelled, nine-fingered woman babbled, and then she grew utterly quiet and a shadow splayed over the fighters which smelled of ale and said, "What's this?"

Both Jert and Nirsen were bloody but Nirsen had perhaps had the worst of it. He was lighter, and anyway Jert was accustomed to fighting.

It was Jert who rose and, with the wife whimpering behind him, he exclaimed, "She screamed out so I come running. He was at her, had her down, and Mrs trying to beat him off and calling for you. Hadn't I come in he'd have done her, your wife."

Nirsen lay stupidly marvelling at Jert's ingenuity, and heard the woman say, "It's true. Ruined I'd have been, you off at your business. But Jert was our friend and saved me."

After which the Kuldhoddr leaned right the way down to the kitchen floor, and he lifted Nirsen up from it with a curious sort of tenderness, all the time peering into his face. The Kuldhoddr did not ask what Nirsen had to say on any of this. Nor did the Kuldhoddr pass any comment. About a minute after he slammed his fist twice into Nirsen, at the heart and at the jaw, and everything collapsed in a storm of black pain and roaring.

WHEN HE CAME to, Nirsen did not know immediately where he was. He had been somewhere similar during the summer, for occasionally in the long fine evenings he would walk out to the edges of the fields, sit on the grass of the pasture and watch the fringes of the forest, where rabbits and squirrels and birds darted in the last westered sunlight. But he had never been out here in winter. Few ever were. It was another country now.

And in the land of full winter, here he lay, and much closer to the wood indeed. Over his very head arched the first deep ranks of the trees, the ash and birch with thick foliage of white snow, and the tall pines and firs beyond, crystallized. Glass beads and pipes and strands of ice had spun all the trees together too. The forest hung now inside the web of some giant ice-spider. Darkness was coming, the sky cold lead, and a thin wind whistled through the forest's avenues.

Nirsen understood well enough what had happened while he was helpless. He had been cast out for his supposed crime of attempted rape. There were stories of such punishments as this. No one would have minded. Why harbour the wicked when the winter would see to him?

He found they had bound his hands and his feet in case he should wake and struggle with them, but he had not woken till now. He shifted round to see and one of the cords on his wrists snapped. His hands were not well tied, both Jert and the Kuldhoddr would have been drunk. Besides, the cold made such cheap rope brittle.

Quite soon Nirsen was free. Then he stood up and looked back from the forest towards the town.

How small and murky it was under its huddle of dirty snow and smokes. The bleak fields between, white as starched table-cloths in rich houses, showed only the trample of the two men's feet and the snake-track of Nirsen's body as they had dragged him.

Without warning Nirsen found he had fallen down again. It came to him how hurt he was, also that he must have lain here most of one night and a day unconscious, for it had been before midnight when he reached the yard and now a second night was just starting.

Surely he should be dead? Perhaps he was. His face ached and gnawed where it was struck and his heart felt sometimes as if it stumbled. His hands were almost numb, the fingers too pale, threatening the awful frostbite. He could feel nothing of his feet — partly the reason he fell. He wore his outdoor clothes but they were not of course of the best. His head was uncovered.

He sat on the white earth under the white trees and the web of the giant spider, and knew if not yet dead still shortly he must be. But he could not go back to the town. Only the forest seemed to offer any shelter. At least it was a better place to perish, cleaner and far more beautiful.

Once again he rose and stamped about until, though no feeling came, yet his balance re-established. Presently he moved forward in among the trees.

Night arrived. The forest sank to dark silver.

AS HE TRUDGED drearily onward, Nirsen heard the sound of darkness begin, the night chorus of owls and foxes, and once maybe a wolf, for in such weather wolf packs might well run this way. But there were stranger sounds also. He started to hear them and put them down to the sudden cracks of branches broken under the snow's weight; frozen streams that had fissured in the greater tepidity of day and now were sealing shut again; the wind, breath-

ing. But really he knew what they were.

He was entering the kingdom of the Ice Maiden.

Those splinterings were the noise of her mirrors smashing; those murmurs like sealing ice were the resonance of draperies drifting over floors of snow. The clink and hush of the wind was an echo of some music played for her. And *there!* That sheer light platinum note — oh, *that* was the Maiden's laughter. Something had amused her tonight. Maybe it was the thought of one more lost outcast stumbling through her world, with Death treading close behind.

Nirsen continued until he could go no further. He was aware that to stop now meant that he must stop living. But finally another footstep became impossible. He took it but never moved. So then he slid down and leaned against the silver stalk of a tree, and watched the forest glowing though no moon had risen, shining from its own deathly whiteness, so the black sky changed to tin threaded with the blue sequins of stars.

But the blue stars were the eyes of the Ysenmaddn. Pitilessly they gazed at him, and yet it was not truly pitiless. How could one like she comprehend that his wretched little existence had been precious to him, or that to lose it was, for him, his greatest tragedy? *Go to sleep*, he imagined that she whispered through the snow-leaves. *Go to sleep like a good child.* And only a slight impatient indifference was in her voice. Nothing sinister or cruel. For she had no heart to be heartless with, the Ice Maiden.

AN ANIMAL CROUCHED over him. This now was what woke him up. He took it for a wolf — perhaps the very beast he had heard earlier in the night. But then his sore eyes, caked with rime, widened and Nirsen saw it was one of *her* creatures.

It was a wolf of ice.

Whiter than any whiteness of the woods, it gleamed with the sleek pure sheen of steel. Every tuft of its pelt was *sculpted*

from ice. Its mask-like face was ice, yet had both expression and potential ferocity, and the profound, solemn wolfish eyes gazed through, the unexpected colour of gold. And then it licked out across its glacial meltless mouth with a living tongue, and he saw its ivory teeth — all that, inside the skin of ice the Ysenmaddn had given it.

The beast will kill me, he thought. He woodenly composed himself, half dead as already he must be, to endure this finish as best he could.

But the wolf only touched his cheek with its rock-hard freeze of muzzle, then raised its head. The howl raked the forest, the sky. The stars shook but did not fall.

Then the others drew near. Nirsen, in his deathly trance, watched. Not for an instant did he reckon he dreamed any of this. There were the two ermines, now ice-clad, their black markings caught perfect in the white slippery glitter of their coats. There was the albino bear, its thick fur all ice and ruffling and combing back and forth as it moved. Some ice-foxes came and played savagely before him as if to demonstrate that even when nipped or scratched their icy overlay was not disturbed. Ice-rats bustled from between the claws of tree roots and stared with chestnut eyes. Last the white owl floated down, silent as a single white feather, and settled on his boot, regarding him from its own round eyes which, in that moment, reminded him oddly of the pale lemon faces of two clocks that showed time had ceased.

Maybe he lapsed; it was like sleep but was it only death? Yet then once more he was woken and he was being dragged again, as his two human enemies had dragged him from the town. Now it was the wolf and the bear that pulled him, their taloned nails, their teeth, fastened in his clothing. The foxes pushed at him. The rats ran by and across him like overseers, and the ermines padded like bodyguards at his sides. The owl flew above them. He observed its metallic solidity passing along weightless just below the web of white quartz branches. Its

wings hypnotized him: every feather chiseled from ice —

Nirsen sensed the earth under his body turning toward morning. He did not grasp what that could be, for he had had no education and did not know it was the earth which turned, as he had never seen that, only the sun rising or going down.

The bear it was who alone hauled him the last distance, bundling him across huge roots that slammed his spine like hammers, so this beating seemed far more brutal than anything Jert or the Kuldhoddr had done to him.

By then a sort of mist or smoke was lifting from the ground. It was like breath on a mirror, and through it the embroidered boughs of the great trees had been unstitched. A view opened. A lake spread before him. It was frozen to alabaster, save now and then you saw thinner places that dully glimmed. In the middle of the lake something rose up.

The bear dropped Nirsen. From behind, the wolf now was pushing at him. He found he had sat up.

The mist rippled and somewhere near a flower-pink stain was seeping: dawn sharpened the scene of the frozen lake, and so Nirsen saw the palace of the Ice Maiden standing at the lake's centre.

It was like a vast crystal goblet, and filled with a fizzing champagne light.

He thought, flatly, *Well, I have seen it. It exists. Hadn't I come here I should have missed it. At least this I've done.*

But then he glimpsed the sled of ice that had appeared on the lid of the lake, and how by itself it glided to the shore. The bear with a grumbling curdle of a growl roll-ed him over on to the sled. How cold the sled was, far colder than the snow. It seared him and he did not care. He would be dead before he reached the palace. Good, good, that was good.

THERE ARE CHIMES all through the house of the Ice Maiden. They depend from all the high, high walls under the wide sky, for here there is no roof. The snow never falls here, or

if it does it becomes simply part of everything else — a curtain, a screen, a mosaic. But the chimes chime with a fearful tinsel deliciousness. It is like sucking raw icing-sugar to hear them. They please, but they *sting*.

There are no windows. The entire edifice is transparent. Any who are inside can always see out. Yet from the outside nothing can be seen within but for the lumination of the enormous chandeliers. These stretch from the roofless spaces above until they reach the floors that are perhaps a quarter of a mile below. Prisms and slender opal pillars comprise the chandeliers, and they convey a candleshine that has no candles, nor, night or day, do they go out.

These floors of the Ice Maiden are laid with circular tiles, each of which is the top of a human skull, remorselessly waxed and rubbed so slim it has become impervious and will magically carry any weight. Who — what — then rubbed them? The refining winter wind, who is never afraid of the prolonged harsh work of brooming, beating, scouring.

There are ice cisterns set in the bone floors where fish, scaled in ice, swim and frisk over little pebbles like polished zircons, which possibly they are.

Then the Ice Maiden comes in.

She is attended by invisible or partly visible beings that are wind-spirits, frothy flurries of light snow, or beasts which have died and become themselves bones, but that still want to remain with her nevertheless.

She is as they say she is. Her skin is like honey, and from a reasonable way off she looks almost like a young mortal woman. Her hair is wavy and darkest blue — that might also seem pale black until you look carefully. She is crowned with a diadem of ice. Her garments are white fur. But her ears are like the ears of no human thing, more dainty, *pointed*, and she wears in them jewels of ice.

Her eyes. Her eyes define and defy everything ever said of them. You believe they may be dark until she looks at you.

Then they are blue as lapis, just as all the legends tell, lapis lazuli behind sparkled casements of frost. And they are terrible. For they have no wickedness in them and know no malignity and no wish to deliver pain. But they know nothing of need, nothing of empathy, nothing of the merest momentary kindness, nothing like that. And they never will.

Nirsen has stood up on the floor of impervious skulls. Thinking he is dead now he feels strong and not unwell.

He bows to the Ice Maiden because he knows one must, with royalty, or they will be angry. But too he senses she feels no anger either. To bow is foolish, but he does.

She says nothing to him. Although he has been shown her eyes, if she even really glances at him he is unsure.

Does she credit he is here? Will it matter to her?

A boar that is made of bones nuzzles at her hand. She does nothing, does not respond, yet a mild flame runs through the skeleton of the beast. It is plainly happy and canters round and about, and all its vertebrae twinkle. Each of the others wants to touch her then, and she seems to allow this, for it happens.

Nirsen though would never dare attempt it.

He stands there and stares and listens to the chimes. Is he now her slave? He supposes she does not require slaves, requires nothing. Even the furs she steals he now suspects are not stolen. Probably they spontaneously fly off to adorn her and then she sighs her fragrant breath and never notices the animals reclad in living ice.

However, since she is there looking at him — or not — and being himself human and a man, in the end he speaks.

"What am I to do, Lady?"

The Ice Maiden answers.

Nirsen lowers his head.

Of course she has replied in her own language. He tries at once to retain and analyse what the words were like. Mostly, he thinks, like the sound of the chimes. He could not and does not understand and doubts he will ever have the means to learn.

Again he speaks. "I'm lost then."

At this, strangely, the faintest glint of something crosses through her gem-stone eyes. But she has no humour, he believes, as no cruelty or compassion. Surely, despite his notion in the forest, she could not be amused.

Besides anyway, this is when she moves on over the long floor between the stalagmite-stalactite chandeliers, her crowd of insubstantial attendants furling round her like a fog. She vanishes somewhere amid the curtains of frost.

Just then Nirsen realizes he has regained total feeling in his feet and hands and ears. His throat is moist and does not hurt, the ache in his face has gone. He has, apparently, eaten and drunk, and he is warm. This must be because he is dead, then. But no. Strong and bravely now his heart is beating in his chest.

He goes to the curving side of the glass of the palace and stares out. He sees the long lake and the tangle of the archetypal forest all around. The sky is golden as the eyes of the ice-wolf. When he puts one finger to the palace glass it gives off a delicate note, as a refined goblet would if tapped, say, with a priceless ring.

There is no way out — or in, that he can detect.

If he is a prisoner he doubts, but nor does he have liberty. He checks every so often to be sure he has not become all bones, or is sheathed in ice, like the animals here. But he is only as he always was, there in his growing beard, and his poor clothes that do not suit the palace (as his beard does not) and his whole skin with his heart thumping rudely and healthily away.

After some hours during which he wanders through the veils and partitions of the seemingly endless chambers, he sits again on the skull floor to look out of the window which is wall. Time does seem to have passed in the normal manner, for now it is evening. A flight of winter swans flies over, real birds whose white is plumage not ice.

The sun sets like a red wound, except now he knows it does not set at all. Instead the earth turns backward, away from it. In the cisterns the glistening fish weave patterns and at last he sees they do not swim in water but in liquid silver. Now this scarcely matters. Night enters the palace and the chandeliers burn no more brightly. Spirits appear to shimmer through the air. An owl of flesh and feathers perches high up on the rim of the tall goblet and calls once in its voice like a ghost, before flying away. Can Nirsen sleep? He will try. Ah yes, thank God, he can.

HOW OFTEN DOES he see the Ice Maiden after that? Does he count? Yes, but then forgets. He forgets.

How can you remember anyway such a visitation? It would be as if a man said *I will count up every occasion I see that star appear in the sky.*

Sometimes she does seem to pause, and to examine Nirsen for a while. Then, as the days and nights continue, he wonders if he can ask her for something, as in stories the woebegone man does ask the supernatural being to grant his heart's desire. But Nirsen has been trained only in sorting and demolishing rubbish into greater dross. He has learned to have no heart's desire, cannot imagine one. Or else he has simply been too *wise* to harbour dreams.

Only one more time does he try to talk to her. He says, tentative, "Here then am I, but why then I, not others?"

And as before she seems to reply. But in her own language like chimes and little bells, and ice that deliberately splinters.

Besides, he knows he is alive. His body works almost completely, breathing and letting him see and think and walk or sit, and even sleep. He needs no food or drink, and therefore the other accessory functions to do with digestion do not trouble him either.

He is warm. Really it would be an imposition to petition the Ice Maiden for any other thing, particularly an explanation. So then he asks no more, only bows to her and steps aside if she enters a part of her palace where he has taken himself. But frequently, too, she passes high up in the air, moving some way off over the floorless space between the upper tines of the chandeliers, the snow and spirits and skeletal animals dancing round her, affectionate and undemanding.

It reminds him a little of some priest's view of God's Heaven. He had never credited that; it had sounded also boring to Nirsen, for he was used to having to work despite the low and ugly nature of his labour. He is not bored in the palace, however, though he has nothing to do. Indeed he does do something, which is that he goes from area to area of it, and he watches the world outside, that is the abbreviated region of lake and encircling forest, and the sky.

In these he finds astonishing constant metamorphoses. They are like books he can read. He studies all the ways that snow comes, and slight thaws, and dawn and day and sunfall, dusk and night, and clouds, and all the stars and planets, and the moon and sun. The lives of the outer animals that survive he is a student of, and also he sees how two die, one a deer and one a hare, there by the lake's margin. But a while after he notices that the blithe and lively skeletons of a deer and a hare have added themselves to the Ice Maiden's entourage. This puzzles him slightly. So many creatures die in winter, seen or unseen, surely there should be more about her. But then it occurs to him not all the dead would want to come to her. Then the other persistent riddle is sharpened, as to how it is he is here alive. Again, despite all evidence, he wonders if he is.

Whatever else Nirsen, doubting or indifferent, goes on with his scrutiny of the outer world. On certain nights he is so emersed in it he forgets to sleep.

But then there is a night when he does slumber and at daybreak he is wakened by a dreadful noise.

He starts up thinking that at last his heart has cracked in two pieces. But it is the lake that has cracked in twain. Black water bubbles up.

Nirsen notices how the edges of the forest are dripping white, cool tears.

IN A DAY or so colossal ledges of snow slide crashing from the trees. Through a shallow place in the lake he catches sight of iceless bluish fish, swimming and rising to a narrow slot where all the frozen lid has gone. On the boughs above, a fearful reddish glint begins to show like fire during the afternoons. Spring is returning.

That evening a bird of bone, perhaps once a sparrow, flies down through the air layers of the Ice Maiden's palace, and sitting on Nirsen's shoulder it twitters in the startling bird-language of the outer world. Is it warning him? He thinks that it is.

Had he a bag he would pack it. He would be ready. He longs to see her one further time, but she does not appear, and by the hour the moon — no longer white, but having a brazen face — crests the trees, the sparrow has flown away. Not upward among the chandeliers, but out through a tiny flaw in the goblet of the palace.

Nirsen does not risk sleep.

He waits, standing on the floor of skulls.

When the wild crunching and crackling begins he is not surprised. It is grief he feels. As if he must truly die now, or worse, for a fact, be *born*.

As the walls liquify and pour in the melting lake, sailing from him in rafts like narrow pearl, the sled is there and he steps on it. It draws him away and away towards the shore.

He stares back. Every bit of the towering crystal of the palace has disappeared.

Of course, where could she go in spring?

Only slowly, as he nears the forest edge, does Nirsen recall the sparrow and wonder if, in the warm weather, the Ice Maiden emerges on to the earth in a different form.

Who then, what then, is she? Is she *spring* now? *Summer* next? He cannot understand. Landing on the muddy shore he observes the sled dissolve. The trees are flitting with birds and somewhere in the forest a stag bellows. Like beads small flowers decorate the ground.

NIRSEN WENT AWAY from the lake and, although he did not properly comprehend it, towards the town from which he had been cast out.

He knew no other place to go. It was instinct, or thoughtlessness.

As he trekked through the green lace architraves of the forest, he wondered where the ice-creatures took themselves in warmer weather. Did their pelts thaw too, and proper pelt grow back? Or did they melt altogether, and were there unseen streams of fox and bear, wolf, rat, weasel, owl, under his weary boots?

He hoped not to see their animal masks when he caught his own image in some puddle, nor did he. He looked as ever, but he had never had much interest in himself. The springing leaves spoke in a foreign tongue. Already they discussed him, whispering.

He dreamed of her when he sheltered by night. When he slept between the paws of tree roots or in skull caves beneath canopies of spreading fern. He saw again her amber skin and her icicle eyes. He was no longer frightened of her, if ever he had been. He felt a sort of cold love, but it was not entirely cold, nor love: it had no name.

Six days, five nights before he reached the fields where they were now sowing, and beyond them the huddle-muddle of the town.

How warm the spring was; the fields steamed. As if under the winter smoke the town was shrouded by vapour. He felt time had played tricks on him. He debated whether, as in old tales, he would find the town a hundred years younger than he had left it — or aged five hundred years into a future he could not know.

But reality is sometimes more unusual than myth.

Once in the town, considering events with greater prudence, he was wary, expecting threats or even a further assault. But those that looked at him seemed only suspicious. This struck him more and more as peculiar. They would, reasonably, reckon him dead.

Then a carter halted his load and strode over. "What you at here, stranger?"

Nirsen recalled him. The Kuldhoddr had several times bought things off the man with Nirsen waiting by. The town was not large. Everyone knew everyone to some extent. But not, it seemed, any longer Nirsen. For having muttered something appeasing to the carter and gone on, other similar inquiries came Nirsen's way.

At length, driven, he even sought the gate by the Kuldhoddr's yard — then shrank back as Jert burst suddenly out. But Jert glanced at and passed Nirsen with just a contemptuous thrust and cursing, "Get from the way!"

Nirsen had seen himself in water on the wet earth, and since entering the town in a window or two. He looked as he had always done.

He wandered through the town and out its other side.

On the track beyond he hesitated, considering. The sun punched down a furnace heat yet he did not sweat. The town too had been like a furnace. The breath of the people there had spooled like fog and had smelled of boiling water or cooking meat to him. Here on the track Nirsen found too something had burnt him on the arm. Lifting back his sleeve he saw a great blistering welt as if from a scorch or scald. It was where Jert's hand had pushed him.

There was pasture ahead with some goats.

As Nirsen traveled on, the animals turned one and all to watch him by. Even from the goats waves of heat emanated, and the tang of smouldering grass.

He trudged all day, away from the town and up into some low hills where the ringing hammer blows of the sun on his head were less bearable, but the landscape was empty of human habitation, and therefore of human incandescence.

When night fell he hoped for coolness, but there was not much difference. A full moon rose yellow and blazing, and he sheltered from its fire.

Through the soles of his boots the ground, in sunlight or darkness, flamed against his feet. If he should brush against a tree or shrub, he felt a surge as if warm steam pressed through his clothing. But when after some further days he went by a single hillside cottage, the heat that gushed from it was like dragon's breath. He had to know, and so set one finger's tip to the wall. It did not blister his skin as Jert's touch had done, yet it burned. It was like a pan just off the stove.

For days and nights again Nirsen went on. The spring was flowering into early summer. The heat of the sun and of most things reached a powerful crescendo, extreme and omnipresent. He could not bear it, but then he could. As with so many bad conditions, he grew used to it. Yet where able, he touched nothing with his unprotected skin. Even the coldest streams that ran down from the circling mountains, still fretted by the recent memory of snow, were tepid if he tried them. But he never drank from them, he did not feel thirsty ever, never hungry. He walked, and studied the book of the world. He was not distressed. Nor in any way exalted. In his life always it had been that he had little or less and must additionally put up with diverse troubles. Nothing had altered for him in that way then, though everything else had changed utterly.

Inevitably he was drawn back sooner or later to the forests. The far-as-space mountains were all that lay beyond and he sensed they, though not of man's making, would be torrid as the lava that once had seethed inside them. They were nearer to God too, presumably, being higher up, and certainly nearer the sun. These features must ensure they were, for Nirsen, killing hot.

Deep in the summer woods he discovered a rock cave. Chill moss smoked with warmth above an icy little stream softly warm as a bath. Here Nirsen took up residence.

Throughout the season he observed the plants and animals. He would sit all day, all night, as he had done on the skull floor of the Ysenmaddn, reading from the forest's pages.

Autumn-fall transmuted the metal of the woods to copper and bronze, and then the cold blew in wild sweet breaths. As the pines put on their white armour, of course he thought of the wide table of the lake. He thought of the palace of glass. He would never seek it save in his mind. He could no more return there than into yesterday.

But as the winter gathered, for Nirsen true spring had come, the time of plenty and of ease.

THERE IN HIS hollow Nirsen lived a long, long life. He seldom stirred from his place, not needing to. Perhaps instead the beasts of the forest, undisturbed by his immobility, carried on their own existences not an arm's reach from him. Perhaps in the core of winter even the ice-beasts came, her creatures, to prowl around the cave, to lick his fingers with pliable cold tongues, to show him things or tell him things, for maybe he learned their language after all of necessity, just as he had, that way, once learned his own. Did the skeleton sparrow sit on a bough, or on his shoulder, and twitter to him and teach him also the secret tongue of birds and bones?

For sure, he never saw her again, the Ice Maiden, save in dreams and thoughts.

But two others saw her once, for the briefest moment, many decades later, and that was because of Nirsen.

IT WAS SUMMER by then, yet some hundred years or more from Nirsen's youth. The two fellows who forged through the forest were not oppressed by the sun at all; they liked it and boasted of it, as if they themselves had invented it, lit it and hung it up on a string to please the world.

But it was a hot enough day, and coming to a shady spot where a stream trickled from a cave, they sat down to eat their midday snack.

"That tree there," said one, pointing with his knife, "that we'll have over for the merchant's fancy door."

They were wood-cutters, sizing up the woods to choose things to slaughter for the use of their town.

The other grunted. But then he said, "That cave-hole there, that's gloomy-chill enough. We might find some rare tasty fungus along in there for the stew."

So when they had eaten, they got up and went over the bank and stood gawping in at the cave.

Cold enough? Oh yes. The cave was very cold. It was a hole back into winter, black and shining with the mail-coat of ancient ice, and spears and daggers of ice pointing downward from its ceiling, dense as iron. Even the stream was frozen over, only thawing once it had escaped the cave.

"I never saw summer such like that," said the older woodsman, "in all my born days."

"Look there," said the other hoarsely, "what's that?"

The bolder older man went in. He leaned forward and beheld a heap of human bones and a human skull sat on top of them. He was not afraid of the dead. He did not understand what dead was, and that it might affect him ever seemed unlikely. And so peering shamelessly through the bones he saw another thing, and, curious, he bent to pick it up. "See here this lying in the middle. It's a chunk of slate, and a picture on it."

But the other would not go in, and then the old man drew the lump of slate from among the toppled bones and brought it outside, into the sunshine.

That way both men saw the picture fashioned on the slate. This was of a beautiful young woman with dark, bluish-greenish locks of hair, and a honey skin, and azure lips, and eyes like the blue icy shadows that gleam behind the face of the winter moon. By this era the stories of an Ice Maiden had been forgotten, or had chameleonized into some other legend, and the wood-cutters did not know what they saw. And it was only for a second anyway that they had the chance to look at it. For abruptly the old wood-cutter let out a yelp and dropped the slate, on which the image of the Ice Maiden was imprinted, down on the earth, where it shattered in a thousand fragments. "So cold — cold as the frost and ice it burnt me — "

And muttering oaths and prayers they hurried away, even sparing the tree they had meant to fell. The older man's hand would carry the scar to the day of his death. But the shattered slate had not been slate.

It was Nirsen's heart. ॐ

Tanith Lee was born in 1947, but didn't learn to read until she was almost eight. Then she started writing at age nine. School, and a number of makeshift jobs — librarian, waitress, shop clerk — interrupted what she calls her insane obsession with putting pen (literally, as she writes longhand) to paper. Tanith lives in southern England with her husband, the writer John Kaiine. She has been contributing regularly to *Weird Tales* since its resurrection in the 1980s.

Creature

BY RAMSEY SHEHADEH

ILLUSTRATED BY RAHUL TIWARI AND MISTER M

IN WHICH ALL
THINGS EBB AND
FLOW, INCLUDING
OUR PROTAGONIST

AND SO CAME Creature out of the wasteland and into the city, bouncing from hilltop to hilltop like a bulbous ballerina skipping across the knuckles of a great hand. He was big as the moon and black as the night, and he came crashing into the city like a silent meteor. The cityfolk watched his approach with wide eyes and open mouths, and then scattered like leaves.

The sun sat smudged and pale behind a grey smear of cloud, and the air stank of scat and putrefaction. But Creature said: "What a fine day it is!" Though he did not say it, of course, he thought it, and so the cityfolk thought it too. And when he released a great bolus of happiness into the air, they paused in their desperate flight, and smiled, and thought: "What a fine day it is!"

Creature surveyed the sea of smiles around him, and was well pleased. He rolled along, growing and shrinking and flattening and widening as he went, dispensing false joy to the destitute and the hopeless, the desperate and the sad. They lined his path like parade-watchers, caught helplessly in his spell.

All except for the Little Girl. He found her standing in the middle of the road, gazing up at him with an expression of puzzled reserve.

She touched his yielding black skin, and said: "Who are you?"

"I am Creature," said Creature. "You are quite happy to see me." Although he did not say it, of course, he thought it, and so the Little Girl thought it too.

She smiled. "Will you tell me a story?"

"Certainly!" said Creature. The sky rained ash and soot, and in the grimy dusk of midday the doomed people of the city rediscovered their despair and slunk back into their slow nowhere peregrinations. "Would you like to hear a happy story, or a sad story?"

"A happy one," said the Little Girl. She was slumped and emaciated, and her features sagged against her bones like melting wax. But her eyes were bright, and the mouth in her face was smiling. Creature looked inside her, and saw the scars where her childhood had been, and felt a cold thrill of sadness. He shied away from it, and began.

"Once upon a time, there was a race of beings called the Lumplorians. Unlike most peoples, the Lumplorians came in all different shapes and sizes. Some of them were tall and bent at right angles, like an L; some were round like cookies, with arms sticking out of the tops of their bodies and eyes in the middle of their bellies. Some undulated like meandering rivers, and some were perfectly square."

The Little Girl giggled. "That's silly."

"Nevertheless," said Creature. "This was the nature of the Lumplorian. And because they were all so different from one another, because no Lumplorian looked like any other Lumplorian, there was no bond between them. This made them sad, because they were all alone. And then it made them angry, because they hated their sadness, and blamed each other for it. There were wars between the Lumplorians, a million million tiny wars, because it soon came

to pass that every Lumplorian was at war with every other Lumplorian."

"This is boring," said the Little Girl. "Can we play now?"

"But it is still a sad story," said Creature, who knew that there are no happy stories or sad stories, only a single tale that stretches across the breadth of time, and happy or sad depends on which part of it you choose to tell.

"That's ok," said the Little Girl. "I don't care about stories anyway."

"Very well," said Creature, and extruded two arms from the front of his body and picked her up. "What would you like to play?"

"Let's play Find Mommy," said the Little Girl.

"A capital idea!" said Creature. "How does one play Find Mommy?"

"You look for Mommy," said the Little Girl, frowning.

"Of course," said Creature. "Where should we begin?"

The Little Girl pointed toward the Pitted Bridge, which spanned the River Sludge. "There," she said.

"Climb on, then," said Creature, and handed her up to a second set of arms, which were emerging a little farther up his body, and they handed her in turn to a third set, higher still, and so on, so that the Little Girl rose toward his summit on a rippling wave of arms.

"And we're off!" said Creature, and surged toward the bridge, undulating around rubble and bridging over chasms and puddling through potholes. Ruined buildings crowded in on either side, staring blindly down at them through shattered windows.

They were nearly there when a black bubblecar, squat as a spider, silent as a whisper, turned the corner in front of them, and stopped. A gun rose from its roof and trained itself on them. Its doors opened, lifting like angular wings, and two blackclads stepped out wearing visors that reflected Creature's shimmering undulate in their mirrored and opaque surfaces.

The first blackclad leveled his weapon at Creature and said: "Halt!" Creature halted. He looked at their weapons, and felt something barbed and murderous rising in the banished parts of his mind.

"Identify yourself!" barked the second blackclad.

Creature extruded a mouth, and said: "I am Creature."

"Release the girl," said the second black-clad, "and put your hands on your head." He said this with some hesitation, because the girl was clearly the one holding onto Creature, and because, in his current form, Creature had neither hands, nor head to put them on.

But Creature devolved into an oil slick, gently lowering the Little Girl to the street. And then he seeped into the cracks in the ground, and was gone.

The Little Girl got to her feet, looking warily at the two men. Fear showed plain on her face. All children knew the dangers of encountering the blackclads, who despise unattached urchinry, and round them up at every opportunity, and ferry them to the Orphan Reprocessing Facility in the center of the city, from which no child had ever emerged.

"You," said the first man, "will come with us."

The Little Girl shook her head, and took a step back.

The first man, who was fond of saying Halt!, pointed his weapon at her and said: "Halt!"

And the girl halted, but not because the blackclad told her to. No. She halted because the bubblecar behind the two men was rising into the air on a surge of black foam. It was rising, and it was rising, and then it was falling. There was a great crash, and the car was lying on its side, where the two men had been.

The black foam fell down to the ground, slapping against the torn tarmac like hard rain, then rose again as ten flat featureless figures with perfectly circular heads and rounded, linked arms, like cut-out paper men. They stood in a circle around the smashed car, their heads bowed, murmuring wordless elegies.

After a few moments, the figures flowed into each other, and became one figure, a giant cauldron that stood on two spindly legs. "I have done a bad thing," said Creature.

"Those were bad men," said the Little Girl, who had seen many terrible things in her short life.

"Nevertheless," said Creature, and sighed. He trundled over to the Little Girl, and unwound an arm and took her hand. "Let us proceed more discreetly."

CREATURE WAS BORN soon after the apocalypse, when the changes beset the world. He'd seeped out of his mother and spilled to the ground, a slick black rill in the muck of the afterbirth, and lay helpless at her feet, listening to the screams. He'd hurt her, clinging and raking and tearing at her body as it tried to expel him. Even then, he knew the horrors that awaited him in the world outside his mother.

The sun was well below the horizon when she died. Creature watched his father, an emaciated halfman in tattered rags, kneeling over her, sobbing quietly. He lowered himself to the ground and pressed his half-body against hers, so that they became one body, three arms and three legs and three eyes. Two of the eyes stared away blankly into nothing, and the third wept.

When the darkness became absolute, Creature slunk away into the night, an amorphous puddle of shadow.

At first, he foraged among the weeds and the thorn-brambles, but he soon learned to lie in wait for more substantial fare. He discovered the secrets of his body: how to flatten it into a dark patch of night, how to rise and thicken and envelop, to crush and consume. Everything in this world seemed bent on his destruction, and so he grew feral, and learned to cultivate savagery. All that had been human about him receded, save one image: the face of the mother he had never seen, smiling at him as she never had.

As he grew, legends sprung up around him, becoming more fantastical with each telling: he was an animate piece of the night, an amorphous devil, a thing of pure evil that consigned the souls of his victims to the infernal realms of hell. The men who lived on the edge of the waste gathered into great hunting parties and came after him, but always to no avail, because he had discovered another talent: he could see their thoughts as if they were his own. He could divine their numbers and their tactics, their plans and stratagems, their feints and their traps before they came within a mile of him. He thwarted all of their efforts, and then he killed them, and then he ate them.

But his ability to read their thoughts was ultimately more curse than blessing. He became entranced by the strange things that he encountered in their minds: wondrous, inscrutable feelings like joy and hope and love and compassion and humility and peace. To be sure, they were rare artifacts in these hard men, but all he had ever known was grief and pain and fear and hatred, and these new sensations, though strange and troubling, were beautiful. He saw the face of his mother in them, and understood that she was their talisman, their fortress and their apotheosis.

He found that he could not destroy creatures who were capable of such wonders. He lurked instead at the edge of their encampments, drinking them in, savoring them. And, one day, quite by accident, he discovered that he could manipulate them, too; he learned how to manufacture happiness in their minds, to sow accord, to soothe despair.

But he could do none of these things in his own mind, try as he might.

And so he conceived of his plan. He would enter the city, and heal its people. He would revive their hopes, scatter their sadness, stoke their love. And then he would wend himself into the fabric of their lives,

and bask in the reflected glow of their joy. He would make himself whole again, through the coerced love of the men who despised and feared him.

THE PITTED BRIDGE rose up from the banks of the Sludge like a leaden rainbow, but plunged abruptly near the midpoint of its arc into the dark waters. Two hundreds yards farther along, it rose from the river again and continued its journey to the opposite bank. Sagging ropes spanned the interval between the halves; from his position on the shore, Creature could just make out tiny figures shimmying back and forth across the gulf, like beads on an abacus.

"All the way to the end," said the Little Girl from her perch at Creature's summit.

Creature stepped onto the bridge, and began his ascent. He moved along a narrow avenue bisected by a fading, dashed yellow line, between dense thickets of shanties, reeking and ramshackle and piled up against the rails of the bridge.

The bridge's residents stopped their milling to stare. Eyes appeared at slit windows, heads poked out of curtained doorways.

The Little Girl waved at a small boy with long thin arms that spindled out from his naked torso like spiderlegs. The boy waved back, beaming. "Hi Ugly!"

"Hi Rat!" said the Little Girl, and laughed. "That's my friend Rat," she said. "We call him Rat because he's always going in dark holes to get food."

"And why does he call you Ugly?"

"Because that's my name."

"Surely not," said Creature. "Who would give such a pretty little girl a name like that?"

The Little Girl did not answer. Creature quickened his pace, because the crowds were thickening on either side of him, and he felt the knife edge of hostility touching the skin of his mind. He sent out balms of goodwill; but he was nearly spent now, and his thin, paltry reassurances served only to dull the rising malice.

"Mommy," said the Little Girl.

"Do you see her, Child?" said Creature, slowing.

"No. Mommy called me Ugly."

"Ah." Creature resumed his pace, and struggled to find the thing to say. "Well, I'm sure she did so in jest."

"She said it's not safe to be a pretty little girl. She said she used to be a pretty little girl too and bad things happened to her and made her wish she wasn't."

A feral dog shot out of the narrow space between two shanties and leapt at them, snarling. Creature extended a protoplasmic tentacle and caught it and held it in midair, speaking tenderness and peace into its mind until it grew calm. Then he lowered it to the ground and released it and molded the edge of a tentacle into a hand the color of obsidian and stroked it behind its ears. It sat on its haunches and watched them pass, sniffing at the air in their wake.

"She wouldn't let me go far away from the house," said the Little Girl. "And after Daddy left she didn't let me out at all. She paid a nice man named Bickle to watch the house when she had to leave but then Bickle didn't wake up one day because of the knife in him and she had to stay with me all the time, because she said she couldn't trust anyone else."

A burly and bearded and shirtless man stepped into their path. Creature slowed, then stopped. The man was fat and large and pink and hairless. He held a book before him, like a talisman, and said: "Leave this place, Demon. You are not welcome here."

"That's Klam," whispered the Little Girl. "He's a crazy person."

Creature touched the man's mind, and recoiled. It was all brambles and barbed wire, and it hurt him just to look at it. He said: "I mean you no harm, sir. I am merely escorting this young lady to her mother."

"The harlot has no place in this House of God," said Klam.

This made Creature angry, and the anger frightened him. It was an ugly and bitter and terrible thing. And so he pressed it into the bowels of his mind, and said: "Please do not speak ill of the child. She has harmed no one."

"Her existence," said Klam, "harms us all."

"Remove yourself from our path, sir," said Creature, his patience suddenly spent. "Do so immediately."

"I do not fear you, Demon. You cannot hurt me."

"I can hurt you in ways that you cannot possibly imagine," said the anger, before Creature could stop it. "I can make you long for mere agony."

And then Klam reached behind him, and drew a shotgun from its holster, and fired.

Creature reacted quickly, bristling into a sudden forest of pseudopods. The onrushing cloud of metal would not harm him, of course, but the Little Girl was only flesh and sinew, delicate and frangible. He lashed out with his extrusions, moving faster than thought, catching the bullets, redirecting them into the central mass of his body.

All but one.

He felt it slip between his fingers and pass over his summit, saw it pierce the flesh of the girl's arm. Heard her scream. Felt her pain as his own.

And then, while he was not looking, the anger rose.

He softened his midsection and moved forward and subsumed Klam into his body and then walled him off into a small compartment, and then shrunk the compartment into a box the size of a coffin, and then shrunk it again, and again, breaking Klam in steady stages. There was a time when he would have prolonged Klam's death, savoring his screams, but that time was past. He crushed him quickly, and heard his thoughts wink out.

The Little Girl was crying, quietly. He lowered her to the ground and examined her wound. The bullet had nibbled at the edge of her shoulder, but had not entered.

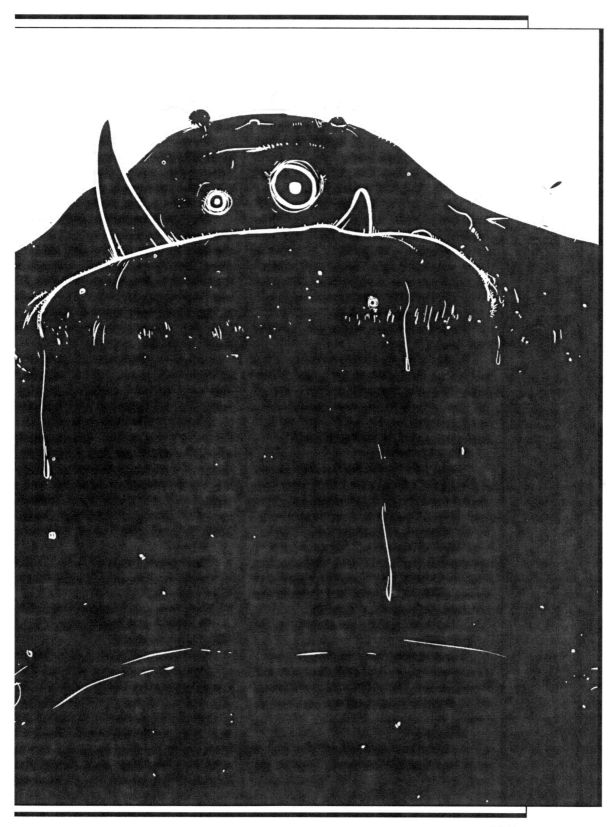

He pressed himself against it, to stanch the flow of blood, and said: "All is well, Little Girl."

They were alone now, all the bridge's denizens having retreated to their shacks. "Come," said Creature. "Let us continue." He took the Little Girl's hand, and they moved through the silence.

After some time, the girl pointed, and whispered: "That's where we lived."

Creature turned his gaze to a collapsed structure of wood and canvas, and then liquified and flowed into it. He found torn shreds of paper, a tattered rug, a toothless comb, scraps of clothing, an empty frame affixed to the canvas; nothing more. He came out again, and said: "There is no one here."

"Oh," said the Little Girl.

"Do you remember where you last saw your mother?"

"Yeah," she said, and turned toward the bridge's summit. Creature followed in her wake. "She woke up really early yesterday," said the Little Girl, "and went outside. She was trying to be quiet, but I heard her so I got up too, and then I followed her."

"Was she alone?"

"Yeah," said the Little Girl, and stopped at the edge of bridge, where it fell away into the brown roil of the river Sludge. "She came here. I thought she was maybe waiting for someone, so I waited too, hiding behind Mr Bickle's house." She pointed at a ramshackle hut behind her. "But she just stood there for a long time, and no one else came, and then she looked back at our house and then she jumped in the river."

Creature was silent for some time. He said: "I see."

"I waited here for a while, and then I went down off the bridge to the river and looked for her. But she wasn't there, and I didn't want to come back up here on my own."

"Of course."

"So I just started walking." She looked up, toward Creature's summit. "And I found you."

Creature stared at the river. Flotillas of muck and jetsam flowed along, teams of wreckage, bobbing and sinking. He said: "Well." In truth, he did not know what to say. The Little Girl affected him in ways he did not understand.

There was a stir behind them, then, small bits of sound running together: curtains drawn aside, shuffling feet, stage whispers. He turned, and saw them: the people of the bridge, massing.

They stood tremulous and resolute and afraid, clasping the detritus of their lives in the hands: long boards with nails hammered into their ends, filed metal rods, rusting butcher knives, ancient firearms. It was a sad and ragtag gathering, and, examining it, Creature could muster nothing more than pity. Not even the anger would rouse itself for this dim spectacle.

A man stepped forward. He was dressed in scraps and tatters, and the left side of his face twitched with a flickering palsy. He said: "We don't want you here, Monster."

He could have killed them all, of course. He could have crushed them against one other, plunged through their mouthes into their bodies and eaten them from the inside, broken the ground at their feet and sent them hurtling into the river. Instead, he moved to the edge of the bridge, beside the Little Girl, and said: "It is time for us to go."

"Where?"

"Someplace that is not here." He folded himself into a broad sickle-moon concavity. "Come into me."

She paused, then stepped onto his body.

"It will be very dark for a while, Little Girl. Do not be afraid."

"I'm not afraid," she said, and lay down.

And so Creature shaped himself a hollow globe, sealing the Little Girl inside of him, and rolled over the edge of the bridge. The brown surface of the river rose to meet him, and he fell into its murk with a great crash, sending up a high torrent of muddy water. They sank slowly into its depths, where the darkness was absolute, and let the current draw them downriver.

When he sensed that the air trapped inside of him was growing scarce, he rose to the surface of the river, unfolding like an opening hand, and fashioned himself into a raft. The Little Girl lay asleep in its center, curled into a tiny ball. He raised a portion of himself into a pillow, and arched a blanket of himself over her body. And they floated thus through the city, with the darkness gathering steadily about them.

THE LITTLE GIRL awoke at dawn, just as the sun was heaving itself over the horizon, a pale shapeless luminescence in the grey soup of cloud. She stretched, and looked around.

"Sir?" she said.

"I am here, Little Girl," said Creature.

"What happened to the city?"

"We have left it."

They were floating through the wasteland now, across a dead plain still scarred with the ravages of the last war: trench furrows had been torn out of the earth, as if by great scythes, and many of the trees were burned stumps, or leafless and shattered skeletons. The air was thick with heat and heavy with moisture. The girl mopped sweat off her brow and surveyed the river. Tourette crabs on either bank followed their progress, spewing unbroken streams of profanity. Jellyfowl floated above them in the soft eddies of breeze, trailing curtains of barbed streamers. A troupe of the soulless trudged the banks, following the scent of life.

The girl lay down and said: "I've never been outside the city."

"The waste is no safe place for little girls."

"Is this your home?"

Creature paused. He had never thought of it as home. "It is where I live, yes."

"Aren't you afraid all alone out here?"

"Not in the way you mean," he said. He had never feared the wasteland, really. But he did not wish to become one of its thoughtless, feral denizens. That, he feared.

She lapsed back into silence, and Creature reached into her mind, and found only sadness. He said: "Do you want to go back to the city, Little Girl?"

She shook her head, not lifting it off his surface. He saw that this was both true, and false. She despised the city, but it was the only home she'd ever known. An intractable dilemma.

Creature prepared a bolus of happiness, the largest he could fashion, and filled it with bright sunlight and green fields, fairytale princesses and caring mothers and endless summers.

The Little Girl said: "Sir?"

"Yes, Little Girl."

"I wish you'd come before. You're nice, like Mr Bickle. I think Mommy would have let you take care of me. And then maybe she wouldn't have gone away."

Again, Creature found himself without words. They floated on in silence.

"I heard her talking to Mr Bickle once, when she thought I was asleep. She said I made her old. She said that worrying about me all the time was killing her."

"Even mothers say things they do not mean, sometimes," said Creature, maneuvering himself around a whirling funnel of piranha clownfish.

"Do you have a mother?"

"I did, yes. She left me a long time ago."

"What was she like?"

Creature did not answer at once. He had two mothers, really: the one he had inhabited for nine months, who'd borne him and then died; and the gentle woman who inhabited him, the light that led him out of his bestiality, that banished his darkness. In many ways, he was glad that he had never known the real mother; it left him free to manufacture the unconditional love of the false one.

"I wish I could tell you, Little Girl. I do not know. But I do know that she watches over me still, and protects me."

The Little Girl turned onto her back, and looked up at the sky. "Your Mommy sounds nice too."

Creature held the bolus of happiness at the threshold on her consciousness, but did not insert it. Its effect would be temporary, and false, an ice sculpture in the desert.

"Sir?"

"Yes, Little Girl."

"Who's going to take care of me now?"

"I do not know. Do you have any uncles or aunts?"

She shook her head.

"Brothers or sisters?"

She shook her head.

"Grandparents?"

She shook her head.

"Then perhaps," he said, almost shyly, "you should stay with me. Until you are old enough to take care of yourself."

"Out here?"

"Yes. It's not so bad, really, once you've grown accustomed to it. Let me show you."

The soulless were well behind them, and the crabs had given up the chase. Creature drifted toward the bank, then rose out of the river as an obelisk, lengthening as he went, thrusting the Little Girl high above the skeletal trees. She squealed, first in fright, then in delight. He extruded eight legs from his base and skittered onto the bank, a tall spider column swaying gently in the freshening breeze.

"I can see everything!" cried the Little Girl. "I can see the city and the hills and the river and everything!"

They walked on. A clod of scuttle earth, the size and shape of a mattress, rose from the ground and shambled out of their path, raining worms from its underside; in the distance, two clouds of semaphore ravens spoke in shifting patterns; a herd of wild rats stampeded across a faraway bramble meadow; a flotilla of sailfish navigated the deeps of the distant oxblood lake.

The Little Girl watched with widening eyes. "This place is weird."

"No stranger than your city, Little Girl. The strangeness differs only in its particulars."

"Where's your house?"

"There is no house." Silence. He lifted the impression of a face onto the flat surface of his summit, and looked at the Little Girl. "Although we could build one. A large house, if you like, with many rooms."

Her expression was composed, and very serious. She was, suddenly, far older than her years. "Can you let me down, Sir?"

"Certainly." He shrank into a disk the size of manhole cover, and, when the girl stepped off, rose into his cauldron shape. "Are you hungry?"

She shrugged, and said: "Sir?"

"Yes, Little Girl."

"Is my Mommy dead?"

Creature paused. He said: "Yes. I fear that she is."

The girl was silent for a moment. She said: "I wish she wasn't."

Creature had nothing to say to this. They stood in silence, listening to the wind rattle the skeletal branches of the trees, the river lap lazily against its banks.

"Sir?"

"Yes, Little Girl."

"My name's Melanie. You can call me Melanie."

He hesitated, and felt the dim stirrings of something unfamiliar in his mind: fear, perhaps, or hope, or dread, or joy. Or none of these things. Or all of them. He said: "Melanie," and extruded an arm, and took her hand. And together they watched the flocks of semaphore ravens converge on the horizon, signaling frantically to one another across the gulf of sky. ❦

By day, **Ramsey Shehadeh** is a mild-mannered Java programmer. But when darkness falls, he sheds his beige corporate uniform, doffs his hat, removes his glasses, and becomes a mild-mannered Java programmer who writes the occasional short story. He enjoys hanging out with his wife, steeping himself in '80s nostalgia, and devising increasingly desperate ways to prevent his beagle from eating him. You can find him at http://doodleplex.com. This is his first published story.

The Yellow Dressing Gown

BY SARAH MONETTE

ILLUSTRATED BY VANCE KELLY

IN WHICH KYLE MURCHISON BOOTH IS NOT THE MOST ANXIOUS MUSEUM CURATOR PRESENT

O F ALL THE curators at the Samuel Mather Parrington Museum, I liked Michael Overton the least. He was a loud, bustling, back-slapping man, red-faced and brash and quite, quite stupid. There was, I believe, no particular malice in him, but there was no particular good, either, except possibly in his odd but entirely sincere devotion to his work. It was the last thing one would expect of a hearty, *manly* man like Overton, but his speciality was eighteenth-century textiles, with an emphasis on women's clothing. We were all indefatigable trophy hunters when it came to acquisitions, but none was as indefatigable as Overton, who spent every weekend attending estate sales and combing through antique stores, and who spent many of his weekdays arguing with Dr. Starkweather about the budget for Decorative Arts. Overton made up in brute persistence what he laced in intelligence, and I believe he was nearly as sore a trial to Dr. Stark-

weather as I was. Perhaps even more so — I did my best to stay out of the museum director's way, while Overton bounded into combat like a particularly muscular Christian hoping for a worthy lion.

The trouble with Overton, as Mr. Lucent said once, was that he was good at his job. He had a special gift for finding clothes that had been worn by famous, or infamous, persons — mostly but not exclusively women — and that, of course, was the best way to make eighteenth century textiles palatable to the general public. Eighteenth Century Afternoon Dress was of interest only to specialists; Eighteenth Century Afternoon Dress Worn by New York Poisoner Deborah Duffy was of interest to everyone.

Overton's provenances were sometimes sketchy (Eighteenth Century Riding Habit Believed To Have Belonged To Notorious Actress Mary Raphael Spence), but they never descended as far as *dodgy*, and Overton himself worked like a maniac — and drove his junior curators like slaves — to improve them, even after an item was acquired and displayed. Overton never gave up.

We clashed, Overton and I, because Dr. Starkweather's habit, when Overton's financial importunings became too much to bear, was to allot him more of the junior curators' time. This practice had several benefits, only one of which was that it would silence Overton for as much as a fortnight, but it meant that when I stupidly broke my wrist, it was Overton I had to fight for Mr. Sullivan's time. Miss Coburn and Mr. Lucent were staunch seconds — especially Mr. Lucent, as otherwise it would be his thankless task to take dictation from me for six weeks — and poor Mr. Sullivan would have stood on his head and recited Coleridge's *Ancient Mariner* in its entirety to get away from Overton, but it was I whom Overton blamed. He seemed to feel I had broken my wrist on purpose to pry Mr. Sullivan away from him, and I believe he came to dislike me almost as much as I disliked him.

This animosity did not, however, prevent him from positively haunting my office, trying to lure Mr. Sullivan back. Overton had the true obsessive's tunnel vision; he could not believe that other persons did not find eighteenth century clothing as endlessly fascinating as he did. Thus, he would "just stop by" to tell Mr. Sullivan about his newest find, or the really clever work Mr. Grice had done on the provenance of something-or-other, and he never once failed to ask if Mr. Sullivan had made any progress in the matter of the dressing gown.

I was keeping Mr. Sullivan sufficiently busy that on most days he barely had time for lunch; thus his answer was uniformly "no." At which, Overton would scowl at me and disappear again, causing both Mr. Sullivan and myself to heave sighs of relief. The particular quality of that relief was such that it was several weeks before I asked what, exactly, the matter of the dressing gown was.

Mr. Sullivan sighed, not in relief, and said, "Mr. Overton has a bee in his bonnet."

"Several," I said before I could stop myself. My wrist ached, sometimes dully, sometimes throbbingly, and the torturous awkwardness it imparted to even the simplest task was making my temper quite alarmingly short.

Mr. Sullivan, though, actually smiled and continued more easily, "This one is about the dressing gown of Ephraim Catesby."

"Ephraim Catesby the artist?"

"If there's another Ephraim Catesby, I've never come across him. He was always caricatured in the papers wearing this extravagant dressing gown, and Mr. Overton is determined to find it."

"It would be a tremendous coup," I admitted. The Parrington had the best collection of Catesby in the country, including the canvas on which he had been working when he committed suicide in 1819: *The Wedding March of Ruin*. The progress of his syphilitic dementia, critics agreed, had not impaired his artistic ability, merely his perceptions. Catesby had been notorious for always, *always*, painting from life.

It was not, when faced with *The Wedding March of Ruin*, a comforting thought.

"But what makes Overton think the dressing gown is still extant?"

Mr. Sullivan all but rolled his eyes. "Mr. Booth, do you *really* want to know?"

"Ah, no. That is . . . where were we when Mr. Overton knocked?"

We returned to our business, and I fully intended to leave Overton to his. But three days later, he burst into my office, without knocking, shouting, "Sullivan! Sullivan! I need you!"

"I *beg* your pardon," I said with a degree of iciness I had never achieved before in my life. Mr. Sullivan moaned and tried to hide behind a stack of bound journals.

Overton did an odd hopping dance step of impatience and frustration. "I need Sullivan this afternoon. You'll just have to do without him."

"How dare you!" I shouted, perhaps a trifle nonsensically, coming to my feet.

Overton at last seemed to recognize that I was not in charity with his excitement. "But it's the dressing gown! I've found Ephraim Catesby's dressing gown, but Sullivan did all the background work, and I need him along!" He blinked at me beseechingly, washed out, pale lashed eyes in a round, red, sweating face. "You can do without him for an afternoon, can't you?"

"No," I said, because I could not. But much as I disliked Overton and much as I resented his high-handed, clumsy efforts to steal Mr. Sullivan, I could not help feeling a pang of slightly envious empathy. I sighed and capitulated. "But I can come with you."

NEITHER OVERTON NOR Mr. Sullivan was pleased with my solution, and I did not like it myself, crammed into the back of Overton's automobile with a musty collection of newspapers and correspondence. Overton drove badly, impatiently; Mr. Sullivan and I were lucky that our destination was less than ten miles from the Parrington.

The person who had lived there, recently deceased, had been Priscilla Fairbody Jones, the granddaughter (Mr. Sullivan whispered to me) of Ephraim Catesby's dearest friend, principal heir, and executor, Robert Fairbody Jones. "I *knew* she had it," Overton kept muttering. "Knew it! But she lied to me. What am I supposed to *do* if people won't tell me the truth?" Mr. Sullivan and I eyed him uneasily and hoped the question was rhetorical.

Miss Fairbody Jones had lived and died in what was obviously a shrine to Ephraim Catesby, a private museum. In the front hall alone, I saw two watercolors for which Dr. Starkweather, on behalf of the Parrington, would give his eyeteeth, and while Overton charged ahead, dragging Mr. Sullivan with him, I took the time to give Miss Fairbody Jones's tired and bewildered niece a business card, scrawling on the back both Dr. Starkweather's name and that of the head curator of Nineteenth Century American Art.

And then, hearing Overton's triumphal bellow, I climbed the stairs to the second floor. I found Overton and Mr. Sullivan in a room dominated by a painting that, the last time I had been au courant, art historians had believed destroyed: *Portrait of the Artist behind a Ruined Mask*. It was a dreadful, brilliant thing, full-length and larger than life-size, and in it Catesby was wearing what was self-evidently the same dressing gown Overton was holding aloft.

I do not know if I can explain how reprehensibly ugly that dressing gown was. It was yellow brocade, a vile, acidic, mustard yellow, faced with white satin. The combination reminded me strongly of drainage from an infected wound. Beyond that, the thing was tucked in at the waist, its shoulders padded and its skirts tuliping oddly to the floor. It gave Catesby a repellantly insectile silhouette, and even suspended meekly from a clothes hanger, it did not

quite look like anything a human being would choose to wear. There were stains on the hem, stains on the white satin cuffs, the white satin lapels, and I tried and failed to remember what method of suicide Ephraim Catesby had chosen. There was no need to wonder if he had been wearing the dressing gown at the time. He had been.

Overton was actually chortling with glee; I suspected it was only conservationist's instincts keeping him from clutching the dressing gown to his bosom. Mr. Sullivan was frankly staring at *Portrait of the Artist behind a Ruined Mask*; he looked more than a little ill.

"Catesby was, er, insane at the end," I said. It was not terribly comforting, but it was the best I could do.

"I know," said Mr. Sullivan. "Don't you think Mr. Overton ought to have that thing fumigated?"

"I'm certain Mr. Overton will, er, do everything necessary," I said, although in truth I was certain only that Overton's transparent delight was appalling and tactless. Not to mention ghoulish.

Mr. Sullivan gave me a dubious look.

"He is *very* good at his job," I said, as firmly as I could.

Mr. Sullivan looked at the bird-skulled monsters beckoning from behind Catesby — so very like the bird-skulled monsters beckoning from behind the wedding party in *The Wedding March of Ruin* — visibly repressed a shudder, and went out to talk to the niece about value and compensation: to do the unpleasant job for which Overton had brought him.

Mr. Sullivan indubitably deserved a raise.

Overton finally came out of his transports and lovingly packed the dressing gown in a box he had brought, much like Mr. Sullivan, for the purpose. On the way back to the Parrington, I had to share my inadequate space with the dressing gown, which even from inside the box smelled unpleas-antly sweet, almost medicinal. Mr. Sullivan was right. The dressing gown needed to be fumigated.

Or possibly, said a darker voice, burned.

I HAVE NEVER been able to ascertain exactly what went wrong. There was no question about the provenance; Priscilla Fairbody Jones had kept immaculate records, as had her father and grandfather before her. There was no doubt about the value to the Parrington of the Fairbody Jones estate; the head of Nineteenth Century American Art had thanked me with tears in his eyes for giving that business card to Miss Fairbody Jones's niece. But the Parrington did not want the dressing gown.

If it had been anyone other than Dr. Starkweather making the final decision, I might have ascribed the refusal to aesthetic principles, but of those I was fairly sure Dr. Starkweather was devoid. The reason he gave, and stood by, was that Decorative Arts already had more than its fair share of display space, but considering the prominence accorded to *Portrait of the Artist behind a Ruined Mask*, that explanation was not entirely convincing. Overton believed — and shouted — that it was a personal slight, but although Dr. Starkweather could certainly be petty, that pettiness was only very rarely allowed to affect the public face of the museum. My best guess (although a guess is all that it is) is that Dr. Starkweather, normally as sensitive to atmosphere as a fossilized barnacle, took the dressing gown in aversion as Mr. Sullivan and I had. Perhaps it was the smell.

Overton refused to relinquish his prize. He reimbursed the museum out of his own pocket and installed the dressing gown in his own house. As he continued to pursue Mr. Sullivan, "just stopping by" my office several times a week, I heard all about his wife's displeasure. She complained about the smell until Overton put the dressing gown, on its custom made stand, in his study, where his wife never went.

At first, Overton campaigned to change Dr. Starkweather's mind, attempting clumsily to enter into intrigues with various staff members, but all such efforts stopped quite abruptly about a month after Overton took the dressing gown into his house. Mr. Sullivan and I were both uneasy about that sudden volte-face, but we spent much of our time, when Overton was not actually *in* my office, cooperating in a mutual pretense that he did not exist, and neither of us was willing to violate the terms of that tacit treaty. Moreover, even if we had, and even if there had been something we could do, our occasional exchange of glances confessed another truth: we did not want the dressing gown in the museum.

But it was at about that same time that Overton began exhibiting signs of nervousness, a thing never observed in Michael Overton before. Instead of leaning in the doorway of my office, as he had habitually done to the annoyance and inconvenience not merely of Mr. Sullivan and myself but also of everyone attempting to use the hallway, he would place himself in the corner behind the door, and there he would fidget, gaze moving restlessly around the room. Other members of the Department of Decorative Arts complained that Overton was "jumpy," and the custodial staff was unhappy about finding him at odd moments, sometimes after the museum was closed, in front of *Portrait of the Artist behind a Ruined Mask*. Michael Overton, surely the last man of whom one would expect it, seemed to be having a nervous breakdown.

Finally, one Friday when Overton "just stopped by" yet again, Mr. Sullivan proved himself a braver and better man than I. He got up, closed the office door, and said, "Mr. Overton, are you all right?"

Overton, backed into his corner, twitched visibly and said, "Yes, of course. Of course, I'm all right. Why wouldn't I be?"

Mr. Sullivan cast me a beseeching glance. "You've seemed, er, awfully nervous lately," I said.

"Nervous!" He barked out a laugh, gaze moving from Mr. Sullivan to me with weak aggression. "*I'm* nervous? That's a fine thing coming from you, Mr. Booth."

It was my turn to cast a beseeching look at Mr. Sullivan. "We're just concerned, Mr. Overton," he said. "Wondering if perhaps something was bothering you."

"Of course something's *bothering* me," Overton said. "This museum's run by a pack of fools. I was mad to think of letting them have Catesby's dressing gown in the first place. Wouldn't know what to do with it. Wouldn't know how to keep it. Not a decent lock in the whole building. Can't keep 'em out."

Now, one thing the Parrington has always prided itself on is its security. Nothing but Yale locks, and the inventory of keys is kept with a strict fanaticism that I often wish we could apply to our actual holdings. Overton's ranting was nonsense, except . . .

"Can't keep *whom* out?" I said.

"Not your fault," Overton said. "Can't see behind the masks. I know. I couldn't either. Can't keep 'em out if you can't see 'em. And they're cunning. They *wait*."

Mr. Sullivan's eyes were wide with alarm, as if he regretted closing the door.

"They know I can see them," Overton said, his voice becoming conspiratorial. "They wave at me. But I know what they want, and they can't have it."

"Er," I said, but there was no way to stop myself from asking. "What do they want?"

"The dressing gown, of course," Overton said.

"Of course," I said faintly.

"They can't have it," he said, his broad, chapped hands clenching into fists. "It's *mine*. I paid for it."

"Of course you did," Mr. Sullivan said, and I thought he meant to sound soothing, though he did not entirely succeed. "You know, if it isn't safe here, Mr. Overton, maybe you should go home for the day. You must be very tired of having to keep watch all the time."

We were nearly holding our breath, waiting while Overton thought that idea over. Finally, he nodded. "Yes. They've been getting closer. Maybe I should — " He darted a suspicious look around my office; it took all my will power not to turn.

"Yes," Overton said, "I should definitely go home. Make sure — " He wrenched the door open and was gone, faster than I had ever seen him move.

Mr. Sullivan and I looked at each other. "I think," I said finally, "perhaps I should tell Dr. Starkweather that Mr. Overton needs a holiday."

BUT I WAS WRONG.

On Monday, every paper in the city screamed the news. Michael Overton had been found in his study Friday night, dead by exsanguination. The door had been locked. He was wearing Ephraim Catesby's ghastly yellow dressing gown, though I was surprised he had been able to cram his shoulders into it. His wrists had been slit, the dressing gown drenched in his blood, and a verdict of suicide would have been simple save for one detail.

His eyes were missing.

According to the coroner, it looked as if they had been pecked out, although there is no bird on the North American continent large enough to have inflicted those wounds. The door was locked; the windows were locked.

Michael Overton's eyes were never found.

Death by misadventure was the eventual ruling.

I wonder about Ephraim Catesby's suicide. I wonder what Robert Fairbody Jones might have hushed up. I look at the beckoning bird-skulled monsters in Catesby's last two paintings, and I remember Overton saying, *They wave at me.*

It was not the dressing gown they wanted. ❧

Sarah Monette lives and writes in a 102-year-old house in the Upper Midwest. Her stories have appeared in *Strange Horizons*, *Alchemy*, and *Lady Churchill's Rosebud Wristlet*, among other venues. Her fourth novel, *Corambis*, will be published by Ace Books in 2009. She does not own a yellow dressing gown.

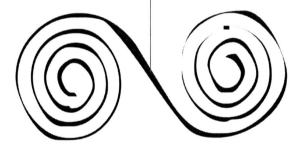

Kyle Murchison Booth's further extranormal exploits are collected in the book THE BONE KEY by Sarah Monette. Read an excerpt online, presented by Prime Books at:

WWW.THEBONEKEY.COM

The Talion Moth

BY JOHN KIRK

ILLUSTRATED BY DANIELE SERRA

IN WHICH A MONK

IN TIBET PROVES

TO BE MORE THAN

HE APPEARS

A T DUSK, A tall man in a sky-blue cloak stood beside a river in Sikkim, India's gateway to forbidden Tibet. The man's name was Harry Talion and he was far from the New York brownstone where he was born. His face was too pale for the harsh sunlight of the Himalayas, but his hair was as black as the hair of a Nepalese child, so black it shined blue in the spots of light reflected by the rushing water.

Behind him, the last slip of gold topped the trees. A bus lay on its side in a clearing at the foot of the wood line, near where the road nested a hairpin turn in the river. The driver had been a proud wheel-man, schooled driving grain trucks over the mountains. He had taken the hairpin too fast during a burst of morning rain, and his face had crashed through the windshield when the bus slammed, careening, into the trunks of the dense pines. On impact, the bus sheared and folded like the pleats of a closing bellows, and the recoil sent it rolling out across the clearing. Now the driver's face lay like a lost glove in the stiff autumn grass, peeled from the bone at his hairline, but still anchored to his chin by a strand of bloody tissue. Momentum had chopped and sliced the passengers on the bus's shorn steel and gathered them, all dead, into a pile. Dangling limbs looked like tendrils sprouted from a monstrous bulb. After a day exposed to the sun and the open air, the ammonia stink of the dead reached Talion at the riverside.

A couple dozen butterflies, vexed by the persistent breeze, scissored their yellow and red wings as they clung to the mangled sheet metal. Talion turned to the bus and opened his cloak. The silk of his shirt grew cold against his skin, and the butterflies stirred and filled the air above the bus. They swarmed Talion, blotting his torso, a few crawling to his legs and throat before they flattened their wings against him. He closed his cloak and turned to look back across the river.

The bank opposite was a sheer rise to a hilltop mounted by a stone house that belonged to a farmer. Talion spotted a procession of monks leaving the house. They walked in single file along the edge of the rise, retreating by the same path they had taken to the front door by starlight early that morning. Talion couldn't hear their chanting over the rush of the water, and soon they reached the turn in the path that led away to the far side of the hill, and one by one they dropped out of sight. They were followers of the Buddha, monks of the yellow-hat sect, called *gelug-pa*, of the same school as the Dalai Lama. Talion's faith, Tibet's nameless faith, the mountain faith of blood sacrifice, was much older, already ancient when the word of the Buddha crossed the Himalayas from India to the land of snows.

Talion waited until the moon was squat and bright above the pines before he crossed the river and climbed the path to the farmer's house. In the courtyard, a small cake shaped in the effigy of a fat man was set on a low oak table, and offering bowls

full of rice were spread about on the ground. A pink-tailed rat tipped a bowl with its forelegs and buried its nose in the spilled grains. More rats poured down the trunk of an oak tree and joined in eating. They paid no attention to Talion as he passed. The door to the house was open, an oblong space filled with wavering amber light.

One hundred and eight butter lamps lit the gathering room, scattered everywhere, each no bigger than a child's palm. Just two steps in from the doorway, a singed photo of the old farmer lay on the floor. He was smiling, his brows and high, fat cheeks swallowing his eyes.

"The photo should have burned up. The corners turned to ash, but then the fire went out." The voice came from across the room, from a woman sitting within the shadows of a doorway that led to more rooms in the back of the house. The flickering lamps lit her creased face and her spotted hands, which were busy twisting a strip of linen. All about the room lamps suddenly spat and surged, brightening the room for an instant, and Talion dropped his eyes back to the photo.

"The monks tried to burn it again," she said, "but it would not take the flame."

"You are the farmer's wife — the one who sent for me?" Talion asked.

"I am his widow," she said.

To ready the farmer's corpse for cremation, the monks had stripped and washed it, then seated it with the legs tucked into a lotus position and the arms bound behind its back. After they wrapped the body in a sheet of white linen, they crammed it into a wooden box, called a *gamti*, with the head poking through a lattice of strong rope meant to keep the dead man from climbing out.

The farmer's adult son sat in a chair beside the box, which was off to one side of the room. He had shaved his eyebrows and scalp to mourn his father in the traditional way. He stood and bowed his head out of respect for their visitor.

"You are the priest," he said to Talion.

"He is the *gshen*," the widow said, correcting her son, using one of the ancient Tibetan terms for "sorcerer." She pulled the linen strip taut, then set to wrapping it around one of her hands as she said to Talion, "My son's name is Rajesh. Please forgive his ignorance. You may well be the first holy man he has ever met."

"Then he must have arrived after the monks did their holy work and returned to the monastery," Talion said to the widow. "Perhaps you both missed them."

The widow leaned back into the darkness, the joints of the chair creaking as she shifted her weight.

"We have always been here," she said.

Talion still stood just inside the front door. The mass of lamps gave off a welcoming heat. But he resisted. Somewhere in the room, feathers rustled.

"My father left a note for us, asking that we send for you immediately after his death. He expected trouble to follow." The son smiled out of embarrassment. "His mother was a *Lepcha*. They believe in the old ways."

"Are you a believer?" Talion asked.

"I am a harvester. My father's son." Rajesh kept smiling, wanting Talion to smile, but the sorcerer focused on the wood floor, listening for the rustle of feathers.

"How was your trip from Kalimpong?" Rajesh asked. "We heard mud slides closed the road."

"There is a bus overturned across the river."

Rajesh looked at his mother. She stopped twisting the linen strip and let her hands drop to her knees. She nodded back at her son.

"We never hear anything up here over the noise of the water," Rajesh said.

"The driver and the passengers are dead," Talion told him.

"There are troops, *Garhwals*, camped in the village. I can drive over and tell them."

Talion raised his head a bit and grinned as he said, "The rats will have the bodies if you don't."

Rajesh peered at Talion, trying to find the sorcerer's eyes in the shallow light, and was about to cross the room for a better look when Talion slipped his hand into his cloak and pulled out a dagger. The steel was forged to resemble the twisting body of a snake, and Talion's knuckles tensed white around the bone handle. Rajesh shuffled back, surprised by the blade, and tipped over the chair beside the *gamti* with his calves. While Rajesh was busy righting the chair, Talion walked to the box and cut the ropes, freeing the corpse.

"Lift your father out and set him on the table," Talion said, stepping back, returning to the doorway.

Rajesh obeyed. After he cleared away the ropes, he pushed the box over on its side and pulled his father's body out. His knees popped as he jerked the corpse off the floor.

"He's stiff like bone."

"He's all fat," the wife said, fishing for Talion's sympathy with a bit of widow's nostalgia. "Imagine, *gshen*, at my age, I still had to carry his weight in bed."

She waited for Talion to respond, but he was studying the lamp light's dance on the flat surface of the dagger.

"Are you shy?" she asked, goading Talion. "Is that why you won't look at me?" The widow leaned into the light. The cataracts, like gnarled shells, should have left her blind, but she nodded as she sat back in the darkness, sure of her judgment after taking a slightly closer look.

"You must be shy," she said

Pumping hot breath from his mouth, Rajesh set his father's body on a long table near the altar the widow had built for the day's death ritual. Paper offerings, inked with prayers and mounted on gold cylinders, covered the altar top. They would burn tomorrow, gifts to protective spirits, in the ceremony that followed the farmer's cremation. If the spirits accepted the offerings, they were obliged to dissolve the ill fortune death had brought to the house.

Talion flipped the dagger blade into his palm and held out the handle to Rajesh.

"Cut off the sheet," he said.

Rajesh looked at the dagger. Sweat greased his face from his struggle with his father's body. He shook his head.

"All I need to do is untie the knot."

One pull on the length of fabric at the back and the sheet came free. Rajesh dropped it on the floor in a bundle. Although his eyes were swollen and blue, the dead farmer's skin still glowed, reflecting rather than stifling the lamp light. His body gave off the tang of green cardamom, the same spice the farmer had raised all his life, the same smell his crops gave up to the night air.

Talion cut the rope that bound the farmer's wrists at the small of his back, but his shoulders and arms held their place. Rigor mortis had set in.

"Did the monks try to liberate him?" Talion asked.

Rajesh nodded. "The abbot performed the 'pho-ba ritual, but he said my father's spirit refused to transfer."

Talion touched the farmer's forehead with the tips of his first two fingers and the body slowly rested back on the table, joints and vertebrae popping as the limbs and spine stretched out. He yanked a tuft of hair at the crown of the dead man's head and sliced it off with a twist of the dagger, leaving a tonsure of clean, gray scalp.

"You have to feed me. And you have to pay me," Talion said, putting the hair into a pocket in his cloak. "You cannot break those rules."

"My mother cooked tsampa," Rajesh said, pointing to a lamp stand near the overturned gamti. A white scarf and a bowl of cold barley mush were set among butter lamps. "I put the coins in the scarf as my father instructed in his letter."

"Go to the village and tell the soldiers about the bus," Talion said. "Take your mother with you. By the time you get back, your father will be free."

"Will you pray for us?" the widow asked from her chair. "Pray for us, so my husband won't haunt this place. He was so attached to his fields, I am afraid he won't leave."

"I will take his soul with me when I go," Talion answered. "Nothing can stop that. I promise you."

The widow smiled, concealing her teeth with her hand as she said, "You comfort me, gshen." She stood, her chair scraping farther into the blackness. She walked on strong legs, legs that had carried her into the stepped fields cut into the slopes of the surrounding peaks, year after year. The farmer had chosen a good wife, Talion could tell, but he avoided this woman's eyes as she took her son's hand. "My son didn't believe you could help us," the widow said to Talion. "But I knew you were the answer."

Rajesh bowed his head in deference to Talion, then let his mother lead him to the door and out to the courtyard.

Talion wasted no time. He put the dagger back in his cloak, then slid his hand under the farmer's head and raised it off the table. Drawing a deep breath, he shouted one syllable — "Hik!" — the intonation that calls the spirit to prepare for its outward journey. In response, a spot of flesh puckered and split at the crown of the dead man's head and a small hole ground open in his skull. Talion slipped the little finger of his right hand into the opening and cleared bits of bone and membrane from the path.

"You will be like a bird set free through an open skylight," he said, resting the farmer's head back on the table. "Come out when I call you."

The chair was rickety. He was surprised it had supported the son without a brace popping out of its slot. He moved it across the room and sat down beside the lamp stand. He found a spoon already dipped in the bowl of tsampa, and he picked up the scarf, set it in his lap and opened it. The payment was generous, even for the family of a wealthy farmer, and Talion put the coins in the same pocket as the dead man's hair, then put the scarf back. He took a spoonful of food without lifting the bowl off the stand. The gruel was thin and cold, and he let it sit on his tongue. Tasting. With a nod he swallowed, then went at the food, as the ritual required, taking up the bowl and eating quickly, scraping the spoon against the bottom and wiping the dregs off the rim with his fingers and licking his fingertips clean.

The bowl was made from cherry wood. His mother had given him a similar bowl for his fifth birthday. It sat now in Manhattan, beside a picture of her on a shelf in the brownstone he had inherited from his father. He remembered how his mother described the nature of the wood's cherry hues after he had torn off the wrapping paper, telling him that red is the color of anger, but cherry is the mellow softness inside the anger, the seed of forgiveness and the promise that the emotion, like all emotions, will transform in time.

His tongue felt thick in his mouth and his teeth had gone dry. He let the bowl and spoon drop to the floor; they hit with a crack. The bowl bounced and rolled on its edge, making one circuit around its circumference, then it stopped and balanced vertically on its rim. Pulling his cloak up past his elbow, Talion shot his arm out and made a fist. When he opened his hand, there was a piece of rice paper in his palm, folded many times to form a packet. Already, his throat burned and his pulse hammered in his ears and sweat purled down his back and the insides of his thighs. He unfolded the packet. Prayers streamed across the paper, written in a careful hand, the ink thin and flecked where the pen had jumped the coarse grains that blistered the sheet. Inside was an indigo powder that Talion fingered and tasted before he closed the packet. He stamped his foot, struggling to drag air into his failing lungs, then popped the rice paper in his mouth and swallowed it — just in time, since his tongue soon swelled and blocked his esophagus. Seeing his hands turning a

deeper blue than his cloak, Talion cupped them in his lap and bowed his head. He was careful to shut his eyes.

His breathing stopped.

The bowl tipped over and swiveled on its rim. It kept on, steadily grinding out a song on the floor. Out in the courtyard, the rats chattered. A few lay on their backs, gorged on sacrificial rice. The weak and the young, bullied from the feast, finally took their turns.

After a while, the chattering stopped. The bowl slapped to rest at Talion's feet. A few butter lamps popped and died, issuing willowy smoke, and Rajesh stood in the front doorway. He walked in, picked up the bowl and set it on the lamp stand, never taking his eyes off the holy man slumped in the chair. The spoon cracked under Rajesh's foot as he stepped up to Talion, took hold of the lashes on his right eye and tried to open it. The lids resisted like a single piece of flesh, so Rajesh pulled at the skin until it was sheer enough to tear. Somewhere deeper in the gathering room, wings fluttered. Rajesh let go of Talion's eyelid and turned to the corpse. He saw the hole in the farmer's skull and decided the eyes of a dead sorcerer could wait.

When Talion was twelve, he learned the nature of demons from his teacher, an ascetic who had spent most of his life praying inside the monastery that fills the belly of Mount Kailash in western Tibet. The nameless religion taught that there were nine types of demons, each with nine sub-groups. They existed in the earth and in the air and in the lower realms. Demons of the earth and air were free to wander and glut themselves. But those destroyed by sorcerers were reborn into one of the nine hells, and they were bound to those planes of suffering for one cycle of existence. In the hells, they burned with the same hungers they knew in the world above, they searched and raged and tore at each other, anything to stop the burning, but their bellies and their hearts still ached, and only the fires were fed.

Standing beside the table that held the farmer's corpse, Rajesh stripped off his clothes and let them gather at his feet. He dropped to his hands and knees and shed his skin in long, wet strips that peeled and fell with a sucking sound. He was a demon of the class called *gshin-rje*, with the body of a giant snow leopard, more than ten feet long from shoulders to mottled tail. Briefly, the demon's head kept the shape of a leopard's, spots converging like a black stain over its face. Then its snout and forehead bloated and its tongue stabbed the air as its jaw bones repeatedly cracked and fixed. Its head became the head of a dragon, with skin like burlap and two rows of sharp, conical teeth. The leopard's spine bowed upward to support the weight of this reptilian head.

Free of the skin it had woven to mimic the son's image, the *gshin-rje* raised a fat paw, curling its tail for balance before it stabbed the farmer's shin with its claws and dragged the body, feet-first, to the end of the table. It rubbed its steaming nostrils over the thick, coarse soles of the dead man's feet, savoring the cardamom sting that rose from the pores. Then it bit, gently, taking both legs up to the knees. The farmer's flesh and bones sizzled in the acids that poured into the demon's mouth, rendering them into porridge composed of fat and marrow and spice. The demon swallowed and purred.

Talion's hands trembled.

He spoke through stiff blue lips, saying, "You will choke, *gshin-rje*." Then he pitched forward and vomited a black mix of *tsampa* and bile, emptying his stomach.

The demon missed Talion's retching. It took its time, pulling itself up onto the table as it crushed the hard bones of the farmer's pelvis with its snout and champed at the spinal column like a piece of waxed cord. Resting its belly in the gore that stained the table's oak planks, it clawed the dead man's shoulders and slid the base of the rib cage to its mouth. One flick of the tongue took the lungs and heart. Spittle bubbled on the *gshin-rje's* teeth.

"No place left to hide," it called inside the empty torso.

Smoke from the butter lamps clouded the air near the ceiling, and thick blue veins showed through Talion's fists as he raised his sword's hilt into the smoke. Lamplight dappled the blade, forged in the same snaking twists as the dagger. He drove the sword down into the demon's back until the tip split the table top and hissed through. Instantly, blood boiled out of the wound and sopped Talion's hands. A shiver coursed through the demon's long leopard body, one last icy message riding its nerves, and then its limbs sagged. Without the blade holding the demon in place like a pin, it would have slipped to the floor.

Talion let go of the hilt. "Calm down," he said to the demon, wiping his bloody palms over the leopard's fur. "You can still speak. You can turn your head."

Tears wet the demon's burlap snout. It tested its neck, rolled its eyes until it found Talion. Aside from his features — those of a *phyi-pa*, an outsider — he looked like a priest, any priest. "We made a bargain, *gshen*. We paid you. We fed you."

Talion tried to clean his hands on the leopard's fur, but blood had already dried in the creases of his palms and the cracked skin between his fingers. He worked at it, digging into the nap and running his knuckles over the demon's ribs.

There was a sound like canvas ripping. Talion looked over at what remained of the farmer's body and saw that an object was rising through the dead man's trachea, swelling his throat. Talion bristled, hating surprises.

"I told you to wait for me," he said to the corpse.

The demon smelled a birth coming. It bucked its head and slammed it on the table, shouting, "Let me up!" The farmer's jaws opened, grinding in the sockets until the lips tore at the corners and the mandible popped free of the joints. His cheeks ballooned. Talion wiped his hands as best he could on his

cloak and took out a white scarf as a raven climbed out of the farmer's mouth.

Cradled by the dead man's lips and tongue, the bird shook thick mucous from its feathers, spattering the wall and floor. Talion wrapped the scarf around the raven's wings, and the bird blinked and cawed in his hands, still craving the dimness of life inside the body. Again, the *gshin-rje* heaved and crashed its head, screaming, "I came here to eat!" Cracks shot through the oak table. Lamps across the room rattled and spilled. The raven settled down once Talion had it tucked inside his cloak. "We missed a feast of twenty souls – more! — from that bus crash," the *gshin-rje* went on. "We missed their screams because we were so anxious to pick this pig's soul out of the air."

"You're hungry — finish your meal," Talion said to the demon, pushing what was left of the corpse, the head and chest, the raw muscle and bone of the upper arms, to its mouth, but the demon spat the remains back on the table.

"Why would you do this?" the demon said. "He promised us his flesh and his spirit to take when he died." Talion ignored the question, keeping his focus on the farmer's torn face, running through a silent prayer. Faced with Talion's indifference, the demon fought back its panic and twitched its mouth into a small grin. "The farmer must have found some magic to lock his soul away until you could open the door. My partner said you would free him for us, and then you would eat the *tsampa*. She said priests are that way — slaves to ritual." The demon expected Talion to challenge the insult, but no challenge came, so it returned to pleading: "The farmer broke his vow. You understand that. A vow is a holy thing."

Talion stepped to the demon's side, rubbing his hands together. Specks of dried blood fell from them like sand grains. The demon's eyes twisted in their sockets, following him. "Something is wrong," it said. "Who are you, *gshen*? I should have smelled your vomit. All I smelled was the farmer's spice."

"I will feed you," Talion said.

"What?"

"I will feed you something pure. I will do it if you answer a question."

The demon swallowed, and strained to keep Talion in its sight. "I want to move again," it said.

"I offered you food."

The demon shut its eyes. "Ask me."

"Where is my father's soul?"

The demon pissed itself, only aware of it by the splutter wetting the table and a sudden, vague emptiness. "Show me your eyes," it said.

Talion leaned closer and raised his head to the shifting light. His corneas were the brilliant white of mid-day snow fields, and rose petals bloomed from pupils flecked like slate.

"You are the *gshen* who hunts the Talion moth," the demon said. "In the hells, they say you are the rebirth of *Khro-rgyal*, the magician who ground demons into dust."

"Where is my father?"

"What will you give me?"

Talion held open one side of his cloak. An Indian girl of high caste leaned against him. She was thirteen and still a year away from menstruation. Her copper skin was bare and hot, and her hair, softened with Brahmi oil and scented with jasmine, spilled over her shoulders. Deep in the past, in the reign of King *Songsten Gampo*, *Khro-rgyal* slit this girl's throat and fed her blood to a river demon that had spread leprosy throughout Tibet. Fulfilling her parents' expectations, the girl welcomed the blade, even tilting her head and raising her chin, and gave her body to *Khro-rgyal* to use as he wished for eternity. The river demon grew so drunk on the girl's ambrosia that it traveled to all the afflicted and bathed their ulcers clear with its tongue. The disease burned out in the fires of its gut, and the victims were cured. The deformed were whole again. Thousands were healed thanks to the butchering of one pure girl.

"Her body is a vessel, *gshin-rje*," Talion said. "She is a holy thing."

The girl rested her head on Talion's chest. "Put me back with the butterflies," she said. She caught the demon staring at her, and she draped Talion's cloak across her hips.

"Ask me again," the demon said to Talion.

"Where is my father's soul?"

"The moth is with the foreigners, across the ocean. It has escaped us for all these years, conspiring with the winds, but we believe it smells its home, the city of its last incarnation. The moth will be there soon." Another grin twisting the corners of its mouth, its eyes leveled to slits, the demon found the girl's scent and inhaled. "You will go back to the city where you were born. My brothers and sisters already expect you. You will empty all the magic from your coat, but your tricks will fail . . . And you will go to the place where you have sent so many of my family."

Talion stepped back from the girl. The edge of his cloak pulled from her hands, leaving her body exposed. Her nipples swelled.

"You see how she wants this?" the *gshin-rje* said to Talion, settling its head on the table. "Take your magic out of me so I can reach her."

Talion's hands were already on the hilt. His fingers fit the grooves in the bone from the forger's polishing wheel. The handle was once a femur, taken from a monk whose skull *Khro-rgyal* had crushed simply by speaking a malicious word. Talion looked at the girl. She wiped a strand of hair from her lips, then rested her hands on her thighs. The skin on her forearms prickled.

"I am glad you came to this lonely place," the demon said to Talion. "I am glad I was able to help you." It raised its massive head, nosing toward the girl. "Now keep your word – give me my meal."

Talion emptied his lungs. The blade slid up and out and dripped blood on the leopard's fur. Nerves in the demon's spine reached and fused. Its limbs shivered. The thick muscles between its shoulders bunched as the claws of its forepaws bit the table. By denying himself air, Talion was able to rise a few inches off the floor and drift back to the girl's side. He opened his cloak with his sword hand.

The demon lunged for the girl, its jaws cranked wide.

Talion spun, sweeping the girl inside his cloak and locking his sword arm open. The demon's teeth shut, taking only a strip of sky-blue fabric, and for an instant it hung its head, anticipating the burst of the girl's juice. But Talion came full circle, his outstretched arm like an iron beam, and his blade shattered the demon's clamped teeth. Shards of enamel and dentin stabbed the floor.

When Talion took a breath, he settled to the floor and the girl was gone. On the table, the demon lay on its side like a foal, blinking, its ribs heaving. Blood seeped from its gums and sprayed from its nostrils. Talion walked to the head of the table and looked into its eyes. The demon whimpered, and the sound reminded Talion of a dying climber he had once tended, perched on a smooth mountain ledge, holding the man's palsied hand. The whimper came at the end, when the climber pictured the faces of his children as he surrendered to the cold.

"You know where I go if you do this," the demon said.

"The same place your family will send me." Talion's mouth rose at the corners. "But nothing is eternal, *gshin-rje*. We must believe that."

Talion braced open the demon's snout. With his free arm, he scooped the farmer's head and torso and shoved them down its throat. He held the bits of corpse in place while the demon choked, its leopard legs dancing, and he balled his fist to keep its throat blocked. The whole time, Talion looked into the demon's eyes, hoping it would carry away a memory of roses.

He had to relax his fist before he could slide his arm out. His sleeve was gone, dissolved along with the remains, and his skin was pallid and streaked with mucous, but otherwise uncorrupted. Feeling tired, tasting the residue of vomit, he let his eyes go out of focus until he saw the river beyond the precipice. He let himself fall deeper, to a place where all he could hear was the rushing of water. And once he settled there, dead petals floated in his eyes while he prayed for the *gshin-rje*.

LIGHT FROM TWO butter lamps split the darkness in the back room. The widow — that is, the demon that had taken on the widow's image — sat in a corner, her hands wound up in the strip of linen. The corpses of the real widow and son were on the floor in front of her. Hundreds of small punctures covered what skin she and the *gshin-rje* had left them. Aside from the chair, there was no furniture in the room, so Talion set the lamps on the floor.

"We came after the monks left," the demon said from the corner. "The wife told us she had sent for a sorcerer. She thought that might scare us off." The demon snorted, remembering the widow wielding her talismans and prayers on rice paper. "She tasted bitter, like October orchids."

Talion knelt beside the bodies, careful not to bury them in his shadow.

"You think if you had come earlier you would have saved them," the demon went on, "but you're wrong."

"You knew the ritual forbid me to enter the house until the moon was up," Talion said.

"Humans do not deserve your salvation, *gshen*. That farmer you freed was one of the worst I have seen. He called us when his crops failed. We told him one fat man would not be enough to save his fields, so he offered us his wife and his son." The demon smiled. In place of teeth, a hundred silver needles filled her mouth. "He sold us his family for leaves on the side of a mountain."

The dead widow's head felt as light as an apple in Talion's hand. The crown of her skull had been ripped off, the flesh around the rim serrated and yellow.

"They are given years in this world to face the truth, but what do they do with that gift? They fuck each other, they kill each other, betray everything they say they love, all to stop from feeling even the smallest bit of their own pain." The demon shook her head, like an old woman telling a story on a neighbor. "You believe you liberate souls.... You shovel shit."

The son's mouth was ripped all the way to his ears. Green and white feathers from a magpie robin covered his face. Talion would have their bodies burned. That was all he could do for them.

"They're children," Talion said to the demon. "They get lost and they look for someone to guide them home. You hold out your hand, but it is your touch that turns them into shit. And then you eat."

Talion stood. The demon tensed at the movement, then caught herself. She let a silver smile ease across her face.

"The *gshin-rje* lied to you," she said.

"How do you know?"

"Years ago, one of my sisters took the shape of a whore, in a house in Ladakh, and the Talion moth flew in her window. Old habits for your father. He landed on her lips, and his energy was so strong that her whore's body erupted. All night his wings marked her with their powder, and her fluid drained through the bed. She said she could hear it, dripping on the floor. In the morning, he rested on her belly like a tattoo, a great Atlas moth, its wings the span of her two hands. She let him rest, because for one night he was good to a whore. Then she plucked him from her belly and impaled him on her teeth and let it take hours for his soul to slide down her throat."

The demon leaned forward, lifting her face. "He burns in the ninth hell, where cowards burn." She sat back with a slow creaking of the chair. "I hope that eases your mind." Talion stayed quiet, letting the demon have her say. "You made your bargain, *gshen*. You tricked the *gshin-rje*, but you are still bound to serve me. Give me the farmer's soul."

Talion nodded, even managed to smile.

"You have eased my mind," he said.

This time when he opened his cloak it was lined with the skin of a white Royal Bengal tiger, an animal poisoned in a zoo in Nandankanan. Talion had cradled the tiger's head and spoke prayers in its ear as it died, and at the end the tiger offered him its flesh as a meal, saying it wanted to see through the flowers in the holy man's eyes.

Talion's cloak rustled, and the tiger's face, flat and broad within the fabric, appeared at his hip. The chair creaked, shuttling backward, but the demon was hampered by her false skin. She was so frightened she even forgot her rending teeth, and slapped feebly at the tiger as it leapt and crushed her in its jaws.

"You poisoned the *tsampa*," Talion said, knowing that the demon was gone, but needing to say the words to fulfill the ritual. "That broke our contract."

He took the coins from his pocket and threw them on the floor. One bounced into a butter lamp and snuffed the flame. At the doorway, he bent and picked up the lit candle. He carried it into the gathering room, setting it on the table beside the dragon's head. In the courtyard, a rat sniffed at the farmer's effigy and took a cautious bite. Talion did not bother to mind the path. He looked at the stars as he walked down the slope. ❧

John Kirk is a screenwriter, and a member of the Writers Guild of America, West, in Los Angeles. He dedicates this story to Jean Munzer and Pema Losang Chogyen, friends who helped to open the door to the farmer's stone house.

Detours on the Way to Nothing

BY RACHEL SWIRSKY

ILLUSTRATED BY FANTASIO

IN WHICH SKIN IS DREAMED & STROKED, AS ARE FEATHERS

It's midnight when you and your girlfriend, Elka, have your first fight since you moved in together. Words wound, tears flow, doors slam. You storm out of the apartment, not caring where you go as long as it's far away from her. When you step off the front stoop onto the sidewalk, that's the moment when the newest version of me is born.

You get on the subway heading toward Brooklyn and ride until the train rumbles out of the tunnels and squeaks into a familiar aboveground stop. The neighborhood isn't good, but a friend of yours used to live a few blocks away, so you know the area pretty well. At least you won't get lost while you work off the rest of your anger. You disembark, let your feet pick a direction, and start walking.

That's how the logic seems from your perspective, but there's another explanation: I want you to come to me.

By a series of what you think are random turns, you end up in an alley between high rise buildings. Reinforced doors protect apartments built like warehouses; skulls grin on rat poison warning signs nailed beneath barred panes. Abandoned mattresses and broken radios decay in the gutter, accumulating mold and rust.

In a streetlamp spotlight, an old Puerto Rican man hurls bottles at a fifth story window. "Christina!" he yells. "Open up!" A voice shouts down, "She doesn't live here anymore!" but the man keeps throwing. Translucent shards collect around his feet. None have flown back into his face yet, but it's only a matter of time.

The distraction stops you, as I intended. I wanted people around so you'd be less likely to spook.

You look up and see me. I'm the girl on the roof. The edge where I stand is flat as the sidewalk and has no guard rail. You gasp when you notice my toes edging over the precipice—then gasp harder a moment later when you see my hair floating in the wind. It looks like feathers. Just like feathers.

The Puerto Rican man runs out of bottles. He rubs his sore palms, repeating, "Christina, my Christina, why won't you open the window?"

Looking up, you gesture between me and the Puerto Rican man, asking: are you Christina? I shake my head and make walking motions with my fingers to say I'll come down. Not knowing quite why, you put your hands in your pockets and wait.

When I get down to street level, you're shocked to see it wasn't an illusion: my hair really is made of feathers. They're bright blue, such a vivid color that it's obvious they weren't plucked from any real bird. They remind you of the ones you and your sister decorated carnival masks with when you were children: feathers dyed to match the way people think birds look.

You reach out to touch them before your sense of propriety kicks in and pulls your hand back. You shuffle your feet with embarrassment. "Hi."

I find your shyness endearing. I take one hand out of the lined pocket of my ski jacket and wave.

"I'm Patrick," you say.

I smile and nod, the way people do when they hear information they don't find relevant.

"What's your name?" you ask.

I step closer. You tilt your ear toward my lips, assuming I want to whisper. It's a reasonable assumption, though wrong. I take your chin and gently lift your face so that your gaze is level with mine, and then open my mouth to show you where my tongue was cut out.

You back away. Another second and you'd bolt, so I act fast, pull a card out of my pocket and give it to you.

"Voluntary surgery?" you read. "What are you, part of some cult?"

It's more a philosophy than a cult, but since it isn't really either, I wave my hand back and forth: in a way.

Debate wavers in your expression. You still might go. Before you can decide, I take your hand and pull your fingers through my hair.

You breathe hard as your fingertips touch skin beneath my feathers. "All the way to the scalp," you murmur. That's when I know I've got you. I can see it in the way your eyes turn one dark color from pupil to iris. You're thinking, how can this be real?

The fantasy has been with you since adolescence. Maybe it started with the feathers you and your sister glued on the carnival masks. They felt so soft that you pocketed a pair—one blue, one white—and took them back to bed with you. Your vision of a bird-woman appeared soon thereafter. Beautiful and silent, she wrapped you nightly in sky-colored feathers that smelled like wind.

In the nearby park, I recreate this. Behind us, a levy of black rocks stands against the East River. Reflected Manhattan lights form a sheen on the water, shimmering like a fluorescent oil spill.

I strip off my clothes and stand naked for you, my shadow falling onto gravel cut with glints of glass. I'm skinny with visible ribs, but soft and fleshy around the belly where you like to stroke your lovers as if they were satin pillows—all the conflicting traits you prefer, combined in one body. Your eyes never leave my feathers.

You will never know how I am possible. My philosophy—my cult, as you called it—is old and secretive. We have no organization, no books of dogma, no advocates to harangue passersby with our rhetoric. Each initiate finds us alone, deducing our beliefs through meditation and self-reflection. Only the magic of our sacrificed tongues unifies us.

Our practices have few analogues in Western thought, though you could call us philosophical cousins to the Buddhists. We believe there is no way to lose the trappings of self so completely as to become someone else's desire.

If you see me again, I will not be a bird. I will be a figure made of jewels or a woolly primate with prehensile lips. My skin will be rubber. My cock will be velvet. Each of my six blood-spattered breasts will be tattooed with the face of a man I've killed. The goal is endless transformation.

I'm still distant from that goal. Though I've been transforming for decades, I'm only inching along the path to self-dissolution. I cling to identity; indulge fantasies like this one of telling you my story. Cutting out our tongues is supposed to silence us. Instead, I speak internally. Can you hear me?

I tease you with my feathers, encompassing your face, hands, and cock in turn. When you tire of that,

you pull me up against the rocks with my legs around your waist. I throw my head back to let my plumage stream in the wind and you come. I don't know if you think of Elka, but don't worry. You can't be unfaithful with a fantasy.

You recline against the black rocks. "Wow," you say, "I'm not the kind of person that would ever do this. Elka and I were together three months before . . ."

Your eyes glaze. This could be bad. There are two possibilities now. You may pull back, stammering her name, or:

You reach for my shoulder. "I know you can't talk, but can you write? Is there someplace we could go? I have so much to ask."

I've done my job too well. It's time to leave. I shrug away from your grip and raise one hand to wave. Goodbye.

"Hey, wait!" you shout.

In your fantasies, when you're done, the bird-woman dissolves into a shower of feathers. Unfortunately, my magic isn't that versatile. I have to walk away.

You try to chase me so I maneuver through sharp turns and unexpected byways. You don't know this area as well as you think you do. Soon, your footsteps grow distant and faint.

I retreat to my rooftop and watch from above as you pace in circles around the neighborhood. I hope you will go soon. If you don't, it may be a sign I've done you permanent damage. Finally, you head back to the subway. I have to admit, I'm a little sad when you go. A little jealous, too.

I climb down the building and discover the Puerto Rican man huddled next to a fire escape, muttering in soft Spanish. Tiny cuts bleed on his arms and calves. I consider remaking myself for him, but all he wants is his human Christina. I catch an impression of her: short and blonde, she hates dancing, speaks seven languages badly, calls him The Man She Should Have Loved Less.

As his yearning for this specific, clumsy, jovial woman flows through me, I realize how little I am to you. What is a fantasy? A scrap of yourself made into flesh. An illusion to masturbate with.

Moving away from the Puerto Rican man, I shelter in a doorway and will myself to molt. My feathers float away on the wind and something I was clinging to flies away with them, carried on the same breeze.

I say goodbye to the girl with feathered hair and wait for another's desire to overtake and shape me. In the few seconds before it does, for one moment, just one, my soul becomes pure essence without form.

It's the closest I've come to nothingness yet. ℮

Rachel Swirsky is a fiction M.F.A. student at the Iowa Writers Workshop and a 2005 graduate of the Clarion West Writers Workshop. Her stories have appeared in publications and anthologies including *Interzone*, *Subterranean*, and *Fantasy: The Best of the Year 2007*.

A TALE OF
ELRIC OF MELNIBONÉ

Black Petals

BY MICHAEL MOORCOCK

ILLUSTRATED BY MING DOYLE

Chapter One:
The Apothecary in Horse Alley

IN WHICH A DARK PAST IS NOT EASILY PUT TO REST

FROM THE SEA the city of Nassea-Tiki was a mosaic of vivid colour, fluttering flags, gilded domes, red battlements, a busy market, tiny black figures. The harbour was vast, serving the trade of the entire South Eastern continent. Foot forward in the prow of the Lormyrian cutter, peering ahead as the late afternoon sun set the great port on fire, Moonglum of Elwher remarked to his friend on the wealth of shining masts which stood at all angles, like the spears of embattled armies, casting a dozen reflections. The sails were furled for the most part, tightly rolled blues and loose-hung russets to match the gargoyles and grim seabulls decorating the hulls. These big ships were local. Others, such as their own, favouring black, dark red, white and silver, were from months away.

The ship's captain came to join them, staring ahead. "What a sight!" He drew in a breath, as if inhaling the entire vision. "After Melniboné they say she's the most beautiful city on four continents."

He looked at Moonglum's companion, as if for confirmation.

"After Melniboné," the passenger agreed.

Throwing back his thick, green cloak Moonglum turned his head, hands around the pommels of his twin sabres. "Who would have thought we'd find such a rich place after all those half-civilised villages we've seen on the way here?" He looked back at his friend, whose blazing crimson eyes seemed to find reflection in the effects of the sun. Set in an intensely beautiful face the colour of bone, the eyes were slightly sloping, like the lobes of his ears. His lips were full. His long hair was like poured milk. His eyes stared into a past and a future of equal tragedy. Yet there was a kind of amusement there, too.

Moonglum's own eyes were troubled as he contemplated his friend. Elric, last emperor of Melniboné, was breathing heavily, having difficulty moving along the edge of the deck, holding tight to the rail. He was hampered by the scabbard of a massive broadsword whose hilt was tightly wired to his belt.

Not for the first time, the Captain turned away, ostentatiously incurious.

"The drugs are ceasing to work, my friend," whispered Moonglum. "Were they the last?"

The albino shook his head. "Almost," he said.

ELRIC OF MELNIBONÉ and his red-headed companion, refreshed to some degree, stepped towards the busy dock while over their heads swung goods of every description. Most eyes were on the cargoes rather than the passengers. Only a few noticed the two disembark, though most had no idea whom they might be.

Nassea-Tiki was not merely busy. The vast port was in celebration. Her very palms seemed to dance. When the two adventurers stopped a passerby and enquired of the uproar seizing the city, the man said that the old system of peacekeeping had, on that very day, given way to the new. The two men were mystified until a passing ship's captain, dressed up in crisp blue silk and black linen on his way to meet a prospective customer, told them the capital city's notorious private, corrupt police force was being replaced by a trained band of municipal employees. These would be free from bribery and arbitrary brutality. "At least in theory," said the Tarkeshite, whose first impression of the albino's identity was now confused and who wanted to be on his way; a desire he indicated by glancing at the gigantic public hour-glass of copper and greenish crystal dominating the busy quayside. A little amused, Moonglum wished him well and the two allowed him to continue.

Feeble as the young albino had become during his long, uncomfortable voyage, on Moonglum's arm he was still able to stumble beneath the blazing brass timepiece of timber and glass and reach the inn recommended by Captain Calder Dulk, master of the Morog Bevonia, as somewhere to find clean lodgings at little risk of being robbed. As they pressed slowly through the narrow streets, full of men and women enjoying a public holiday, he was noticeable as being taller and slimmer than the average. Though his cloak's high collar was raised about his face, it was clear to which race he belonged. The local people paid him no special attention but those from nations closer to his own gave him a respectful distance.

Paying for a quiet room, with two hammocks and a window overlooking the inner courtyard, Elric tipped the servant generously when hot water for baths was brought. Moonglum sighed. His friend was too generous with the little money they had remaining. After washing and grooming themselves, they donned fresh linen and went back downstairs. Looking around at the other guests, they judged Dulk's advice reliable.

Moonglum's thieves' eyes brightened with curiosity when he saw that main hall of the inn was full of well-dressed merchant seamen already engaged in the business which brought them half across the world and might take them still closer to the edge. Some men were running impromptu auctions with those who had waited days for ships, delayed by bad weather. Even Elric, who had travelled widely on dreamquests over a hundred thousand years of history and seen much, was surprised by the amounts of money changing hands on speculative bargaining.

They sat together, under a window in the quieter part of the hall, drinking the local wine and studying a map they had bought in Thokora. The albino was having difficulty focusing. He muttered that the livestock the ships had brought in was in considerably better health than himself.

"Aren't you at all tempted to untwist those supernaturally intricate lengths of brass and copper which lock your sword to its scabbard?" Moonglum whispered, holding a blank scrap of velum up to the light because he thought he might confuse a potential observer while he had the chance. Shaking his head, Elric seemed utterly unaware of what two men in a harbour tavern poring over a map might signify to the crazed, treasure-hungry denizens who hung around these merchants like carrion birds.

Moonglum knew that Elric feared his blade Stormbringer quite as much as any potential enemy. Indirectly, it was their chief reason for risking this long journey from the few remaining sources of Elric's drugs. In Melniboné's past, before such drugs were discovered, silverskins like himself had led short, painful lives usually ending in madness and self-destruction. Only by resorting to the darkest sorcery and trading their souls for supernatural aid, could the enfeebled creatures hope to live like others. While the drugs sustained Elric, they did not invigorate him as the sword had. Yet he wished never to draw it again and have more souls pay the terrible price so many had al-

ready paid for his own life. To that end, he must find the legendary *noibuluscus* plant.

For the first time in months, the pale prince, reassured that, in Nassea-Tiki, his reputation was no more than a distant legend, relaxed a little. Thankfully, the Bright Empire of Melniboné had never extended this far. And the *noibuluscus* could soon be his. He had bought the book and map in a market; they had been in the middle of a vast pile of manuscripts, any valuable decoration already removed, looted from somewhere by illiterate nomads who brought the stuff to market only in the faint hope someone would put value on it.

Map and herbal had told of the so-called Black Anemonë which grew in a temple's *lunarium* at the centre of an ancient jungle city, upriver of Nassea-Tiki. The plant had all the properties Elric needed to sustain himself. But, another grimoire he had consulted reminded him, the black flower only bloomed once a century; and in full moonlight. So he had gambled on finding it and forever protecting himself against the sickness brought by his rare form of albinism.

A dozen dark legends surrounded the Black Anemonë. Truth could not be told from fable. What all his sources agreed, however, was that the time of the Black Anemonë's blooming grew close. Their departure from Lormyr had been hasty. At certain moments, when the seas grew stormy, they feared they would arrive in Nassea-Tiki too late and Elric would be forced to fall back on the power derived from his sword. As it was, the ship had docked with only days to spare. Now they had to get upriver to the mysterious city marked on the map. Ancient Soom was now said to lie in ruins, deserted by its folk.

Relaxed and wearing the loose silks of Aflitainian gentleman captains, Elric and Moonglum completed their supper. Then, with his friend at his side, Moonglum at the bar enquired of his friendly, corpulent host if he knew the whereabouts of a certain apothecary with the unlikely name or

Nashatak Skwett, said to reside in the older part of the port. This brought a broad smile to the landlord's face. "So old Nashatak's found another customer, eh?" Even here, so far from the Dragon Isle, they spoke a form of Low Melnibonéan.

Elric raised a white, enquiring eyebrow.

"Nashatak has a bit of a reputation as a quack in these parts," explained the innkeeper, "though I'll admit I've met a few wise medical men and women from abroad who seem to respect him. And you, no doubt, are one of them, sir. He wrote a much-copied book, I hear. It's often said that local wisdom gets no respect until it's traveled a ways. He's eccentric, I will tell you. He comes and goes a bit, but when he's here he is generally to be found at his shop in the Moldigore. That's the area sometimes called the old fortress. A fortress no longer, but it's where the robber-captains who founded Nassea-Tiki built a great stone keep and what became a self-sufficient village, for when the lords of Soom came a-visiting, impatient with their thieving. Long ago, when Soom was still powerful, the lords brought an army downriver. They razed the keep but, having no quarrel with ordinary folk, left the outer walls and the village standing. Anyway, it's in the Moldigore you'll find him."

To Moonglum's further disapproval, Elric put down generous silver. "But Soom, I gather, is itself a ruin. What became of her folk?"

"Nothing pleasant, sir, that's for sure. A few of her lords settled here and rebuilt the harbor. Some members of our present ruling council claim them as ancestors, for they were a learned and brave people according to legend. Others, however, say their blood turned bad with arrogant pride and they took to perverse teachings and strange practices. All we do know is that Soom is shunned by wise folk, not so much because of any supernatural curse upon the place, but because it is periodically occupied by a nomad tribe of cannibals during certain seasons of the year. I heard that the King of the Uyt was the last to go there, seeking some fabled treasure. Neither he nor his men are yet returned."

Fearing that his loquacious landlord was about to launch into a series of local stories, Moonglum interrupted gently to ask the way to the apothecary's. The man raised a finger then led the pair back to his nook behind the bar, reached under a cupboard and unrolled a local map. "There it is — just off Horse Street." He waited patiently while Elric took a piece of charcoal and, borrowing Moonglum's scrap of vellum, made a quick copy of the map. Then, with a word of thanks, the exiled Prince of Melniboné and his friend left the inn, pushing through still-celebrating crowds packing streets of multi-coloured stone and brightly painted wood whose ornate frontages rose eight or ten storeys into the glaring, blue-gold sky. They followed the harbour wall until they found the turning into Moldigore's alleys and were soon at Horse Street.

The apothecary's sign was prominent at the far end of the narrow cobbled way, painted on the fading white wall of a tall old house whose black timber beams looked hard as iron. Now that they had at last found the apothecary's, the pair found themselves approaching with a certain reluctant caution. For too long Elric's quest for his ailment's remedy had ended in failure. Moonglum knew his friend had gambled everything, this time, on what he had read in Nashatak Skwett's *Herbal and Magical Remedies for Rare Diseases and Conditions* and was almost afraid to proceed. What did it matter that a few good folk had died to feed him their energy? After all, most of those his sword killed deserved their fate. But then he remembered his betrothed cousin Cymoril, who had died, albeit accidentally, on the point of that blade. Elric's pace quickened. Slipping his silver hilted dagger from its sheath, he rapped on the door with its hilt.

The door was almost immediately opened. A pink-skinned, bright-haired child of indeterminate gender opened its mouth in a question.

They gave their names. Moonglum asked for Master Nashatak. The child disappeared, then returned to hold out its hands to lead them through ill-lit halls and passages, up flights of crooked stairs. A mixture of smells struck their nostrils — chemicals, animal odours, a sweet stink reminiscent of rotten flesh. But, entering the room at the end of a long, twisting passage, they were impressed by its orderliness and the cleanliness of the relatively young man who rose to greet them. He was rerolling a parchment and set this down as he opened his arms to them. "I have your letter, my lord. Let me tell you how honoured I am to receive one as learned as yourself. And, of course, you too are welcome, Master Moonglum."

"Ah," said Elric, embarrassed, "such learning was commonplace in my homeland where we absorbed it on our dream couches. I can make no claims for myself . . ."

"As you please, prince." Master Nashatak's lank fair hair was pulled back from his lugubrious dark brown face and secured by a fillet of copper. He wore a long velvet gown which had been recently washed but on which the stains remained. He looked curiously at Elric. "We have an acquaintance in common. Doctor Cerlat Vog . . ."

"Who sent you this letter?" The walk had tired him. Breathing with some difficulty, Elric reached into his purse and brought out a sealed packet.

"My old friend! Was he well?" Nashatak accepted the letter, breaking the seal. "His teeth?"

Moonglum answered. "They were little better when we left Noothar. But his feet showed some improvement. He enquired after the health of your wife." Still enough of a Melnibonéan noble to find such pleasantries at conversation irritating, Elric disguised his impatience.

"She is well. I thank you, Master Moonglum. Visiting her mother on the other side of the river. This is our child."

They still had no clue as to the little creature's gender. Its large, hazel eyes continued to regard them from the shadows.

Master Nashatak read the letter carefully, holding it close to one of the lamps and occasionally nodding to himself. "So you've heard of the *noibuluscus* by its true name. In your original letter you spoke only of a black flower. And you've come seeking it in the right season of the right year. But I fear there's another searching who has gone ahead of you. Do you know of Tilus Kreek, King of the Uyt?"

Moonglum shrugged. "We were told he died in Soom seeking a treasure."

"He has not returned, that's so. But I heard it from a friend that Tilus, too, sought the *noibuluscus*."

Elric turned, hearing the child utter a deep, throaty chuckle.

"The flesh-eaters caught him and ate him," it said. "And almost every one of his mercenary army was killed or captured."

Moonglum swore. "Where did you get such intelligence?"

"The streets. It's common knowledge."

Elric laid his hand on his friends arm. "Nonetheless, I would go to Soom and find the Black Anemonë. Where can I employ a guide with a boat to take us upriver?"

"I suspect it will be difficult. There are other terrors, they say, in Soom."

"We've dealt with fierce beasts and men in our time, Master Nashatak." Moonglum told him gently. "And supernatural horrors, too."

"I believe you have. You are evidently soldiers of great courage and resource. Indeed, this letter speaks of your bravery and wisdom. You performed Cerlat Vog a considerable service, I gather."

Elric restrained his impatience. "If he says so. I must have that boat and a guide, sir. I have little time remaining."

"If it's true," added Moonglum, "the black flower blooms only once in a century at this season when the moon is full, you will appreciate . . ."

The apothecary shrugged. "Nonetheless, it is unwise to go at this unprepared. I myself am curious, as you can imagine, but I could not afford the small army needed."

"Unless you can discover the whereabouts of the Uyt king's twin daughters and their escorts," murmured the child almost to itself. "I heard…"

"Heard? Where?" Its father frowned and Elric gave the child his concentrated attention.

"They came this morning, seeking audience with the Council. They met with one of your race, Prince Elric."

"A Melnibonéan?" asked Moonglum.

"Aye. And I heard that some of the same folk were in King Tilus Kreek's band."

They became still more intrigued.

"How could I find these sisters and the others?" Moonglum demanded

"If the street speaks truth, then they no doubt lodge at the great Council House as guests of the city."

"Where's that?"

The apothecary interrupted. "Prince Elric, I would not have you go to Soom alone. I will write you a letter. My boy will take you to the Council House. Certain members of the Great Council are good customers of mine. You will need to be introduced. But first — " He crossed to one of several tables covered in all kinds of curios, many whose function was completely mysterious. He opened a box of ivory inlaid cedarwood and took out of it a short string of amber beads which moved like sluggish flames in the lamplight. He handed this to the albino who, puzzled, turned it over and over in his long-fingered bone-white hands. The amber felt warm, almost like living flesh. It seemed to vibrate as if to the beating of tiny wings.

"You might not need it now, but you might need it some day. It is in acknowledgement of the service you did my old friend. Put it on," said the apothecary. "Place the beads around your neck."

To humour him, Elric did as he was asked.

"Wear it until you have the opportunity to use it," Nashatak told him. And when Elric sighed, he added: "I can tell that you are one who does not value his own life overmuch. But that thing might prove useful to you, for I know you have a destiny and a duty to live. I have no personal use for the charm. I wish you good fortune, sir, for I suspect you carry a weird which few would envy."

Elric's smile was thin. "My folk had lost any sense of sin they might once have had. It was my poor fortune to rediscover it. My destiny is a result of my actions, I suspect. Nonetheless, I value your good will. There are few in this world, I suspect, who share it. I thank you."

While Elric waited with growing impatience, Nashatak Skwett went to his desk and began to write. Meanwhile, the strange child continued to watch them through those laughing, hazel eyes until its father folded and sealed the letter, handing it to his offspring. "Go in peace, gentlemen." The apothecary made a sign to his child who again took their hands to lead them from the house.

Outside, the sky had darkened. Looking up, they saw a three-quarter moon above the rooftops and heard a distant sound, like the cawing of a crow. For an instant they saw black wings outlined in the moonlight, then they were gone and the city, which on their way here had been so raucous, was momentarily silent.

Chapter Two:
Two Princesses ~ A Pair of Dukes

THE CITY CONTINUED its celebration. The new peace-keepers had not had time to lose the citizens' good will. Somewhat cynically, Moonglum reflected on the many times in his journeying through the world when a change of government had been greeted with the same joy only to be followed by disappointment and anger when the new proved no better. "People hate real change," said the stocky Eastlander, "and are usually only satisfied with superficial and momentary differences. At least when Law controls the Balance. Remember how the Young Kingdoms, even as they recovered from their own terrible losses, took pleasure in the collapse of your Bright Empire. Now they grumble and curse their own leaders as they once cursed Melniboné. Some even long for the stability they knew under the Sorcerer Emperors. No doubt this republic's satisfaction will last as long."

The child led them deeper and deeper up the twisting, cobbled lanes of the port away from the sea until they looked back at the dark, crowded masts below and the glinting water, like ebony, beyond. To their left they followed the silhouettes of warehouses and other buildings on both sides of the river as it wormed out of sight into the distant jungle, seemingly impenetrably dense. They would have to go to those upriver docks in the morning, either alone or in company, depending on what transpired at the Council House.

The night stank of wine, burning wood and moss, of sweating bodies, roasting meat and other less identifiable things. Men and women linked arms and stumbled past singing. Although they had to pause occasionally while Elric rested, the three ignored the crowds and their friendly invitations, walking until the child brought them in sight of the gates of a vast and beautiful building, low and wide, with a tall irregular roof topped by masses of miscellaneous towers, drawbridges and battlements, all in different styles yet strangely unified, each patrolled and guarded.

"There," the child pointed to tall towers framing glittering gates. "The entrance to the Council House."

As they approached they saw that the entrance was festooned with a thousand flags and coats of arm. Again, Moonglum

found himself marvelling at the wealth and strength displayed. Before he could call out in Low Melnibonéan, to announce themselves, the child shouted something in the local dialect and instantly received a reply. A further exchange, followed by the slow rising of a great gate. At which point a liveried officer strode forward to receive the letter handed him by the child. The mismatched trio were left to stand in a circle of brandlight while the officer took the letter away.

A short while later a voice spoke from the darkness, asking their names and business.

"I am Moonglum of Elwher. This lord's companion. And he is Prince Elric, Sadric's son, of Melniboné. We seek audience with the Republican Council concerning a proposed expedition to the ruins of Soom."

And then the child had vanished. Surrounded by soldiers in rather intricate and impractical armour, with plumed helmets hiding all but their disciplined eyes, they were led into the depths of the great palace. They allowed themselves to be marched into a great hall. A celebratory banquet was clearly just ending. Diners fell silent as the two entered. The women in particular found them interesting. Male curiosity was warier. Rows of tables bore the remains of the elaborate meal. At the head of each table sat a man or a woman wearing identical blue and yellow robes. These were evidently members of the Council. A table at the far end of the hall was set cross-wise to the others. At its middle a tall, burly man, in the same livery but wearing a conical black cap, rose to greet them.

"Good evening, Prince Elric. Forgive our hesitation. We heard you were either a legend or a ghost. Two such distinguished travellers are most welcome here. I am Juffa, privileged to be this city's Chief Councillor. Please come and be comfortable at our table. We'll have fresh meat and wine brought. Tonight we are graced with not a few people of high degree. Our nation, being a republic, still recognizes those of rank. You

are not the first of ancient blood to honour us." He spoke as an habitual diplomat.

Two women sat to Juffa's right and two men to his left. From their clothing, they were clearly visitors. But it was not their dress which impressed the newcomers. For a long moment Elric stared into the face of the stranger furthest on the Chief Councillor's left. The man had risen from his seat, his face pale and his lips pursed, a gleam of hatred in his eyes. From his high cheekbones, slanting eyes and ears almost coming to points, he was clearly of Elric's unhuman folk.

Elric bowed first to the women, then to the Chief Councillor, then to the bearded man and lastly to the one who directed a look of terrible intensity towards him then raised a piece of meat on his table dagger. Placing it in his mouth he began to chew with fierce intensity. He took his time swallowing.

"Greetings, cousin," Elric said. "I did not know you still lived."

The man controlled himself. At that moment he was almost as pale as Elric. He was Duke Dyvim Mar, one of the few Dragon Masters to survive Elric's betrayal of their nation to the Young Kingdom reavers. Trained from birth to betray no emotion, he barely kept the tremble from his voice.

"Greetings, Prince Elric. Sadly, I survived where my brothers and sisters did not."

"You are countrymen, I take it, from your appearance." The Chief Councillor seemed unaware of any tension. "Well met, eh?" He waved the letter the apothecary had sent with his child. "And with common interests, I gather."

The other male visitor, with thick blue-black brows, full red lips smiling from within a square, divided black beard, his oiled black curls falling to his shoulders, stared with some amusement at Elric and then at Dyvim Mar. He clearly knew more of Melniboné's recent history than did Juffa.

"Forgive me," said Councillor Juffa, rising a little unsteadily. "May I introduce Prince Elric? The Princesses Apparent of Uyt, Princess Nahuaduar and Princess Semleedaor." Elric and Moonglum bowed. "And this is Duke Orogino, Senaschal of the Shanac Pines, also of Uyt." Bearded Duke Orogino rose, his palm outward from his forehead in what was clearly the normal gesture of greeting of his people. The two princesses were both of exceptional beauty. Nahuaduar was pale-skinned, with wide black eyes and black hair curling to her shoulders. Semleedaor was of a rosy complexion, her auburn hair cut short against her oval face. Both were frowning, not quite able to understand what was happening.

Breaking this tension, two huge ginger dogs came to sniff at Elric, growling softly in an almost friendly way and wagging their tails.

Duke Orogino turned to Dyvim Mar and made a joke, but the young man did not respond. His eyes were still fixed on Elric.

Councillor Juffa continued. "The princesses are the twin daughters of Tilus Kreek, King of the Uyt and these gentlemen are in their service. Duke Orogino was in the late king's household . . ."

"Last king," interrupted dark-haired Princess Nahuaduar in low tones. "We have no proof of his death." She stared steadily at Elric from beneath half-closed lids, her full, sensual lips curved in a sardonic half-smile.

The regent bowed his head, acknowledging his mistake.

"We have come because your countrymen failed to protect our father on their recent expedition to Soom," said Nahuaduar icily. "We had hoped to recruit other soldiers who might not have his portion of ill-luck."

At this, Elric's kinsman turned away, his eyes hardening. He had been insulted.

Duke Orogino cleared his throat. "But it seems only Dyvim Mar's Melnibonéans and a few Lormyrians had the nerve to go to Soom. In spite of offering generous wages, we have been unable to raise soldiers for a second expedition."

Elric glanced at Dyvim Mar. His cousin spoke evenly, controlling any anger of con-

fusion he felt. "I lost twenty six brave Melnibonéans and seven Lormyrian archers. The jungle around Soom teams with dwarfish cannibals. We suspect more than one tribe has been travelling for weeks to get there. They attacked us. One Lormyrian and I escaped in the river, carrying our wounded, and those who died. I believe some of our men were taken alive. I suspect we were allowed to escape, perhaps as a warning to others not to attempt a further expedition. The Lormyrian is also dead. What brings my kinsman to Nassea-Tiki?" He clearly had some notion of Elric's intentions.

"I seek a flower said to bloom in Soom once a century under the light of the full moon."

"You are a botanist, sir?" This from an apparently innocent Princess Nahuaduar. "My father also studied plants."

"A curious coincidence." Elric inclined his head. There was still considerable tension in the air. "But what of these savages? I was told the city was deserted."

"So it is." The Chief Councillor was almost amused. "Unfortunately, the surrounding jungle is not. It is full of wily, brutal cannibals thought to be the stunted degenerate descendants of the Soomish people. Perhaps they regard the city as sacred. They appear to have been gathering all this year. We know not why. Usually the individual tribes war amongst themselves and offer us and the river traders no serious danger. But clearly I would fail in my duty if I did not keep all my people here to defend our own city against this horde, should it choose to attack."

"Aye." Elric drew breath to continue but was interrupted by a young man who rose from the end of the table. Like many locals,

he had deep brown skin and long black hair. He dressed simply, conservatively in black, while the collar and cuffs of his white shirt were exposed at throat and wrist. He carried a heavy, scabbarded sword of antique design.

"I am Hored Mevza, son of Councillor Menzi of the eighth ward. I have already volunteered to return with the new expedition, no matter how small."

Elric guessed the handsome youth to be enamored of the sisters. Moonglum did not smile when he enquired: "How many do you command, sir?"

"None." Hored Mevza sat down again. "But perhaps a few of us can reach Soom where a larger party would be more readily detected."

"True." Elric looked enquiringly at the others.

"It's as good a logic as any other," said Duke Orogino. "I'm willing to put it to the test."

Princess Semleedaor rose suddenly. "Then shall we to our beds, my friends? Will you be ready to begin moving upriver in the morning, Prince Elric, Sir Moonglum?"

Taken aback, but impressed by her decisiveness, Elric smiled. "If there are no objections to my joining your party, my lady, at least until we are all arrived at Soom." Then looked directly at Dyvim Mar, who said softly:

"I see no reason why you should betray us on this particular occasion, cousin. We have a good-sized boat in readiness. You will find us at the river harbour soon after sunrise."

Elric bowed his head again. "I look forward to it."

He fought to repress the sense of foreboding which filled him. Not since he had led the attack on his homeland had he felt so unwell. But he had no choice He would free himself of the black sword's power or die in the attempt. Besides, he felt an obscure compulsion to aid his kinsmen if he could. He knew it was guilt that drove him,

but this time he would allow his guilt to rule. Careless as he was of the opinion of the world, which could not hate him more than he hated himself, he would follow these most unMelnibonéan urges. Part of him was curious to explore such feelings. Moreover, he found Princess Nahuaduar singularly attractive. He guessed that, were he to succeed and choose to take it, the fruit of the Black Flower would not be his only prize.

As they turned to leave, Princess Nahuaduar's voice came sweet and clear from behind them. "Do you know what they call that black blossom, Prince Elric?"

"I have heard it called by several names, my lady."

"The Blood Flower. They say it yields a sap which can be dried and from which a drink can be distilled that will give a sickly silverskin the strength he naturally lacks."

When Elric looked back at her, he saw that she was smiling directly into his eyes. Again he offered her a brief bow. "I had heard that, too, madam. But, as one wanders the world, one comes across many unlikely tales. A man would be a fool to believe them all."

Chapter Three:
Upriver

ELRIC AND A grumbling Moonglum arrived at the river dock in the cool air of early morning when dew brightened every leaf and gaudy piece of wood. Cocks still crowed and the languid smoke of breakfast fires rose from a thousand chimneys. Carrying a long bundle under his arm, Elric paused in surprise, seeing five figures standing near a big single-masted scarlet-painted boat anchored between several much larger inland barges which, they had been told, traded between Nassea-Tiki and the interior cities beyond Soom. Normally Soom was easily avoided, the river captains had said, but their traffic had stopped since news of the gathering savages had come. Now, said the landlord, only fools would risk the journey, or those whose greed outstripped their common sense. When Elric asked him 'why greed?' he replied with some old, familiar tale of lost treasure.

The people waiting to go aboard the vessel, whose only shelter was a small deckhouse set amidships, were Dyvim Mar, wearing the formal light battle armour of the Dragon Master, Duke Orogino had intricately carved wooden armour which made his body bulky and seemed cleverly designed to protect the wearer from arrows and yet keep him afloat in water. The councillor's son, Hored Mevza, had equipped himself in a coat of light brass mail and an elegant conical helmet. To Elric's mild surprise, the two princesses were also present. Their armour was wooden, like their countryman's. Elric greeted them with a bow. Princess Nahuaduar met his gaze with that same almost mocking directness while her sister dropped her gaze and seemed almost to blush. They greeted each other and, at a signal from Dyvim Mar, who led by common consent, began to cross the narrow, bouncing gangplank from quay to boat.

"We are grateful for your company, Prince Elric," said Princess Semleedaor as they boarded.

"We are at your disposal until we reach Soom," he replied. "And from then until the moon turns full. Then we have our own business to follow."

She looked curiously up at him, clearly restraining herself from asking him any further questions.

The tide and wind were in their favour. Within moments Hored Mevza had untied the boat and they were carried by the current towards the centre.

As the women watched, the men unshipped oars and set the single sail, following the tide while it ran upstream.

Soon they had rounded a curve and the city was lost from sight behind a curtain of lush palms and thick foliage. The rowing grew harder. The familiar stink of the forest almost clogged their lungs. The air filled with the calls of myriad birds and all the grunts, barks and bellows of the diurnal jungle. The journey to Soom would take several days. None showed the same impatience to reach the city as Dyvim Mar, whose eyes never lost their haunted quality and rarely looked directly at Elric. The titular Emperor of Melniboné felt an equal discomfort, though for opposite reasons. Dyvim Mar hated him for the doom he had brought to Imrryr, a hatred Elric also felt; yet the Dragon Master still knew respect for a name and lineage which had ruled the Bright Empire for ten thousand years.

Dyvim Mar had no Phoorn to command and was by nature laconic, when not speaking to his dragons. Phoorn and Melnibonéans, it was said, had once been of the same race, in a time before time began, and still spoke the same language. But the dragons needed decades, of sleep to restore their energy and their powerful venom. Almost all the dragons had been used in Imrryr's defence, destroying the invaders even as they fled with their booty, and none remained for a Master to command. This, Elric knew, was a further source of Dyvim Mar's frustration. The dragons slept in their deep caves, beneath the ruins of the city. The surviving Dragon Masters, Elric among them, yearned for the moment when they would begin to wake again. The very things which had once bound Elric to his cousin were those which kept them apart. He noticed that Dyvim Mar also tended to keep his distance from the others, as if he in turn considered himself guilty of betraying those he had first led to Soom.

In contrast, Duke Orogino and Hored Mevza seemed positively loquacious, talking almost to take their minds off the dangers ahead. Elric and Moonglum sat in the stern, taking the tiller whenever possible, and the two women, when not doing their share of the steering, sat near them. Princess Semleedaor, as she became used to the company, seemed direct and open compared to her twin, who was full of smouldering, secret

humour and enjoyed baiting the men whenever the opportunity came to her.

At noon of the third day, as they lunched off local meats, breads and wine, Princess Nahuaduar turned her hard, sardonic stare on Elric: "A question I have been meaning to ask for some time, my lord emperor."

"Lady?"

"I wonder what it is that brings so many exiles from the Dragon Isle to these shores?"

Elric shrugged. As was common, Moonglum spoke for him. "I would imagine they need employment, my lady, and soldiering is the thing they know best, now they have no empire to defend."

"But the women? Are they soldiers, too?"

At this, Dyvim Mar growled: "There are few women. The reavers either slew them or took them as prizes. Then — " He lowered his eyes. "Then our dragons pursued the reaver ships."

"And?" She genuinely did not know the answer. Dyvim Mar turned away.

"They died aboard those ships," said Moonglum. Then Elric spoke: "My cousin would want you to know that it was as a result of my betrayal. They had sworn they would take only inanimate treasure. Perhaps we were all betrayed, one way or another, that day." Instinctively, his hand had gone to his black sword, Stormbringer, so tightly bound to its scabbard.

"We are from the Uyt, as you know, and have no direct experience of events surrounding your nation's sudden fall but I heard — a noble woman, was there not, to whom one of your princes was betrothed? I seem to recall a tale . . ."

"I doubt it's a tale my lord the Emperor would care to hear retold," interrupted Dyvim Mar bitterly. And Elric stood up suddenly, finding some work in the bow of the boat. In spite of Moonglum's warning glance, Princess Nahuaduar called after him. "There's a sword involved in that story, too, my lord."

He sighed, his eyes clouding as he drew his brows together. "Lady you'll have heard no doubt that my betrothed died by my own sword . . ."

"Is that why you keep it so thoroughly bound?" With slender fingers, she gestured towards Stormbringer.

"Oh, 'tis best you ask no more questions concerning this sword, your highness." He pretended further interest in the boat's equipment. On both distant banks of the river, under the blaze of the noonday sun, the dark jungle moved slowly by. "Indeed, it is in none of our interests for me to release this sword."

Enquiringly, she looked up directly into his own ruby eyes. "Then why carry it?"

"To placate my own patron, I suppose." His returning gaze was as direct as her own. "Be warned, lady. Few have ever been glad to have such questions fully answered."

Nahuaduar made to speak again. Then her twin called from where she sat in the prow. Semleedaor pointed to their left, to a long sand bar on which several large crocodiles basked. Among them was an object reflecting the sun. Metal washed by the river and polished by the sand. A large piece of armour. As they drew nearer, Moonglum recognized it as a breastplate of Melnibonéan workmanship, similar to that worn by Dyvim Mar. The two kinsmen turned away, frowning.

"Was it here?" Princess Semleedaor's voice was sympathetic.

Dyvim Mar shook his head. "Further upstream. It must have been dragged down this far by the current. And perhaps by those reptiles . . ." He lifted his head and stared into the middle distance.

Duke Orogino murmured: "I never knew a people so racked by guilt. And yet which never knew a moment's self-doubt before their diaspora." He spoke ostensibly to an embarrassed Hored Mevza, who pretended to stare down into the water.

For some little time the party sailed on in silence. The heat had caused the men to discard much of their own armour. The sluggish water was thick with strange leaves, boughs and exotic, brightly coloured blossoms. The two women murmured together, but as evening came and the sun sat atop the silhouetted jungle, the atmosphere aboard became significantly more relaxed. Duke Orogino and Hored Mevza fell into a political conversation, The notion of a republic was foreign to the Duke. He found it difficult to understand how such a thing functioned. He was used to the state embodied in the person of a king, reflecting and exemplifying his nation's virtues. A nation run by a set of institutions and elected officials seemed to him to be a strange, even sickly affair, no longer dependent on the virtue and honour of its hereditary leader; prey to the basest desires of people who would promise anything to an electorate in order to be placed in high office.

The princesses speculated on the wild life to be found in the jungles and of the ancient, perhaps unhuman people who had built the city and ruled the land of Soom, occasionally asking Elric or Dyvim Mar for their opinion.

'The savages, though ugly and stunted, seemed human enough to me," Dyvim Mar said.

The women spoke of their father who had hired the Melnibonéans. Tilus Kreek had been obsessed with learning Soom's secrets, they said. He was convinced the city had been the centre of a wise civilization almost as old as Melniboné. Its treasure might have been knowledge or gold, he had not known from his reading. It might even have been the Black Flower, said to confer power on its kings. Ancient manuscripts had spoken of it in mysterious terms. Whatever form it took, that treasure could have revived his own nation's fortunes. The Uyt had suffered a great plague, taking a huge proportion of the population, making it weak and liable to being preyed upon by stronger neighbours.

"My father was obsessed with the stories he had heard of Soom," said Semleedaor. "He believed the older civilization

would save ours. We belong to a race of scholars and it is our wisdom alone which has kept the worst predators at bay, even though we lost a number of our vassal states. Our war engines are sophisticated, our magic, too, is feared. We have made none of the alliances which, by all accounts, made ancient Melniboné great. We believed that the crisis was over, that we had been able to resist the worst of the threats. There were other plans in place which did not depend upon discovering the secrets of Soom. But his curiosity, we suspect, began to drive him more than any immediate danger."

"You say he was a botanist, also?" Hored Mevza asked. "Perhaps this wealth he coveted was in the nature of rare spices? Our own city's fortunes were based upon the spice trade."

"Perhaps." Princess Nahuaduar was looking at Elric, as if to discover his reaction. Her own expression indicated that she did not welcome this suggestion.

Night fell for the third time since they had left Nassea-Tiki. The men drew an awning over the deckhouse and set up nets against the biting insects, tying up to a large tree trunk wedged where the river curved and the current ran slowly. They all slept soundly, save for the albino whose occasional groans and mutterings reminded Moonglum that his friend still relived those events surrounding the fall of that great capital. He had rarely slept in peace since the death of Cymoril, his betrothed.

Dawn came again and they rowed on upstream. By noon the sun was a throbbing, glaring eye gazing pitilessly down on them as they sweated to force their course on a river grown increasingly difficult to navigate, whose bends twisted and snaked, narrowing then widening unpredictably at every turn. Dyvim Mar warned them not to drag their hands in water now seething with poisonous reptiles and giant cephalopods. "And all are hungry for our flesh, or blood, or both." As he spoke, to illustrate his warning, a great coiling serpent leapt from the

water to snap at a bird skimming the surface in pursuit of a giant dragonfly.

Moonglum murmured to his friend; "What could have possessed the Uyt king to leave his country and his daughters and mount an expedition here? You at least have a far better reason for seeking Soom."

Somehow, they survived yet another day and a night until at last Dyvim Mar stood up in the boat to point at something the colour of dried blood stretching out into the water. Clearly of sentient manufacture, it had the appearance of a ruined mole, of worn, red sandstone with rusted iron rings still set into slabs casting black shadows on thick, unpleasant water.

Moonglum, half-certain that intelligent eyes were watching them from the dark green jungle depths, made to draw one of his curved swords from its sheath. At any moment an arrow or a spear would come flashing out of the shadows and plant itself deep in soft flesh. Then a worse thought came to him — *What if they want us alive?* For what? For bait? In spite of all his experience, he caught himself shuddering. Now he wondered about more sinister projectiles. A net, perhaps? Or a poison dart?

Pulling on his armour, Dyvim Mar said: "If they act as they did before, they'll wait until we reach the city proper until there is little chance of escape to the river." He turned to Elric. "Others beside me have noticed how well secured that blade is, cousin. It might be wise to have it more immediately to hand."

Elric reached down and picked up the long bundle he had brought aboard. He raised his eyebrows. "You'd risk that?"

"No choice is palatable, but, having experienced what these savages are capable of, I'd take my chances with Stormbringer. Assuming you plan to remain on our side . . ."

This further stab at his conscience froze

Elric's face into a familiar expression of hauteur. "Why, cousin, would you trust my word, even if I gave it?"

Buckling and knotting, Dyvim Mar peered into the forest. "Cousin, I trust nothing. But at least I know you…" With Moonglum at the tiller, he took an oar and, in unison with his kinsman, began to row towards the overgrown quay, murmuring: "It was no idea of mine to bring women here. But I was allowed no say in the matter. I understand why they want to find their father, but he is a fool. Haste and stupidity led us to that doom. Some of my own men might somehow have survived. I hope to save them. But you, Elric, what do you really seek here?"

"I seek to free myself from the weakness which made Yyrkoon believe he could usurp my power and put his sister, my cousin, into a trance."

Dyvim Mar nodded, adding: "Which led you to rely upon the stolen souls the black sword harvests."

Elric sighed. "The *noibuluscus* is the five-fingered flower whose petals are the colour of jet. It grows only in Soom. They say Soom's soldiers drank its distilled essence and thus imposed their authority upon the world."

"And do you recall the rest of that story?" his cousin asked.

"There are many versions."

"Most agree that the black flower poisoned the people of Soom, so that they relied upon it merely to survive."

"I should fear that?" Elric smiled more broadly than he had done for many years. "I should fear reliance upon a potion rather than upon a sword?"

His cousin shrugged. He could think of no suitable answer.

Chapter Four: Soom

SLOWLY, THE THICK foliage parted to the careful blades of the seven oddly matched men and women, each of whom carried a small, brass-studded shield. Duke Orogino exclaimed at what they saw. He was still the only one of the company not apparently affected by the atmosphere of danger. Elric unwrapped the long, simple Jharkorian blade he had carried aboard. A thoroughly practical weapon. Dyvim Mar was disappointed. "I would have preferred a bow or two or perhaps a javelin." If attacked from cover at a distance, they would be unable to reply.

"Gods! What minds designed such architecture?" Moonglum peered ahead.

Young Hored Mevza gasped. "Not human, whatever they say. Now I truly believe the stories are true and these buildings were raised even before fabled Melniboné thrived." He looked to Elric as if for confirmation.

Elric's expression had become sardonic at this reference to the fabulous nature of his homeland. Carrying slender scimitars like those of the Fookai pirates Elric had fought when employed by Ilmioran sealords, the women stepped onto a weed-grown pavement through which old trees now pushed up trunks, some grown almost as high as the great red ziggurats which stretched before them, carved with bizarre figures and shapes. Elric had some dim memory of this place. Perhaps he had visited it on one of his dream quests as a youth. But the association was in no way pleasant. On instinct, he turned suddenly to look backward. He saw nothing but the jungle through which, as silently as possible, they had trekked for the past few hours.

Duke Orogino lowered his own longsword and rested his gauntleted hand on the haft of a busily-engraved battle-axe of silver-chased steel more commonly associated with cavalry fighting. He allowed a look of skepticism to spread across his bearded face and he shook back his head to rid it of the damp locks obscuring his vision. Dyvim Mar pointed a slender finger towards the centre of the ruined city and its crumbling pyramids. "That's where we were am-

bushed — as we entered yonder square overlooked by that ugly building — palace, temple, whatever it is. We had made too much noise and I think we were followed."

"You say you could not count them. A fair-sized tribe?" Princess Semleedaor pushed golden hair back from her damp forehead.

"A party of perhaps a hundred." With his soft doeskin boot, Dyvim Mar indicated fairly fresh bloodstains on the paving. "Perhaps a few more. We dispatched half that number—"

"Before you let them take you prisoner?" said Princess Nahuaduar sharply.

Dyvim Mar bridled. "I am a hired mercenary, madam. We followed the king's commands!"

"To do what?" The question was rhetorical. Elric suspected she had heard the answer before.

"As I said, lady, your father was anxious to reach that sandstone pyramid there, the one they have made some crude attempt to restore. He called it a palace, but I think it was some kind of temple. He took the majority of my men forward and left me to protect the rear with some Lormyrian archers, a few lancers and my chief lieutenant, Agric Inricson. The last we saw of the king he had disappeared into the palace. We fought off the savages for several hours until they fell back. Then we moved to try to rejoin the king and the rest of our men. We got as far as yonder house — the one with the walls still intact. A trap. They were waiting for us inside. Fresh warriors. I saw half my men butchered. Most of us were overwhelmed. Then we thought we saw a way free. We got almost to the river before they began shooting at us. We carried the wounded with us into the river. I now think they intended to let us go, maybe as a warning to any other expedition. That is why I think we have not been attacked. They believe no one else will dare come to Soom."

"Or they have moved deeper into the jungle," said Moonglum, "taking their prisoners with them."

"Or they completed their business in Soom and returned to their tribal homeland further upriver," suggested Duke Orogino. "I agree it is most likely they would have attacked us by now if they were still in the city."

"Should we try to follow them?" Hored Mevza did his best to hide his disquiet.

"You may do as you please," replied Elric. "My business is in Soom."

"We need all the swords we can muster," Princess Nahuaduar glared at him.

"Indeed, my lady." Elric acknowledged. "But we agreed to lend you our aid until Soom and the rising of the full moon."

"There is some hope that Melnibonéans are still alive," said Dyvim Mar softly.

"And I hope to be again at their disposal once the moon has risen," said Elric. "A matter of hours." He reached into his pouch and drew out the map he had bought in Thokara. Beside what the king had called a palace was some kind of garden, perhaps the *lunarium*, what Elric's people had called a night garden, judging by the iconography on the map. The *noibuluscus* appeared to have a religious function. Perhaps the black flowers had grown there. While the others debated, he marked out the site in his mind. Timing was important. The flower had to be picked at the moment of its blooming. He and Moonglum moved away from the others. "This is where I guess the site to be."

They had gone only a few steps when the brooding air was cut by a terrible sound — a high-pitched wail of agony which was suddenly cut off. The others stopped talking and listened carefully. Elric turned, questioning, into a sickening silence.

"It came from inside," Moonglum said. Duke Orogino began to cross the square at a run, heading for the huge pyramid, the women behind him.

And then, from out of a dark, ragged hole in the pyramid's wall, a scarlet figure came stumbling. Even Elric, versed in the refined tortures of his people, could not disguise his horror.

The figure might once have been a naked man. How it continued to move Elric could not guess, for every inch of skin had been flayed from scalp to feet. The red mouth moved. The throat gurgled with blood. Blue eyes, from which the lids had been removed, stared blindly before it. Every movement must have been a century of agony as it raised bloody hands before it, groping for unseen help.

The party stood stock still as the flayed man approached. He screamed, leaving a trail of thick strings of blood behind him. Moonglum ran forward with the intention of helping the man. Instantly, an arrow thrummed from somewhere and took him in the shoulder. He fell to his knees, an almost ludicrous expression of surprise on his face. But the arrow had failed to penetrate his mail and dropped to the ground even as he raised his hand towards it. He stood up, sheepishly, drawing his long curved sword.

"Form a square!" Elric, Moonglum and Dyvim Mar took charge, showing the others how to raise their small shields to protect their faces and upper bodies. Moonglum ducked and picked up the long barbed arrow, darting a look of enquiry at Dyvim Mar. He nodded, confirming that it was the same kind of shaft which had killed so many of his men. Then a whole rain of arrows came from the same direction, thudding into their shields.

"I suspect they don't plan to take casualties or seek confrontation," said Moonglum. Elric nodded.

"They might even have released that flayed prisoner to encourage retreat."

Moonglum was puzzled. "Why, when they clearly outnumber us, would they avoid conflict?"

Still screaming, the flayed man stumbled on.

"Use the black sword, Elric! Use it now!" cried Dyvim Mar.

Everything in the albino told him to do as his cousin demanded, yet still he resisted. His hand fell to the scabbarded blade.

"No!" cried Moonglum. Then he murmured. "At least, not yet."

Dyvim Mar made to go after the flayed man. Elric stopped him. "No one can follow him. If we break ranks we are dead."

"Then use the damned sword!"

Instead, Elric reached down and pulled a spear from his shield. Now he had a more useful weapon. Stormbringer stirred against his thigh. He heard it murmur but he deafened himself to its voice, to the tones of Arioch, Duke of Chaos, urging him to do as Dyvim Mar demanded. They were looking to him for leadership, even as the bloody figure, still intermittently screaming, disappeared into a jungle opening like a maw to swallow him.

Duke Orogino stood trembling, his eyes blank, maybe mad. The stink of the skinned man's bloody flesh was in their nostrils. Seeking the best cover, Elric made the small party fall back towards the pyramid and the high walled annex from which the man had come. He had his own motives for investigating the compound. As they crowded in one of the women screamed and the lad fell back retching.

Princess Semleedaor turned her head away but her twin sister, pushing black hair from her face, forced herself to stare down at the blood-soaked ground. Laid out on it, like a suit of clothes, was flayed man's skin, neatly separated from the body by an expert hand, including the hair of the head and the man's private parts. The operation would have taken a long time. Looking at the pelt they imagined the victim's horror and pain. But Elric saw something else, pushing its way through the dark mud created by the man's blood and urine. He barely resisted falling to his knees and staring at the small, dark shoot exactly the same as the one he had seen in a dozen grimoires and herbals. The *noibuluscus*. The Black Anemonë.

"So your instincts were right." Moonglum spoke so softly only Elric could hear him. They stood in Soom's ancient *lunarium*. From the histories and geographies

Elric had read, he had expected something larger. Clearly, the compound, now roofless, had been roofed in crystal, perhaps even a great prism concentrating the moon's rays, used to grow the sacred flower which blossomed once every hundred years. And would bloom tonight, if the scrolls and books he had consulted told the truth. Then Elric was struck by a realization. The arrival of the savages was no coincidence. "The man's flaying, the draining of his fluids into the ground was a ritual. Those degenerates, doubtless descendants of ancient Soomians, were here to witness the black flower's blooming." The shoot was growing before his eyes, a tightly closed bud surrounded by black, spikey leaves.

Moonglum reached his hand towards it but his friend stopped him.

"The *noibuluscus* must be plucked at the optimum moment. We must wait until the moon is full. It's not even twilight. We must somehow hold out against the savages until midnight." He had waited so many months, he could feel the last of his strength ebbing out of him. He thought only of his own needs.

Dyvim Mar stared at his cousin in contempt. The princesses, too, knew what they had found, for their father had spoken of it, hoped to find it. Perhaps the *noibuluscus* was the treasure their father sought? Even Moonglum was troubled.

Elric cared nothing for what any of them thought. At last he need depend no longer either on herbs or hellsword. This, in turn, freed him from Arioch, from all those hideous pacts which had led, in his mind, at least, to the death of Cymoril. He knew a deep satisfaction. Everything he had hoped for was coming true. After tonight, his dependence on the supernatural would be over. All he had to do was survive.

"We're heavily outnumbered, Elric." Moonglum was reminding him. "We're trapped."

"This place can be readily defended," Elric replied. "The only entrances are that gap in the wall, through which we came and that smaller opening — " he pointed to a small, square, regular opening in the main structure of the great pyramid itself. "It seems to be some sort of outlet, perhaps for water, used in the original construction." The battle-leader he was trained to be, he positioned Dyvim Mar and Duke Orogino at the small, regular opening. The others were told to watch for activity beyond the wall. Any attackers could only come through one at a time. The walls themselves were too high to permit spears or arrows to be aimed at them.

When Elric turned to Princess Nahuaduar to explain this, she looked directly into his eyes and said firmly: "We are here to rescue my father, Prince Elric . . ."

". . . and to save any of my men who survive." Dyvim Mar added, peering down into the square opening and then leaning to look up, as if it was, indeed, some kind of sluice from above. "If only we could calculate the enemy numbers, we'd be better able to determine our strategy."

Elric ignored them. He had already told them his purpose. While their mutual interests coincided, he would work with them. If they conflicted, he would have to concentrate on the black flower's blossoming.

Moonglum went to stare through the gap in the wall at the horizon. The sun was already setting. He had long since accepted that Elric was driven by his own needs, but he had thought there was another quality in his friend, something which might just possibly on occasions put the greater good above his own. He shook his head, trying to clear it. Then he had a new thought. What if the savages, who had already demonstrated their sophisticated strategies, did not want to frighten them from the city at all? Perhaps the party had been deliberately offered this route. He whirled and as their eyes met, it was clear Elric shared the same suspicion.

Elric cursed his desperation and need. "Is there time for a new strategy?" Hadn't he already found what he had come to Soom to take? Why not do, however, what the mysterious tribesmen least expected and attack the pyramid? Apart from himself, there were only two experienced soldiers amongst them. True, the women were brave and willing, even trained to arms to a degree, yet they were scarcely strong enough for an assault. Not unless most of the defenders were already dead . . .

Suddenly a shout came from above. Elric could not see who it was but Hored Mevza, furthest away from the main wall, looked up and Princess Semleedaor exclaimed. "Father! We are here to save you!"

A distant voice replied. "Fools! Now we are *all* doomed. Get out of here while you can. You men have brought my daughters into danger!"

"He lives!" Princess Semleedaor hardly listened to her father's words. "Oh, thank Yenob! He lives!" She and her sister stared upward with radiant faces.

"Great king!" cried Duke Orogino. "If they speak a civilized tongue tell them we'll pay any ransom they demand."

"Get out of that cursed compound if you can. Now! Get into the jungle. They do not want our gold. They want our flesh — ah!"

"Father!" Princess Nahuaduar was beside herself with emotion. "He's gone. They took him back!"

"He's right. We can't stay here." Dyvim Mar feared more for his men than for the king. "We must help them, Elric. Draw the sword! You are the greatest sorcerer in our history. You can help them! You owe them that!"

Moonglum said quietly. "Elric. Friend. You must."

"I am losing strength. It's almost gone. If . . ." But he realized he could not continue as he had. Every instinct was against it. Cruel his people might be, but they had loyalty one to the other. The last of his herbs were gone. His only hope now was that he could live until the *noibuluscus* bloomed. Even then, there was no certainty. A spell of the kind they wished him to cast would

drain any vitality left him. If the spell failed, would he be too weak, then, to help his countrymen? Could he do nothing while another victim was flayed alive? Yet he had vowed never to draw the black sword again . . .

His cousin was yelling something at him. Beyond the tall, red walls of the ruin the blood-red sun was beginning to sink behind the dark jungle foliage. Twilight was coming. In a short while the full moon would rise and, if Elric's understanding was right, the black flower's petals would open and begin almost instantly to fall. At that point, they must be gathered. He must collect the seeds so he could grow fresh plants somewhere. Or was this red mud the only kind in which the plant would grow . . . ?

Still he hesitated. It would be worse than ironic if, only an hour or so before those petals opened, he lacked the energy to pick them.

"Elric! Do you not owe us *something*?" Dyvim Mar's bared sword almost threatened his cousin. "Do you want to see your remaining kin slain as — as that poor wretch — " and he pointed at the skin laid out on the wet ground — "was slain?"

Moonglum was silent, but it was clear he shared the Dragon Master's opinion.

Elric lowered his eyes.

"No," he said.

From somewhere above came another prolonged and terrible scream.

The albino drew a deep breath. His eyes stared as if into a vision. His lips began to move, silently forming the words of a tongue more ancient than that of Soom, more ancient than Melniboné's. Words he had learned in a dream quest, long ago, sleeping upon the dream couches of Imrryr, when he had forged a certain alliance. His mind began to travel out along the strange network of roads that had once taken him through the many dimensions of the multiverse.

He lifted his head, his eyes now shining with an alien brightness. And he shouted a word which burst like a blaze of voices upon the agonized ears of all near him. Yet the

others could not make sense of the word they heard. They did not recognize the name. Only Elric heard and recognized it. And it drained his life force from him even as it left his lips.

"*Saaasuurrasssh!*" he said.

chapter Five: Kalakak

SOMEWHERE UNDER THE river, in a dimension of waters and dank foliage, Elric's voice found a supernatural resonance, stirring the memory of a creature which opened its jaws a fraction and passed a long, leathery tongue between pointed teeth. Its eyes were shut in the sleep of centuries and would not open. The creature's curiosity was not yet aroused. Indeed, it still dreamed dark, sluggish dreams of death, of things devoured and things to be devoured. It was some time before it recognized the word which had awakened it and some further time before it recalled that Sasuras was perhaps one of its waking names, though not the name by which it identified itself. That name was Kalakak and it knew that somewhere it had kindred which spoke to it, called to it. But Kalakak still dreamed that it lay curled in the egg its mother had laid somewhere in the multiverse, so many millennia ago. Kalakak lay safely in the mud on the bank of a vast river, whose further bank could not be seen. The world river wound between mud flats and beyond the mud flats was the rich warmth of mile-high thick-boled trees, branches twisting and curling and full of living things, all of which tempted its appetite.

Kalakak remembered its appetite. It began to salivate. It remembered Sasuras . . . that name . . . the name which called it not to feed but to serve and it was therefore somewhat slower in its response . . .

Saaasuurrasssh

Kalakak's tale twitched. Its limbs began to sting and its eyes moved beneath heavy lids.

Saaasuurrasssh

Kalakak's nostrils moved and tasted murky, amniotic air. Something flickered in the darkness; veins of red fire, streaks of deep green and blue. And Kalakak took a massive breath.

ELRIC LAY IN Moonglum's arms. Dyvim Mar looked on, almost sympathetic. Somewhere, near the ruined gap in the wall, Hored Mevza thrashed and groaned and clawed at an arrow which had found a gap between his helmet and his throat. Princess Semleedaor stood beside him, trying to stop him from moving while she attempted to snap the head of the arrow from the shaft. It stuck out from the side of his neck. She spoke to him as soothingly as she could. Elsewhere Duke Orogino and Princess Nahuaduar peered around their shield rims. A makeshift brand in her hand cast sputtering light across the compound. Out in the square, shadows shifted, running swiftly here and there, shooting arrows, flinging lances. Only by accident had an arrow struck Hored Mevza. The young man dropped to one knee, his eyes wide with horror as the princess at last managed to get the shaft out of him and staunch the blood with his own torn shirt. The arrow had not struck the jugular.

Weakly, Elric climbed to his feet, balancing with the spear, the steel sword in his right hand. From above, men's voices were shouting and it seemed to him that the captured Melnibonéans had broken free and were fighting their captors. Certainly, something was happening up there. He looked over to where the Black Anemonë grew, its tendrils pulsing and lengthening with every passing moment, the flower not yet opened. His mouth was dry, his arms and legs shook. He had difficulty breathing.

"Elric, you're too enfeebled" Moonglum spoke reluctantly. "The spell did not work."

Dyvim Mar was grim: "There is only the black sword now."

Still Elric shook his head. Trembling, he steadied himself with the spear and, sword raised with difficulty, turned to Princess

Nahuaduar. "I led us into a trap, I admit. But I promise I will do all I can now . . ."

She cursed a soldier's curse and all but spat in his face. "I thought you, of all men, would be the one to help us. Now my father faces dreadful death and your own people, too. You carry an unhappy weird upon you, Elric of Melniboné. Oh, how I wish I had not let you join us . . ."

He managed to respond, his smile ironic, panting. "Madam, you must try to wait until midnight before you condemn me entirely . . ."

Another flight of arrows came pouring through the gap. By now they had taken cover. Hored Mevza had stopped screaming and now sat against a wall breathing rapidly, the rag pressed on his wound which no longer bled badly. Princess Semleedaor, sword in hand, darted a quick glance around the ragged gap. "I can see little in this blackness. It sounds as if they've gone back into the ruins or the forest."

Then, as if to contradict her, from above several spears rattled down uselessly. The object of both attacks was to demoralize them. Moonglum's attention was on the *noibuluscus*, "It's bigger! Look!" It reached towards the starlit sky now touched by the first faint traces of the rising moon. Even though Elric had studied all there was to study about the plant, its rate of growth astonished him. Was he going to die there, with the object of his quest so close? Watching it go through its entire cycle while unable to make use of its petals?

"Elric! Take the buds!" Moonglum helped his friend to his feet. "The attempted summoning weakened you too much." Yet still he refused to untangle the wire binding his sword.

The long stem of the Black Anemonë stretched high towards the night sky and then curled downwards. It was only as it reached out towards the wounded Hored Mevza that Elric realized the thing seemed to be questing for something. Questing for fresh blood.

Moonglum cried "No!" and leapt forward, twin sabres whirling, slashing at the plant, which reared back, hissing.

Blood had stimulated the plant's growth. "It needs more blood! It's feeding." Moonglum's shout stimulated the albino who cursed himself. That was why they had been tricked into entering the compound. They were food for the black flower.

This knowledge seemed to stimulate the albino. Shouting an oath, his voice quavering, Elric shook his fist up at the window — to be answered by a haphazard rain of missiles. "Those savages want us wounded but not dead. That's why they took so many prisoners. To feed the plant!" A plant which drank blood and souls as thirstily as his runesword.

Above him scarred, wicked little faces glared down at them. Out in the night the other savages prowled, their only intent being to keep the party inside the compound.

As it had dawned on Dyvim Mar that they were the intended food of the black plant, he began to whistle an old, complicated Melnibonéan melody: The Drowned Boy.

"What do you say, cousin?" Elric asked. "Would you wait like a pig in the slaughterhouse? Or would you die fighting these filthy little devils?"

His kinsman darted him a look of approval and began to move towards the ragged gap in the wall.

Before he could reach his object, he drew a startled breath and stepped backwards, staring. Turning sideways on to the plant, Moonglum peered into the gloom.

There was something else out there now. A much larger, heavier shadow. Some kind of beast?

And then Elric collapsed and Duke Orogino came blundering past them, screaming, to flee into the night. They looked back. "Gods! It's so fast!" Moonglum gasped. He tried to help, but he was already carrying Elric. The plant writhed and

shifted on the ground. It had seized poor young Hored Mevza who now struggled in its coils. It was squeezing him so that his blood streamed from his orifices to be sucked up by the plant's tapering bud. "Ugh. The poor bastard's dead already!" What had been a thin stem was now a fair-sized trunk and as they watched, horrified, it thickened visibly, sucking the flesh and blood from the youth's now limp body. Then it dropped back to the ground, slithering into the spread-out skin of the flayed man, filling it.

A travesty of a human creature now swayed before them, its tendrils occupying the skin like legs and arms. And from each branch now, more tendrils sprang, like fingers and toes, reaching towards the five who remained in the compound. The plant, distinctly manlike in form, continued to grow.

And still, as Elric knew, it was not yet moonrise. Still the plant sought more sustenance.

With a yell, Dyvim Mar now flung himself forward and began to hack at the disgusting limbs. The sisters imitated him, their scimitars flashing in the growing light from the sky. Moonglum tried hard to hold his friend upright. Elric did his best to summon the last of his strength. He fell forward, stabbing at the monstrous thing. Anger and disappointed rage empowered him. He had wanted no more than a normal life of the kind enjoyed by others. Again and again he thrust the sword, but he made no impression upon the thing.

A noise behind them. Duke Orogino came shrieking back into the compound. His armour was pierced in a dozen places by arrows. His helmet had been knocked from his head which streamed with blood. He gibbered and pointed behind him and then fell to the ground.

They tried to pull him free of the Black Anemone, but the gigantic plant was too strong. Its tendrils wrapped around the duke's body and dragged him to itself. He gave one last, long yodelling cry as he was lifted into the air and then suddenly the full moon rose above the high wall and illuminated the scene, the struggling Duke Orogino, the five figures, weapons in their hands, gathered around the swaying, manlike plant.

Then they turned to see what Duke Orogino had seen. What had caused him to flee back into the compound.

"Kalakak," said Elric.

And he smiled.

Chapter Six:
The Black Flower's Blossoming

THE TWO WOMEN stared in horror as the creature Elric called Kalakak pushed its massive bulk against the gap in the compound, breaking down the ancient brick, its cold green eyes glaring, its long snout opening to reveal teeth the length of swords and the thickness of a man's arm. In the moonlight its scales glistened with water. Its massive tail thrashed this way and that, scattering the corpses of the savages who tried to attack it. When it saw Elric, it lumbered towards him and from its vast, red throat something like language sounded. Only Elric could understand everything it said, but Dyvim Mar recognized a form of High Melnibonéan which he and the Phoorn dragons spoke between themselves.

The monstrous reptile looked down at Elric, who was again supported on Moonglum's shoulder. Its eyes were full of profound memory, of old wisdom and a new thirst. "You summoned me, old friend?"

"I thought you had not heard me, Lord Kalakak. I called to you in the name of our ancient pact. I presumed you still slept." The thing looked like nothing as much as a gigantic crocodile, but its snout and tail were more slender, its legs and webbed feet longer. Like certain dragons, it had a tall, spiked crest on its neck and head. Its colour was neither green, nor black, nor brown. It

was not an earthly colour. As it moved, its scales clashed softly, the sound of wind over drying leather.

"True it will be a millennium or two before I am fully rested. Now I am at your service. At least before sleep claims me again. Unlike our mutual kin, the Phoorn, I need rather more sleep than a mere century." The jaws clacked and smacked almost as if Kalakak joked. "Remember, I cannot kill for you. Otherwise, you must tell me what you need, before I return to the river below the river and close my eyes. There is a dream I need to continue."

As the manlike plant, distracted, began to devour Duke Orogino, Elric pointed towards the high window. "We need to reach that opening, yonder. Can you help us?"

"Use my crest to climb." Steadying his scaley bulk with his tail, Kalakak lifted himself on his huge hind quarters, his snout extending to the window from which the Uyt king, Tilus Kreek, had last called to his daughters. The black flower swayed in the background, unable to assess this new potential danger as if for all the world a sentient thing. The albino was dangerously weak, but he could still call out instructions to the others. They began to clamber up the reptile's massive back. Below them the black plant thrashed and screeched. Above them the dwarfish cannibals crowded to the window and stared in disbelieving consternation. With a yell as bloodthirsty as any warrior's Princess Nahuaduar led the way through the window, her scimitar taking off a head as smoothly as if she were cutting daisies in a field. Then she disappeared inside, Dyvim Mar and Princess Semleedaor behind her.

Elric and Moonglum were the last to reach the window. With a word of thanks to Lord Kalakak, the albino dropped into the room. The princesses and his cousin had already taken their toll of the savages. Bodies lay everywhere. Red revenge had been taken at last. The remaining savages scrambled into the outer corridors and scattered as fast as they could go. They left their prisoners bound but otherwise unharmed.

Weeping with joy, the princesses ran towards their straightbacked but naked father. As they cut his bonds he stared at them in astonishment. He, like the captured Melnibonéans, had not expected to survive this night.

Rubbing circulation back into limbs, King Tilus Kreek crossed to a corner of the room where weapons were stacked and found his own sword amongst them, returning it to his scabbard. He was a tall, old man with a short grey beard and long hair. He drew on a padded surcoat over mail and sweated in the heat of the night. Moonlight streamed into the room, showing Moonglum, Elric and Dyvim Mar the captured warriors, whom they set about releasing. Elric leaned beside the window taking great gasps of air, scarcely able to stand. Below, the ground shuddered. Presumably, Lord Kalakak had dropped back to all four gigantic legs. Looking down, Elric saw that oddly-coloured tail disappearing from the compound. Out in the moonlight, the black flower still hissed and slithered and quested for fresh blood.

Swiftly, the released warriors recovered their weapons, then embraced their commander, Dyvim Mar. To Elric, they offered more formal thanks, clearly surprised by his ruined condition. Some showed concern as he leaned weakly against the window frame, still gasping for breath. The summoning of Kalakak had exhausted what was left of his strength and the climb had taken the rest.

"We owe our lives to our Emperor," Dyvim Mar explained. "Without him, gentlemen, we should all be dead."

The fine-featured Bright Empire soldiers remained reserved in their greetings, but some were prepared to accept the truth of their captain's short speech and bowed briefly to the Prince of Ruins, best known as 'Kinslayer', whose treachery had destroyed their homeland. Elric expected nothing from them, save acknowledgement of his rank, for none denied that he was their rightful Emperor, named by his dying father as the true inheritor of the Ruby Throne.

"How easily can we leave Soom?" said Princess Nahuaduar. "We are still outnumbered by the savages. Has your reptilian ally departed the city, Prince Elric?"

"He was the best I could summon under present conditions. He helped us but he is forbidden to kill, which is the thing he yearns to do most. Like our Imrryrian dragons, he must sleep a year for every hour or so that he's awake. He returns to his rest."

"So we have no other ally against the savages?" asked Princess Nahuaduar, glancing significantly at his sword.

"Only our own courage and cunning, my lady." Elric turned again to glance through the window and stumbled suddenly backward. A thick, black tendril appeared. Next moment it was curling through the opening. Moonglum yelled to his companions. "Quickly. Back down the stairs. We'll fight our way through the savages to the river." Already the tendril had come snaking in as if scenting blood. Elric cocked his head. He could almost hear it sniffing out his remaining lifestuff.

Led by Dyvim Mar and Tilus Kreek, with the twin princesses following close behind and Elric leaning on his friend, the Melnibonéans poured from the room and down the broad deep winding blood-stained stone steps within the pyramid.

It was almost with a sense of anticlimax that they ran out into the open square to find no enemies. Warily, back to back, they moved slowly out through the alien ruins towards the jungle. Half-fainting, entirely dependant on the stocky Eastlander, Elric came last. From the darkness, spears and arrows flew. A Melnibonéan sobbed with pain as a spear took him in the arm. Without another sound, he pulled the arrow through and discarded it. The remaining Lormyrian archer gathered the arrows for

his own quiver. Their shields absorbed the worst of the onslaught, protecting Elric and Moonglum. With a hissed curse, the archer fitted an arrow to his string and sent it back into the invisible pack.

Two more men were lost to enemy spears before they reached the edge of the jungle. In the moonlight they could retrace their original progress from the river. The undergrowth remained dense. With Dyvim Mar leading, they moved slowly on.

For the first time, the savages made a direct attack. Tattooed faces, white, glaring eyes, ochre skins and an assortment of cruel axes, spears, swords and lances suddenly surrounded them. No longer was the strategy to herd them into the compound to become food for the Black Anemonë. Now the cannibals sought only to kill the survivors, so that the man-flower would not devour the degenerate Soomians themselves. Their caution was gone. Moonglum, guarding Elric who was still barely able to hold his blade, did his best to fight back. Then Princess Nahuaduar took the albino's arm onto her own shoulder and helped defend him as they stumbled on. Mostly, the enemy's weapons fell on shields or were blocked by steel. Every so often one of Elric's party would groan and blood would flow. But they could smell the river now. If the savages had not destroyed their boat the remains of the two expeditions might still escape.

Then the remaining savages had fallen back. For a moment the jungle was still. No animals called, nothing moved. The brilliant moonlight cast deep shadows. Some of them seemed to shift and curl into alarming shapes. "Maybe," murmured Moonglum, "They've lost their stomach for the fight?" King Tilus Kreek let out a long relieved sigh — just as a huge, manlike shape loomed up behind them. A giant, with long, curling fingers waving as, momentarily unsteady, it balanced itself in their wake. The Black Anemonë lumbered relentlessly after fresh food. Any food so long as it pulsed with

human blood. Then, suddenly, a dark arm shot into their ranks. The last Lormyrian archer shrieked and beat at the huge shape as he was lifted into the air.

They watched helplessly.

"We are finished," murmured King Tilus. "We cannot defeat that thing. I know its power. I should never have led my men here. Now my daughters will die obscenely, thanks to my folly. You go on. I will stay here and try to slow it." It was clear he had no hope of defeating the hugely bloated manlike tree. Only a few hours before it had been a tiny shoot. Now it came swiftly after them, gaining speed with every kill. Whenever it paused it plucked another man from the jungle. It was indiscriminate. Savages, too, were lifted kicking and shouting into its maw. They had no chance of reaching the river before they were caught and their lifestuff added to its size, speed and energy.

"We will fight together," said Dyvim Mar, coming to stand beside the king.

Moonglum drew his twin sabres. "Rest your back on mine, friend Elric. Sadly, we'll die disappointed deaths. Killed by the very treasure we sought."

"No," said Elric. He sighed. "Get the women and the rest of our fighters to the boat. I will stay to slow its advance."

The savages had not fled after all. Realising that they were now also food for the *noibuluscus*, they flung themselves again at the Melnibonéans, perhaps hoping their blood would satisfy the Black Flower. This time Princess Semleedaor gasped as a sawtoothed blade slashed her arm. Her father roared his anger and his sword took the attacker in the throat. Blood spurted. Another black tendril came out of the night and seized the slain savage.

"Go!" cried the albino, almost falling. "All of you! Go!" And his fingers began to fumble at the copper wire securing his sword.

Seeing this, Moonglum gripped his shoulder. "Elric. We may yet . . ."

"No. We'll all be slain. And for what? Take everyone and hold the boat for a little while. I'll try to join you. If not, well then, I'm missed by one friend, at least. And a debt will be partly paid."

Like five long fingers, black petals, a hideous, grasping travesty of a massive human hand reached for his arm. He drew back in horror, his own feeble fingers trying desperately to untie the thongs securing his sword's hilt to his belt.

Moonglum paused and helped the albino to untie the wire. Then he turned and with a shout began to run into the jungle, herding the little party of survivors before him.

The Black Anemonë rose up out of the tangle of silhouetted forest, the full moon outlining its writhing head, while moonlight revealed its broad, waving arms and hands. A thin, terrible whistling noise escaped the cluster of long leaves surrounding what resembled a mouth. From under its feet, a score of savages rose to surround Elric.

For a moment the tattooed cannibals stood there confronting him. The silvery light emphasized the whiteness of his skin. No doubt they saw him as some kind of phantom, the chief source of their plan's failure. With deliberate movements, they began to close in on him, watched by the creature they had created through their barbaric blood sacrifice.

Elric grinned.

Reaching for the great broadsword at his hip, he drew it from its scabbard. So finely balanced was the black blade, he could hold it easily in one hand, almost like a rapier. The sword murmured and whispered in his grasp and he felt a sudden rush of energy suffuse him. A thrill of ecstasy that others might feel in lovemaking.

Then he began his work.

Elric's eyes blazed with red, unholy light, reflecting the flickering runes which ran up and down his blade. He swung Stormbringer first one way and then another, as if to display its power. His lips twisted in crazy delight as he stepped towards the savages, now standing between him and the creature they had raised. His chest rose and fell with deep, strong breaths. He knew a pleasure he had all but forgotten. And, as that familiar black radiance poured from the blade and its song rose and fell in a melody that to him at least was beautiful, he remembered why the Black Sword had been so hard to put aside. Why his addiction had taken so long to conquer. "Aaaah!" Again he swung the blade, but this time it was not in display.

"Arioch! Arioch! Lord of the Seven Darks! Arioch! *Blood and souls for my lord Arioch!*" This time the black, strangely wrought metal sliced into flesh and bone. Heads sprang from necks like so many weeds in a hay field. Arms flew into the foliage. Legs buckled and torsos were hacked in half. Terrified savages tried to flee, but were now trapped between Elric and the Black Anemonë, drunk on the smell of ruined flesh. It was down on the jungle floor, sucking the blood which pumped from the remains of their bodies. It clucked and yelped with dreadful glee. A few men managed to scuttle past the monster they had brought into being, only to be snared by its prescient tendrils.

Elric yelled his mockery at the creature. "Come, Black Flower! Come to me. My blood is thin, but it is yours if you can take it!"

The *noibuluscus* paused, staring from its strange head, around which great, spiked leaves curled like a living crown. It bent, reaching out its long branches towards this laughing, white-faced, puny little thing of flesh and thin blood which challenged it and which, perhaps, it sensed as the agent of its own frustration.

Voicing the ancient battle-yells of his ancestors, Elric ran at the Black Anemonë. "Arioch! My lord Arioch! Blood and souls for thee and thine! I present thee with this sacrifice!" The lifeforce of all those he had killed seared through his veins, filling him with preternatural energy, with a wonder-

ful lust he had almost forgotten, but always craved.

The tendril hands reached out to seize him. Elric dodged them, hacking at legs like two trunks standing across the path above him. The hands curled down to try to grasp him. A weird shriek escaped the monster as the black blade slashed at the writhing fingers, sending them flying into the undergrowth.

"Arioch! Blood and souls for my lord Arioch!" The albino's features were contorted in unhuman delight.

And from somewhere in the darkness came a low, mocking chuckle, as if Elric's patron demon had always known that he and the sword would feed again.

At last the black flower was down, but still the arms whipped and thrust and grasped for the albino. Still the black sword sang. Monstrous branches transformed themselves into snakes, coiling around his body, his arms his legs. But too much energy now pulsed through him. He easily broke free, the blade rising and falling, rising and falling, like a woodsman's axe in the forest. Suddenly, he was tireless. With every blow the albino's energy increased, while the plant weakened. The head darted at Elric, the cluster of long, tough leaves spearing towards his face, trying to suck it from his shoulders, but he dodged it cleverly, still laughing with that wild, maniacal glee, as much in his blade's power as it was in his.

A huge blow. Another. Squealing and chittering, parts of the plant tried to escape now, slithering off into the undergrowth. From head to toe, Elric was covered in black sap, but still he hacked at the thing, finally pausing to reach out and rip the crown of leaves from around the ruined head. To snatch a handful of large seeds, beating like so many hearts, from the centre. He stepped back, panting. His body sang and thrilled with the force pouring through it. He lifted his head in exultation, shouting his mocking triumph at the moon.

"ARIOCH!"

A tendril began to curl itself around his leg. To his horror, he realized that the plant was reforming itself. He stepped back and with the point of his sword threw the branch as far as it would go. Then he turned and ran towards the river.

Epilogue

THE FULL MOON still brightened the dark waters as they rowed out into midstream and began to follow the current away from Soom. Dyvim Mar, seven Melnibonédans, the King of the Uyt, his two daughters and Moonglum. In the stern of the boat, taking no part in the rowing, sat a solitary figure, washed clean of the filth that had covered it, its pale hand resting on the pommel of a scabbarded black broadsword. Crimson, gloomy eyes stared into another world, seeing nothing of the others.

After some time, Tilus Kreek made his way to where Elric sat and placed a hand on his shoulder. "I must thank you, prince, for all you did tonight. I know from your friend and your kinsmen that it was no easy decision. You saved our lives. Perhaps, too, you saved our souls. I can only imagine the cost to you."

Elric turned those brooding eyes upon the Uyt. He nodded slowly. Then he reached into his purse, feeling what writhed there, almost like human flesh. He drew the stuff out. A bunch of already drying black petals which still moved with a life of their own. A few large pods. which also had a fleshy look to them. "Here," he said. "I have no further use for these. I sought an impossible remedy for my condition. I should have known the only real remedy is the one I carry with me." He held the petals and spoors of the *noibuluscus* towards the king. But Tilus Kreek shook his ageing head.

"I thank thee, Elric. We both sought to save something by the cultivation of the Black Anemonë. And both of us risked far too much in its pursuit. Perhaps we are lucky to have learned something and still have our lives?"

"Perhaps." With a sudden movement, the albino took the petals and scattered them overboard onto the murky, glistening water. For a moment they wriggled on the surface, like fish, and then sank out of sight. He threw the pods after them. It was just possible the current would carry them downriver and even out into the sea. One day they might even find fresh soil in which to take root. Whether they would ever again be nurtured by human blood, find form in human skin, however, was unlikely.

As the king moved discretely back to join his other daughter amidships, Princess Nahuaduar came to sit beside Elric, her face flushing as she looked boldly up into his dangerous eyes. "And will you seek a substitute for the black flower?" she asked.

Taking her hand, he shook his head. "My lady, the sword will have to serve me for my usual sustenance. Meanwhile, I have other consolations."

Yet, even as she responded to his touch, he looked away again, as if still hoping to see something familiar in that dense, unpleasant forest. ℮

Michael Moorcock is an iconic figure in literature, having written in perhaps every genre as well as producing such mainstream classics as *Mother London*. A multiple award winner, he lives in Bastrop, Texas, with his wife Linda and several oats. Moorcock has been honored as a SFWA Grand Master and has received the World Fantasy Award for lifetime achievement. *Weird Tales* names him one of "The 85 Weirdest Storytellers of the Past 85 Years" on page 35 of this issue.

The publication in 2000 of English author China Miéville's second novel, Perdido Street Station, *galvanized and challenged the fantasy field with its potent mix of pulp and literary influences, fantasy, horror, and SF; its commitment to "the Weird"; and its epic scope.*

Since then, Miéville has given us two more novels set in his New Crobuzon milieu, The Scar *and* Iron Council, *along with a young-adult novel,* Un Lun Dun. *Along the way, he has won the Arthur C. Clarke Award and the British Fantasy Award — and has been a finalist for the World Fantasy Award and the Hugo Award,*

Interview | BY JEFF VANDERMEER

China Miéville: Capitalizing Weird

among others. Many critics consider Miéville's contribution to modern Weird fiction (and the "New Weird movement") as important as Clive Barker's in the 1980s with the Books of Blood.

Author and anthologist Jeff VanderMeer recently caught up with Miéville on behalf of Weird Tales *via instant messenger. The chat meandered . . . oddly . . .*

First off, thanks for agreeing to be interviewed for *Weird Tales*'s 85th anniversary issue. Can you tell readers a little bit about where you are as we're having this conversation? Please, it's an honour. *Weird Tales* is an indispensable part of my history, and Happy Birthday to it. I'm sitting at my desk, looking out over my North West London street, with a stack of students' stuff to read, sipping a cup of tea. That's just how I roll.

Now, because it is the 85th anniversary, there will be a lot of questions with the word "weird" in them, but the word "new" will be nowhere in evidence. So: "What does the word 'weird' mean to you?" I've been thinking about this a lot recently. I'm teaching a course in Weird Fiction at the University of Warwick, so this has come up a lot. Obviously it's kind of impossible to come to anything like a final answer, so I approach this in a Beckettian way — try to define/understand it, fail, try again, fail again, fail better . . . I think the whole "sense of cosmic awe" thing that we hear a lot about in the Weird tradition is to do with the sense of the numinous, whether in a horrific iteration (or, more occasionally, a kind of joyous one), as being completely embedded in the everyday, rather than an intrusion. To that extent the Weird to me is about the sense that reality is always Weird.

I've been thinking about the traditional notion of the "sublime," which was always (by Kant, Schopenhauer, et al) distinguished from the "Beautiful," as containing a kind of horror at the immeasurable scale of it. I think what the Weird can do is question the arbitrary distinction between the Beautiful and the Sublime, and operate as a kind of Sublime backwash, so that the numinous incomparable awesome slips back from "mountains" and "forests," into the everyday. So . . . the Weird as radicalised quotidian Sublime.

So theoretically people should see "the weird" in everyday life. But most don't see it — or aren't prepared to see it, possibly because they're too inward-turning, not really experiencing the world moment-to-moment? Is that what you mean? Or is that too New Age-y for what you're talking about? I'm talking about it as a literary/aesthetic effect — my impression is that a lot of us do experience it quite a lot, in everyday life. But given that part of its differentia specifica is that it is AWE-some, beyond language, expressing it is very difficult. I think a lot of what we admire in

Weird fictioneers is not that they see, but that they make a decent fist of expressing.

That's the theory side, in a sense, but expressed on a more personal level, what appeals to you most about the weird tale? The awe, the ecstasy. I was reading Blackwood's "The Wendigo" the other day, and the moment when Defago is taken by the Wendigo and wails from above the trees this astonishing moment of unrealistic speech — "oh, oh, my burning feet of fire! This height and fiery speed!" — the strange poetry of it, I found very affecting. Of course we all have our favourite iterations of Weird, and for me it dovetails a lot with a love of teratology, so I also hugely love when the Weird is expressed by radical monster-making, the strangeness of strange creatures, but some of my favourite Weird tales contain no monsters at all. It's the awe and ecstasy that gets me.

But not necessarily epiphany? I.e., this awe and ecstasy is a cumulative effect of the story or it's what it culminates in? I don't think I can distinguish [between] the two. I think for me the best Weird fiction is an expression of that awe, which permeates the whole thing, but because you can't structure a story as a continual shout of ecstasy (at least not and expect many readers to stick with you) it sort of pretends to be an epiphany. But I think it's the epiphany of realisation — that the real is Weird — rather than change or irruption — that something Weird occurs. Lovecraft, for example, is always back-projecting his

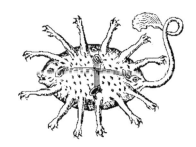

"I hugely love when the Weird is expressed by radical monster-making . . . It's the awe and ecstasy that gets me."

mythos into history. We don't know it, unless we're one of the select unlucky few in his story, but it's not that these things have suddenly arrived to mess about with previously stable reality, but that we're forced to realise — there's the epiphany, it's epistemological, rather than an ontological break — that it was always Awesome.

Yeah, but you are talking about visionary fiction to some extent — some of it is hardwired with ecstasy, and that's why the best examples are short stories, no? Because you can't sustain that "reverie"? I think that's true — it's much harder to maintain Weird, or, certainly, ecstasy, over a longer form. Which is why these stories are about the revelation — not because it's a surprise (we expect it) but because it's a necessary kind of bleak Damascene moment. There are Weird novels and some brilliant ones, but they're harder to sustain.

What do you think most surprises your students studying weird tales? I think for a lot of people who don't read pulp growing up, there's a real surprise that the particular kind of pulp modernism of a certain kind of lush purple prose isn't necessarily a failure or a mistake, but is part of the fabric of the story and what makes it weird. There's a big default notion that "spare" or "precise" prose is somehow better. I keep insisting to them that while such prose is completely legitimate, it's in no way intrinsically more accurate, more relevant, or better than lush prose. That adjective "precise," for example, needs unpicking. If a "minimalist" writer describes a table, and a metaphor-ridden, adjective-heavy Weird fictioneer describes a table, they are very different, but the former is in absolutely no way closer to the material reality than the latter. Both of them are radically different from that reality. They're just words. A table is a big wooden thing with my tea on it.

I think they also are surprised by how much they enjoy making up monsters.

Who doesn't? But you say they're surprised? They think that's too childish to start? Yes, to some extent. It's something you need to grow out of. Or your monsters are only legitimate to the extent that they "really mean" something else. I spend a lot of time arguing for literalism of fantastic, rather than its reduction to allegory. Metaphor is inevitable but it escapes our intent, so we should relax about it. Our monsters are about themselves, and they can get on with being about all sorts of other stuff too, but if we want them to be primarily that, and don't enjoy their monstrousness, they're dead and nothing.

Right — nobody likes a monster piñata. Yeah — it's what Toby Litt brilliantly called the "Scooby-Doo Impasse" — that people always-already know that they'll pull the mask off the monster and see what it "really" is/means. The notion that that is what makes it legitimate is a very drab kind of heavy-handedness.

Do you think a lot of writers create monsters, though, that they don't mean literally? I mean, do you think writers sit down and go, when writing the rough

draft, "This is going to be a metaphor for 9/11?" Or is it just that readers and academics think they do? Well I think this is one of the big distinctions between genre and non-genre traditions. I think, for example, that when Margaret Atwood invents the "pigoons" for *Oryx & Crake*, part of the problem with them for me is I think they are primarily a vehicle for considering genetic manipulation, and only distantly secondarily scary pig monsters. I think plenty of monsters get hobbled by their "meaning." The Coppola *Bram Stoker's Dracula* vampire had to shuffle along, so weighed down was he by bloated historical import. None of this is to say that monsters don't mean things other than themselves — of course they do — but that to me they do so best when they believe in themselves.

Good point — and of course writers often look at their rough draft and like oracles pull things out that look like they have meaning. [But going back to the metaphor-for-9-11 thing,] I haven't seen *Cloverfield* yet so can't judge.

Yeah — I was thinking of *Cloverfield*, although handhelds for a whole movie make me nauseous. I gather a lot of people have had that problem. I'm fully expecting to dislike it. I don't enjoy many films these days.

Anything you have particularly enjoyed, in any genre? Good question. Nothing recent is coming to mind, to be honest. I've largely stopped going. Lots of things I haven't enjoyed. Hello *Transformers,* you despicable piece of shit.

Impressively bad? I have to say I think part of the problem here is that we don't have a precise enough vocabulary. I think a lot of the time when people complain that a film was "bad," we need to unpick what it means. What is the purpose of big films? To make money. If they make a lot of money,

they succeed. In what sense are they bad? Well, they may be aesthetically incoherent, offensive, anything like that, but that's contingent to their purpose, whatever the intent of the director. So I think *Transformers* may well have done exactly what it set out to do: make a load of money and push an aggressively crass, offensive agenda. So was it "bad?" Well, I loathed it, but that's not the same thing. Oh, I know what I liked: *Pan's Labyrinth* I thought was terrific.

Yeah, me, too. Wow: consequences to actions. And I disagreed with lots of people who enjoyed it — our readings of what went on seem radically different. I liked *Pan's Labyrinth* because it was so merciless about fantasy. I didn't think its ending was "uplifting" at all, I thought it was admirably unsentimental and unforgiving.

This does actually bring me to one of those "weird" questions I'm contractually obligated to ask for this interview: What's the weirdest (in any sense) movie you've ever seen? Weirdest movie? Probably either a Jan Svankmajer — *The Flat* — and/or a Jean Painlevé, *Le Vampire*. Also, *Terror in a Texas Town*. [And] Yeah — *Pan's Labyrinth* — this is spoiler territory — but I know a lot of people who said they thought the end was a lovely escape into the healing power of fantasy and I was thinking OH REALLY?!?! I had a similar argument with those people who thought the ending of [Steven Spielberg's] *AI* was "sentimental." I was thinking, fuck, did we see the same film? That was some sadistic shit I just saw. Not that I much enjoyed *AI*, but I was fascinated by the astoundingly cruel last half-hour.

Do you find that some readers, related to what you're saying, don't recognize a monster, a human monster, when they see one? And I agree — *AI* is a very cruel movie, unnecessarily so. Whereas *Pan* is cruel only because it has to be.

China Miéville

Perdido Street Station

"An astonishing novel, guaranteed to…enthrall." — *Times Literary Supplement*

I totally agree — *AI* sadistic, *Pan's Labyrinth* politically unsentimental. Very different. What do you mean [about not recognizing a monster]?

I have a current theory that writers become so in love with their characters that they don't always recognize when they've written a sociopath, for example. And then their enthusiasm blinds readers who aren't careful and who go along for the ride, thinking, "Oh, this person is great." Ah. It's an interesting question, and I've not thought of it in those terms. I've certainly been aware of the consideration of certain characters as admirable, or, in other ways, as despicable, when read from a different optic, they are not. I loathed *Tess of the d'Urbervilles* because I got the strong impression that Hardy and I disagreed about Tess. Similarly Simmons' *The Terror*, with several of his characters.

Did you like *The Terror*? No. I kept wanting to find out what the giant polar bear was. When I discovered it was, indeed, a giant polar bear, I was deflated. I found it fairly page-turny, but I found it much too long, too bogged down with its historical research for its narrative, its disclosures and teratological money-shots too contingent to its narrative, and its embedded politics — particularly vis-à-vis homosexuality — offensive.

You don't believe those embedded politics were part of the historical research? No, because I'm not talking about the politics of the characters, but about the politics of the text, as I read it.

At least he was honest. In that sense. Specifically, the obsessive locus of the evil character's evil in the fact that he was an engager in anal sex. I know lots of people point to the fact that there's a "sympathetic" gay character too (who reads, incidentally, to me, very like someone invented because an editor said "we really need a counterbalance to the evil gay") but that character is explicitly defined as a goody because he doesn't have sex on the ship. That's nothing to do with historical research or attitudes (and parenthetically, the idea that in a crew that size only two men would be fucking is ludicrous) but to do with the text's pathological Terror of anal penetration which is (spoiler! — hello *The Sparrow*) the usual way culture gets to have a deep-seated pathologising of gay sexuality alongside putatively liberal attitudes to desexualised gay men.

You've just ruined the innocence of perhaps 85 percent of *Weird Tales* readers. Hurrah! My work here is done.

Please take a bow. I really liked the book, but I didn't catch the subtext you're talking about, in part, probably, because I was turning pages too quickly. I'm very aware, by the way, that loads of readers of this may think I'm being

a humourless or po-faced dick about it. This is how it reads to me, and I have a big problem with it. And I think arguments about "what the writer really means" or thinks are very point-missing, because this stuff isn't reducible to "intent."

True, but — and I'm not saying in this case — but in some cases, don't you have to be forgiving? It depends of what. Give me an example?

For example, Philip K. Dick was a raging misogynist. But if you unravel the stuff about his work that is bad in that sense, you also unravel the good stuff. In a sense I'm playing devil's advocate because I do believe writers should think these things through, because it reflects on whether they've really created well-rounded characters as opposed to stereotypes. This is not about pissing and moaning just because I disagree with the writer's politics — I love passionately Gene Wolfe's work, for example, far more than the writing of many people whose politics are more congenial to me. It's about saying that as a matter of reading, of literary response, when the politics or concerns or whatever of a particular text impinge on it in certain ways, make it pull in certain directions, interfere with other aspects of it, etc. etc., and in my opinion make it not just politically objectionable but work less well as a text, then I feel perfectly free to criticise it on those (politico-literary) axes.

Sure — I mean, what you're saying about *The Terror* makes sense in that — does it make any difference whether the evil guy is gay or not? To the story? Not really. So then you have to ask yourself why it's there. I don't think there's such a thing as "the story" disembarrassed of the other stuff, basically. That's why I think about "texts" or works rather than the story, versus/and/or the writing, versus/and/or the characters, etc. In

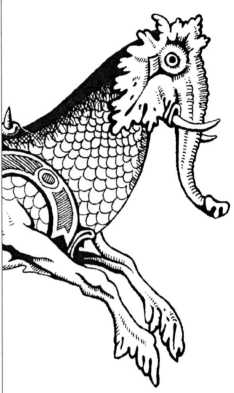

art these things are intertwined. Not reducible to each other, sure, but not little just-add-and-stir packets of sauce that you can choose one but not the other. Did I want to get to the end of *The Terror* and see the bear? Sure. Still, though, I stand by what I said, and I think there's no contradiction. I don't mind people disagreeing at all, of course, that's the point of debate. I do get frustrated when — and maybe it's my fault for not being clear — people take what I'm saying as "he doesn't like books by people he doesn't agree with." As the Lovecraft, Celine, Machen, Blackwood, Ewers, James, Cordwainer Smith, Blyton, et many al, on my shelves indicate, this isn't so. And it can operate the other way round too. For me, *The Sparrow* was a big thing there — that's obviously a book that intends to be very progressive about homosexuality, but in my opinion it, whatever Russell's beliefs and intents, is deep-structured by anal-penetration panic.

Since we seem to be approaching this territory anyway, here's another contractually obligated question. What's the weirdest book you've ever read? God, that's a merciless question.

All the weirdest questions are merciless. *Un Semaine de Bonté*, by Max Ernst. Which means that "read" is a bit of a tendentious verb in this context, but fuck it, I'm sticking with my answer.

Shifting gears just slightly, in doing some research, I came across an *Interzone* from the early 1990s, I think, that contained a letter to the editor from you commenting on a couple of stories in the previous issue. How early on did you get hooked into genre magazines, and did you read any besides *Interzone*? AGH! Please eradicate from your memory. I was reading *Interzone* from about 1987ish onwards. I dipped into a few more, but that was my main one. I wasn't part of the fanzine scene at all, for example.

Right. But it was kind of nice to see that letter, to see that you didn't just pop out of a volcano or something. No. I sent poor *IZ* several lamentable stories in the early 90s. Luckily all rejected.

What else did you read growing up, if you don't mind me asking? In terms of magazines, etc. Magazines not many at all. It was really just *IZ*, plus occasionally I'd buy an exotic copy of *Locus* or *Back Brain Recluse* or whatever, but in terms of the field, that was kind of it — plus old *Galaxies, Weird Tales*, old pulp stuff as and when I came across it, but not collected with any rigour. I mean I loved oddities like that when I came across them, but wasn't systematic about them.

What about reading habits more generally? You're seen as a fiercely intelligent reader — I mean, the comments in this interview and others support that. **But what do you read for escapism? Or do you? I know I have times when I cannot focus on something serious or deep and I need my schlocky noir mysteries, for example.** On the whole I don't tend to have "escape" and "non-escape" reading, except that I find fiction in general a lot easier to relax to than non-fiction. Certainly I have plenty of pleasures that I think are less skillful in certain ways than other favourites — Lloyd Biggle Jr, for example — but that's not quite what you're asking. I'd say when I'm trying to be "on" I read non-fiction, and I find fiction much easier to kick back to. Which doesn't preclude getting angry about it, of course, but that's part of the pleasure, often. The only qualification I'd add is about use of Language — some writers who have very intense knotty language — Beckett, Iain Sinclair, older books which read less naturalistically now — I wouldn't crack open when exhausted, and would be more likely to read a simpler-written YA book or a PKD or something — but that's not about a hierarchy of quality than about a stylistic tendency. Sometimes books that demand a lot of effort from the reader are just what you want, sometimes you want it to enter your eyes easier.

Right — and that's actually a more precise and useful explanation of what I meant. It isn't necessarily a hierarchy of quality, that's true. I think *Skellig* by David Almond, a book for children, limpidly clearly written, one of the most sophisticated and daring books I've read for some time, for example.

Okay, so we've talked about weird books and movies. What's the weirdest place you've ever been? Probably the East Anglian coast, where M.R. James set loads of his ghost stories, and which I have a long family connection with. Very freaky places — Cove Hithe, Dunwich, Walberswick. Second, the outskirts of a big factory

in the outskirts of Bulawayo in Zimbabwe. But places are all *so* weird, that's a real embarrassment of riches. Ever been to the coast of the Netherlands? Weird.

Speaking of strange, have you followed the U.S. presidential race at all? Sigh. Yes, somewhat. It is at least rather more interesting than I'd thought it would be.

I assume you're a huge Huckabee supporter. Yah! Totally. Go Huck! Me and the karate man [Chuck Norris].

Now that is weird. But not in an awe way. Maybe an ecstasy way, however. LOL. I preferred it when Vin Diesel was the guy about whom all those memes were spread. You know, when VD does a press-up, it isn't him going up, it's the world being pushed down, etc. I really like Vin Diesel, but he's not done anything I've enjoyed for a long time.

His *XXX* movie is a guilty pleasure, I have to say. Look at you pretending you don't remember the name, like you don't have a T-shirt, the limited edition DVD . . .

Well, I stopped with the plushy Vin Diesel dolls. It had to stop somewhere. He's a good actor. And a committed D&D player. Wrote the foreword to a collection marking its something-or-other's birthday.

Not something I would have expected. On that note, let's wrap things up with a "weird" speed round or two. I'm going to list two "weird" writers at a time and you'll tell me which you like better with maybe a sentence on why, if you want. Ready? OK, cool. I *love* the either/or game. People who say, "Ooh, can't I have both?" are terrible cheats.

Here goes. Jack Vance or Robert E. Howard? Vance because of *Dying Earth.* Dying. Earth. And big dying sun.

Vance or Lovecraft? Lovecraft — damn you for making me choose! — because i) the monsters are revolutionary, and ii) the prose is totally weird. And Weird.

Lovecraft or Clark Ashton Smith? Lovecraft. Because CAS, to whom all honour and respect, has a post-Dunsanian sort of slightly sentimental archaic singsongism that doesn't freak me out as much as Lovecraft's hysteria.

Surprise! Lovecraft or Ursula K. LeGuin *or* Ray Bradbury? A troika? That's cheating, surely! Lovecraft *ow* sorry sorry LeGuin and Bradbury. Because he reshaped a form more radically than either of them (to whom infinite burnt offerings and love).

Lovecraft or Tennessee Williams? (Both of whom appeared in *Weird Tales*.) (NO! REALLY???) Lovecraft. Though TW [comes] close for that weird play where the guy gets eaten by children — *Suddenly Last Summer.* Also, William Hope Hodgson is pulling ahead of Lovecraft in my head, increasingly recently, workmanlike prose or not. But that's another discussion.

And, finally, mammals or reptiles? Please. *Please.* Mammals schmammals. In ascending order, it goes Mammals and birds equally, Reptiles, Amphibians, Insects, Fish, Cephalopods. ℮

Jeff VanderMeer is the World Fantasy Award-winning author of the novels *City of Saints & Madmen, Veniss Underground,* and *Shriek: An Afterword,* as well as coeditor of such anthologies as *The New Weird, Best American Fantasy,* and *The Thackery T. Lambshead Pocket Guide to Eccentric & Discredited Diseases.* His next anthology, due in May, is *Steampunk,* coedited with *Weird Tales* fiction editor Ann VanderMeer.

Lost in Lovecraft

A GUIDED TOUR OF THE DARK MASTER'S WORLD

BY KENNETH HITE

"*N*ow *I found myself upon an apparently abandoned road which I had chosen as the shortest cut to Arkham . . .*"
—H.P. Lovecraft, "The Picture in the House"

WITH THOSE WORDS, Lovecraft introduces his signature setting to the rest of the world. Five of Lovecraft's tales are set primarily in Arkham — "The Unnamable," "Herbert West — Reanimator," "The Silver Key," "The Dreams in the Witch-House," and "The Thing on the Doorstep" — more than Boston, or New York, or even Providence. Arkham also serves as a major counterpoint to the primary setting in "The Dunwich Horror" and "The Colour Out of Space," and takes a turn as the backdrop in "The Shadow Out of Time." It has become a permanent part of the atlas of the imagination, alongside Hobbiton and Atlantis and Trantor.

"[My] mental picture of Arkham is of a town something like Salem in atmosphere [and] style of houses, but more hilly [and] with a college . . . I place the town [and] the imaginary Miskatonic . . . somewhere north of Salem — perhaps near Manchester?"
— H.P. Lovecraft, letter to F. Lee Baldwin (1934)

But it differs from those storied locales in that Arkham, like Ruritania or Gotham City or Yoknapatawpha County, though technically fictional, is clearly part of the real world, not a hidden valley like Hogwarts, a philosophical phantom isle like Lilliput, or somewhere "long, long ago" like Camelot or Tatooine. You can buy a bus ticket there, or come upon it if you take an apparently abandoned road. This sort of fictional-factual setting is a creation of the railway-obsessed and urgently domestic Victorians, with Elizabeth Gaskell's *Cranford* (1851), Charles Dickens' *Coketown* (1853), and Anthony Trollope's *Barchester* (1855) as the first examples. Their novels dealt with

real, even quotidian, concerns, but something led them to expand the map a bit and disguise their fantasies in timetables and tour-guides. Lovecraft, for all his expressed contempt for Victorian values, recognized a good trick for achieving simultaneous verisimilitude and phantasy when he saw it.

His acolytes, not content with climbing Federal Hill or exploring Red Hook, have tried to pin Arkham to their own maps as well. Will Murray presented an ingenious argument that Lovecraft initially sited Arkham in central Massachusetts — specifically, where the similar- sounding town of Oakham once sat before being flooded by the Quabbin Reservoir. And indeed, any ordinary reading of "The Colour Out of Space" (speaking of reservoirs) implies an Arkham amid the wild hills far from the sea. But against that, we have numerous descriptions of Arkham as a river port hard by coastal Kingsport and Innsmouth, and Lovecraft's own description in letters (to Wandrei in 1927 and Derleth in 1931, among others) of seaboard Salem as "my Arkham." Perhaps it's not entirely the narrator's fault, in "The Picture in the House," that he gets lost looking for Arkham.

"What lay behind our joint love of shadows and marvels was, no doubt, the ancient, mouldering, and subtly fearsome town in which we live — witch-cursed, legend-haunted Arkham, whose huddled, sagging gambrel roofs and crumbling Georgian balustrades brood out the centuries beside the darkly muttering Miskatonic."
— H.P. Lovecraft, "The Thing on the Doorstep"

Though it's not quite clear why one might be in a hurry to get to Arkham at all, given its unpleasant associations with "traditions of horror, madness, and witchcraft," in Nathaniel Peaslee's words. Even its creator seems repulsed by the town: Lovecraft calls it "terrible," "haunted," and "crumbling," a "black city" with a "brooding, festering horror" to it. Arkham's

"centuried gambrel roofs," those "huddled, sagging," "tottering," "hoary," "moss-grown," and "clustering" constructions, signify the horror in tale after tale. They, and Arkham, are crouched and old in the way of the Old Ones and the cannibal in the woods, a baleful "hoary" age. In "The Dreams in the Witch-House," Arkham's gambrel roofs are explicitly linked with Arkham's other great evil, witches: they "sway and sag over attics where witches hid from the King's men in the dark, olden days of the Province." Arkham is "witch-cursed" or "witch-accursed" or "witch-haunted" (twice in "The Silver Key") or "whisper-haunted," or "legend-haunted," where children disappear every May Eve. This connection, by the way, points to the special horror of the gambrel roof; it is a relic of the "ghastly, festering" Puritan seventeenth century, not the glorious Augustan eighteenth, where Lovecraft fancied himself at home.

"[T]he pastures slope up to the ridge above the Miskatonic and give a lovely vista of Arkham's white Georgian steeples across leagues of river and meadow. Here he found a shady road to Arkham, but no trail at all in the seaward direction he wished."
— H.P.L., "The Strange High House in the Mist"

That century, however, Arkham also represents, significantly in its "white Georgian steeples," and even the "crumbling Georgian balustrades" in "The Thing on the Doorstep." Arkham is part of the "breathlessly lovely panorama" in "The Silver Key," and part of the Sunset City likewise seen by Randolph Carter in *The Dream-Quest of Unknown Kadath*. But it is not merely lovely in the dream or Dunsanian tales, it is representative of order and sanity in the later Miskatonic stories. In "The Shadow Over Innsmouth," Arkham is the bright mirror held up to Innsmouth's even more shadowy and decrepit nature. The Arkham-born grocery clerk shows "brightness and affability" and attends a decent church (Asbury Methodist Episcopal) in

Arkham rather than the debased cults of Innsmouth. Even in a "dark Arkham" tale like "The Thing on the Doorstep," Innsmouth is still worse; as Upton reminds us, "Arkham folk avoid going to Innsmouth whenever they can." In "The Dunwich Horror," Arkham is not merely the "good twin" to decadent Dunwich, but its antidote: Arkham kills both sons of Yog-Sothoth, and "the Arkham men" are embodiments of order and reason. Meanwhile, "The Festival" tells us that compared to Kingsport, Arkham is "broad-minded," with better hospitals. Not only is Arkham wise and caring, but it is conventional and even bland, uncomprehending of Kingsport's temporal drifts. "They must have lied when they said the trolleys ran to this place," muses the narrator, prefiguring the contrast in "The Whisperer in Darkness" between remote Vermont and Wilmarth's native Arkham, part of the "mechanised, urbanised" region of New England. By this tale, even the trains run to Arkham; there's a stodgy, respectable commuter train into Boston (the 8:07). "Changeless" "hoary" Arkham has become one of "the sections which modernity has touched," no doubt featuring "foreigners and factory-smoke, bill-boards and concrete roads," a sea change from the "shadowy tangles of unpaved musty-smelling lanes where eldritch brown houses of unknown age leaned and tottered and leered mockingly through

Even Arkham's creator seems repulsed by the town. Lovecraft calls it a "black city" with a "brooding, festering horror."

narrow, small-paned windows" where Walter Gilman studies hyper-modern mathematics and medieval metaphysics alike.

"About 'Arkham' and 'Kingsport' — bless my soul! but I thought I'd told you all about them years ago! They are typical but imaginary places — like the river 'Miskatonic,' whose name is simply a jumble of Algonquin roots."
— H.P.L., letter to August Derleth (1931)

Perhaps we can resolve this dilemma not by locating Arkham the place, but by reading Arkham the sign. Robert Marten believes that "Arkham" comes not from the location "Oakham" but from the name of the Rhode Island township of "Arkwright," in metropolitan Providence, named for the proto-industrialist Richard Arkwright. Lovecraft may or may not have taken his fiction's name from Arkwright, but unlike Dunwich (a real town in Suffolk), he could not have taken it from England, either. (The closest homonym is the tiny living of Arkholme in Lancashire.) It's perhaps more likely, and certainly more interesting, that Lovecraft built the name deliberately. Let's start with the easy half, *-ham.* It has two possible Anglo-Saxon derivations: from *hám,* or "home," as in Nottingham; from *hamm,* or "enclosure" (cognate with "hemmed in"), as in Oakham. (As the Puritans came mostly from East Anglia, we can omit the derivation from the Norse *holm,* or "island," most common in the North, as in Durham.) And then there's the *Ark.* Here, also, we have two options: the Ark of the Covenant, preserving Law and Order against the wilderness; and the Ark of Noah, carrying bestial survivals away from righteous wrath and disaster. Is Arkham the enclosure of the Ark, the shelter for ancient lore safe from mundane gaze? Or are its "ancient, cryptically brooding hills" the resting place of those who fled the Flood, the home of primordial evils and ancient witchcraft?

"It may be that centuries of dark brooding had given to crumbling, whisper-haunted Arkham a peculiar vulnerability as regards such shadows ?"
— H.P.L., "The Shadow Out of Time"

Arkham is "crumbling" and "changeless," rational and mad. It is what Robert H. Waugh has called the "double city," both ideal and shadow, both personal and fancied. In "The Dreams in the Witch-House," it stretches back into "the monstrous past," and perhaps its shadow extends immemorially farther back as the quote above hints in "The Shadow Out of Time." In Lovecraft's apocalyptic 1925 poem "The Cats," Arkham is a necropolis some time in the dead future. And intriguingly, in *At the Mountains of Madness,* the brig that transmits Dyer's (the one who dies?) messages from the camp at Kadath to academic civilization, the intermediary between Hell and the waking world, is named the Arkham. The eponymous city likewise speaks to two realms, even as its name carries two burdens. Perhaps, much as Arkham switches from rustic backwater to bustling coastal railhead, and from witch-haunted blight to Georgian bulwark, it is both home and enclosure to both Arks.

Lovecraft begins by littering the hinterland of Arkham with unnatural survivals — the immortal cannibal, Herbert West's zombies, the Unnamable in the burying ground — like jetsam on the slopes of Ararat. (The *Arabian Nights*-obsessed HPL would perhaps have known of the Arabic legend that some monsters survived the Flood by clinging to the Ark in the darkness.) But soon enough, Arkham becomes a shelter, an enclosure, first against the chaotic floodwaters underlying Kingsport and later, literally — like the Biblical Ark of the Covenant — against the hosts of Dagon. The sign changes, or is lettered on both sides, but the name remains the same. ❧

Next Stop on the Tour: *Dreamland*

The Cryptic

BY DARRELL SCHWEITZER

TIME TO GO TO THE FESTIVAL

I TOUCHED THE original Blob! It didn't even crawl up my hand or try to devour me. It must have been sleeping, lying contently in its five-gallon drum where it has been residing (so its current custodian told me) peacefully since 1965.

I mean *the* Blob, the title character and star of the 1958 cult film of the same title. That one. It wasn't like shaking hands with an old-time movie star, because this particular star didn't have any hands. Touching it is not normally encouraged, but since I was a purported Gentleman of the Press, present in my professional capacity, I was allowed. It was a bit rubbery under my fingertip, room-temperature and vaguely yielding. I did not press hard. No sense pushing my luck.

But I'm getting ahead of myself. What I'm talking about is the eighth annual Blobfest, held in scenic Phoenixville, Pennsylvania, at the Colonial Theatre, where a very famous scene from *The Blob* was filmed.

Phoe-nixville is a quiet little town about an hour and a half west of Philadelphia, four miles beyond Valley Forge. It's one of those old industrial towns along the Schuylkill River since turned to other purposes, unremarkable enough that for all I had been going to its outskirts for the past thirty years to visit a used-book store, I had never actually been into the town center until it occurred to me that Blobfest might be a suitably illuminating subject for one of these columns and an excuse to freeload a press pass.

The Blob (shot in 1957, released in 1958, directed by Irvin S. Yeaworth Jr.) is the ultimate 1950s science-fiction B-movie, about an oozing, gooey Thing that bursts out of a meteorite; oozes over the hand, then the forearm, then the whole body of the foolishly curious Earthling who first pokes it with a stick; and subsequently grows bigger and bigger and Can't Be Stopped until, at last, it is. But before that, a bunch of hot-rodding, small-town teenagers led by Steven (later Steve) McQueen in his first starring role try to convince the authorities of the (literally) growing danger. But nobody listens to them because they're teenagers, and so the film gains a purported sociological significance (not to mention audience pandering) when, *for once*, the sort of wild, car-crazy kids who, in those dim days, usually ended their high-speed adventures wrapped around telephone poles or otherwise messily demised in cautionary novels by Henry Gregor Felsen . . . these kids are right and save the world.

Or at least they make a significant contribution, as do the obnoxious cop everybody teases (who thinks the kids are jealous of his war record; but he proves an able marksman when one is needed), the high-school principal (who defies decorum by actually breaking the school door open with a rock), and, last but not least (this being a '50s monster

As long as the Arctic stays cold, we're told, the Blob should stay put. Hello, global warming? Time for a sequel!

movie), the U.S. military. When it is discovered that the Blob is repelled by cold and can be brought to bay with the aid of large quantities of CO_2-type fire-extinguishers (which is what they were breaking into the high school to get), the military then transports the now inert Blob to the Arctic. It can't actually be killed, you see, but, as McQueen portentously intones in the final line of dialogue: as long as the Arctic stays cold, it should stay put.

Can you say "global warming"? Isn't that an obvious opening for a sequel? Once again, if we want to take it more seriously than it will really bear, *The Blob* assumes a whole new degree of relevance, as if the original allegory of how American society can pull together and overcome generational differences in a crisis were not enough.

More than that, *The Blob* — even after all these years — is still cheesy fun. Not great cinema, but it moves well. Things happen fast enough that, while you're watching at least, you don't really care that this isn't *Citizen Kane*. Admittedly, if you look at it now, you realize that McQueen was the only

actor in the cast who was obviously going somewhere. The others are routine B-movie character players. Most of the "teenagers" look to be about thirty. The role of the Blob itself is played by what I encountered in that five-gallon bucket: a large mass of silicone, acquired by the producer from Union Carbide, and dyed bright red. (This was one of the first color '50s monster movies. The red made a difference.) The present owner of the prop (the eminent Blobologist, Wes Shank) bought it from the producer about 1965, and has been its keeper ever since. A chemist assured him that it is likely to retain its blobbishness for years to come, and so there it . . . sleeps.

Of course, as we all know, Hollywood seldom comes up with a new idea. There have been numerous blob and giant amoeba stories published in *Weird Tales* over the years, ranging from Anthony M. Rud's "Ooze," the cover story on our very first issue of March 1923, to Joseph Payne Brennan's celebrated "Slime," which inspired the Virgil Finlay cover that graced our March 1953 issue. But we must admit that *The Blob* rang new changes on its amorphous theme by giving the story a distinctly late-1950s context. This may be one reason why the movie itself seems as unstoppable as its subject matter, fifty years later.

The reason it's celebrated in Phoenixville is that once of the most memorable scenes in the film takes place right in the Colonial Theatre. After the teenagers have been scoffed at, ignored, and told to go home by the authorities, the Blob, which has now devoured several more hapless townspeople, comes oozing right through the projection booth into the theatre — which must have been a wonderful novelty at the time, the cinematic equivalent of breaking the "fourth wall" of live theatre, involving the audience directly in the story, or at least pretending to. Of course, back in 1958, nothing actually came oozing out of that projection booth, in the Colonial Theatre or elsewhere. It remained for schlockmeister William Castle to

really involve the audience by such gimmicks as wiring the seats to give a mild electrical shock in *The Tingler* (1959).

In any case, it was great fun to watch the movie from the balcony, right below that very projection booth. I looked behind myself a couple times during the famous scene. No gelatinous monsters, but the little windows are configured exactly the same way they appear in the film, and the paint scoured from the walls might well be a sign of Blob damage.

The other famous scene in the theatre comes immediately thereafter, the "run-out," in which patrons stream screaming into the street. Nowadays, for Blobfest, this is lovingly re-enacted with the help of the local police who close off the street, and a couple Blobfest staffers directing human traffic with glowing batons to avoid a pileup. I got to participate in this Friday night event. I had been in the balcony. It was announced that the lower theater was full, but it didn't look full, so I went downstairs, slipped in through a side door, and found that there was indeed room for one more. I may even have gotten on local TV for my trouble, because as soon as I emerged out onto the street I was face-to-face with a TV cameraman. Maybe as press I wasn't supposed to participate, but how else was I to report on the complete Blobfest experience?

Other activities Friday night included a screaming contest (won by a girl about five or six — the cute kid will get it every time), a tin-foil hat competition (some very elaborate creations, to prevent aliens from beaming mind-control rays into your noggin) and the showing of two award-winning amateur "blob" films. One looked to me like a typical high-school effort, but the other was quite clever, a period "commercial" for Blob Jelly, which cheerfully assures us, "There's no trouble spreading it" on bread or anything else. There was also a Fire Extinguisher parade, in commemoration of how the Blob was brought to a halt before it could devour Steve McQueen and his co-stars in the nearby Downingtown Diner at the film's climax.

I even wandered into the projection booth whence the Blob oozed in the film.

Saturday morning, Blobfest turned into a street fair, announced by a big banner as you drove into town. Several blocks of the town's main street were closed off. There was a large, inflatable Blob over the marquee of the Colonial Theatre. Below that, you could pose with a cutout of the Blob. Rock bands played. Ghoulish goodies of all sorts were for sale, including such oddities as Turkish Dracula films. Inside the theater, there was a panel discussion featuring some of the people involved in the original film, including producer Jack H. Harris and co-scripter Kate Phillips (Kay Linaker), both of whom are now 94 and surely did not imagine that fifty years later they would be back in the same theater celebrating *The Blob*, with or without the presence of the Blob itself in a bucket upstairs.

Another panelist was Howard Fishlove, a crew member on the original film, and an easy to spot extra in the famous "run-out." (The big guy in the white T-shirt.) Also present was the woman who (quite accidentally) tripped during the "run-out" scene. Fifty years later, she was presented with the Golden Crutch Award. There were also the inevitable lines for autographs. You could buy Blobfest t-shirts, posters, and pens. I even wandered into the projection booth whence the Blob oozed in the film. Also in attendance were a local scary storytelling troupe, the Patient Creatures. When I encountered a nearly 8-foot-tall Grim Reaper in the balcony, in the dark, I was able to say, "Ah, nice to see a familiar face." (We *Weird Tales* folks have connections, you know.) There were also characters from a local children's TV show called *Ghoul A-Go-Go*. I am not familiar with the show, but they had an impressively hulking hunchback. One other film was shown, *Angry Red Planet*, presumably because it has a (Martian) blob in it, but this is a film that is so low-budget that, next to it, the 1958 *Blob* looks as a elaborate as the Peter Jackson *King Kong*. (They couldn't even afford matte paintings. Mars seems to consist of black-and-white drawings.)

What is notable about all this is that Blobfest isn't just a gathering of film buffs. It's a genuine community event. Most of the people there were way too young to have seen the film when it was first released, and they brought their children. There were whole families in Blob-centric costumes, particularly headgear. The grandchildren or even great-grandchildren of the original *The Blob* audience were being turned on to that throbbing red ooze. But for a couple Phoenixville denizens I passed pitching pennies in a back alley on my way from where I'd parked my car, the whole town seemed to have turned out. It was a big deal.

Maybe, you might say, that's the only thing this town has to celebrate, but that can't be the whole story. The film *Taps* was made in and around my (nearby) hometown of Wayne, Pa., and nobody much cared, save to be glad when the helicopters stopped flying low overhead at all hours. Certainly there were no commemorative street fairs. But as producer Jack Harris said on the panel, when someone asked him in 1957 why he was wasting his time on this junk, he replied, "This movie will outlast us all." Mr. Harris is still with us, but, undeniably, *The Blob* has lasted.

Why? We can only guess. Maybe we look back on it nostalgically, as typifying a more innocent time when it was still possible to believe that alienated youth, parents, teachers, police, and the military could join together to defeat a sticky menace from outer space. There is, admittedly, an appealing idealism there.

Maybe it's just an excuse to be silly and wear funny hats. Or maybe it's because not *enough* people are wearing tinfoil hats — and the alien mind-rays have taken control. You'll never know . . . ℮

Darrell Schweitzer is senior contributing editor to *Weird Tales* and *H.P. Lovecraft's Magazine of Horror*.

WHEN WE DEBUTED the new *Weird Tales* nameplate last spring, it was the latest step in a calligraphic and typographic evolution that began with the first issue in March 1923. While it's true that the magazine's geometric, "Big W" look is the one that stuck around the longest, the first ten years of *Weird Tales* history saw no fewer than half a dozen logo changes — though three of those were part of the first-year fumbling before long-running editor Farnsworth Wright took over in 1924. Nobody has ever admitted liking the inappropriately goofy comic-bookish lettering atop the very first issue, but we *will* confess to a fondness for the elegant script that adorned fourteen *Weird Tales* throughout 1924 and 1925. The simple, serifed look that ran from 1926 to 1933 was strong and bold, albeit as un-weird as lettering can be. The classic logo debuted in May 1933 —— the same spring that began artist Margaret Brundage's long run of sexy cover paintings. Coincidence? We think not. Readers knew they liked those covers for *some* reason. —— *S.H.S.*

 IN OUR PAGES, NEXT ISSUE . . .

BE THE FIRST to read an exclusive excerpt from **Stephen Hunt**'s upcoming steampunk novel from Tor Books, *The Court of the Air* — a fantastical adventure of orphans on the run from an ancient power. Then there's science-fiction legend **Norman Spinrad** dipping his toes into the pool of fantasy, with a tale of the most perverse princess-rescue any of us can remember! PLUS: mythic alien nightmares, Lovecraft on tour, and much more . . .

Lightning Source UK Ltd.
Milton Keynes UK
14 September 2009

143710UK00001B/66/P

9 781434 450302